MAGGIE

MAGGIE

CATHERINE JOHNS

hachette
AUSTRALIA

hachette
AUSTRALIA

Published in Australia and New Zealand in 2023
by Hachette Australia
(an imprint of Hachette Australia Pty Limited)
Gadigal Country, Level 17, 207 Kent Street, Sydney, NSW 2000
www.hachette.com.au

Hachette Australia acknowledges and pays our respects to the past, present and future Traditional Owners and Custodians of Country throughout Australia and recognises the continuation of cultural, spiritual and educational practices of Aboriginal and Torres Strait Islander peoples. Our head office is located on the lands of the Gadigal people of the Eora Nation.

NATIONAL
LIBRARY
OF AUSTRALIA

A catalogue record for this book is available from the National Library of Australia

ISBN: 978 0 7336 4471 9 (paperback)

Cover design by Christabella Designs
Cover image courtesy Trevillion
Author photo: David Johns
Text design by Simon Paterson, Bookhouse
Typeset in 12.7/18.4 pt Baskerville MT Pro by Bookhouse, Sydney
Printed and bound in Australia by McPherson's Printing Group

MIX
Paper | Supporting
responsible forestry
FSC
www.fsc.org FSC® C001695

The paper this book is printed on is certified against the Forest Stewardship Council® Standards. McPherson's Printing Group holds FSC® chain of custody certification SA-COC-005379. FSC® promotes environmentally responsible, socially beneficial and economically viable management of the world's forests.

For my daughters, and in memory of my younger sister.

PROLOGUE

. . . we possess nothing certainly except the past . . .

EVELYN WAUGH,
BRIDESHEAD REVISITED

For more than twenty years after I left school, I put up a shield against memory.

I couldn't bear to listen to certain music: The Beatles; Beethoven's Symphony Number 6; Christmas carols sung by a choir.

If I brushed against a cluster of star-jasmine flowers, I inhaled with the scent an unblemished, forgotten bliss, and I was no longer on a Melbourne footpath but beside Delia in the line of boarders, waiting to go in to mass at the convent in Cumberland, the air sweetly spiced from the old jasmine vine arching on the cloister: beyond it the chapel's shadow lay blue-green on the lawn, the garden was golden in the early morning sun. Or if I heard the shrill, ratcheting sounds of plovers, I was in the bottom paddock with Delia after school,

1

talking in the peaceful air, she eating her orange and I my apple, blameless and content.

Other times, I heard the querulous calls of doves outside my window in the morning, and I was in the room in Abernant I shared with Anne, waking to the cold stone of dread in my chest, fumbling beneath my pillow for my book.

And for years I couldn't sleep in a motel.

But it was the memories of my years at the convent before I met Lloyd that left me winded, stranded in the space between present and past.

❖

Then one morning I open the door and see Delia on the verandah. I hug a ghost and touch flesh, solid and warm. We stand back and look at one another.

Delia says, 'You look just like you did when you were twelve – as if . . .'

'. . . the wind would blow me over! You look the same. For goodness' sake, are you going to stand there all day?'

In the kitchen, we sit opposite each other at the table. The grey stippling Delia's hair, the shallow furrows between her eyebrows and at the outer corners of her eyes, one moment cause me pain, the next are as light as a layer of dust.

After almost twenty-five years, she is the same: her rapid speech and staccato laugh, her practical haircut, her shirt collar folded over her crew-necked jumper. She still wears no make-up, no adornment. For this reason, the slim, gold chain that slides in and out of her left sleeve is invested with a subtle, mysterious meaning. I try to picture her with her husband and children, but I can't.

She unpacks from her briefcase the papers she has to put in order for her conference in the afternoon. I can't stop looking at her hands, which are knobbly-knuckled, more square than oval, and as familiar as my own. But they belong on the scarred surface of a school desk, on the basket-weave pattern of a laminex table in the refectory. On the official papers I see her name: Dr Delia Cusack. She's famous, in her field. She travels the world. The work she does betters people's lives. I'm proud of her, as though we were related.

When she leans back in her chair I wait, and yes . . . she tips it onto two legs and balances, her fingertips gripping the edge of the table. Delia was never afraid of falling, and she never did.

Which of us gets a word in first? So many years sketched in over an hour at my table. I picture the old farmhouse she lives in now with Martin and their two small children – her youngest has just started kindergarten, mine Year 12, while my two older ones have already left home. While we talk, I'm aware of the incongruity of Delia's presence in my kitchen, as if she travelled here across time as well as space.

Then she says, 'It wasn't easy to find you. I knew you were probably still living in Melbourne, that was all.'

'I heard you'd gone to study overseas after you left Sydney. I used to send letters care of your mother, but you never

3

replied. I thought she might've thrown them away when she saw my name on the back of the envelope.'

'Why?'

'The big scandal. The scarlet woman.'

I remember Lloyd's silhouette against the window of the senior library, when he stopped beside me where I was drawing alone at the big table: his round collar shiny and white above the black suit. Delia was in the classroom next door: the day, the moment my life took off in the opposite direction I'd planned, right off the edge of the map, like falling over a cliff.

Delia says, 'That was hard for me, having to keep it a secret.' It's not an accusation; it's a fact.

I asked too much of her, but she was loyal. Giving in to the need to tell someone about him – it could only have been her – was selfish. I told no one else about what led me into the false starts, the wrong turns, the dead ends – the way I see my life now, sitting opposite Delia. 'I know. Now I do. I'm sorry.'

For a moment neither of us speaks. Then I say, 'I have dreams about trying to go back to school. But there aren't any uniforms to fit me, or there's some other reason I'm not allowed back in. In one of them Sister Theresa looked angry and bitter. I said, "I was young, I didn't know anything." But she just laughed a mocking laugh. The other night I dreamed I was standing in front of a big cupboard. I'd left all these things behind and I had to face the mess, it was stacked to overflowing. I didn't know where to start, or where to take the stuff. All I knew was I couldn't take it home.'

'Oh, Maggie.'

I can't tell her how I wake from these dreams with a grief as sharp as physical pain.

I don't know what else to say, and as though she senses this, Delia says, 'I'm glad they're holding the conference here. I wanted to see you, of course – and Melbourne's a lovely city.'

'I can see it, but I can't feel it. I think it's because I didn't choose to live here.'

'Why did you stay?'

'My children were born here, I didn't want to uproot them. And their father lived here.'

Delia looks up at the unframed painting on the wall, the blue outline of a nude woman. 'Is that you?'

I laugh. 'No, I painted it in a life class a long time ago. I never finished it.'

'I thought you might have become an artist.'

'I never studied art.' It feels as hard to explain to Delia about my life since school as it was to explain to her then about Lloyd.

When it's time for her to leave, Delia packs her briefcase, and we walk together down the hall and out onto the foot-path. The life in her still burns and warms the air, it seems, on this cold Melbourne day, as it did on winter mornings at St Dominic's, standing beside her waiting for the click of the wooden clapper – the signal to enter the chapel, or after mass to walk along the cloister outside the hall to the refectory. Now she walks ahead of me with the same gait, springing on each foot – almost bouncing: I remember telling her once that she looked airborne, as if she touched the ground only lightly, without depending on it.

A taxi slows for her and stops. 'I'll see you tonight.' She slips inside the taxi and I lose sight of her in moments.

I go back inside and wander through the house as if seeing it for the first time. It's another rented one. Beyond the front room on each floor it is dark. Some of the plaster is peeling and cracked; the paint is flaking on the window-sills. I have an image of the house where Delia's children will live until ready to leave: the trees planted when they were babies, the nurtured garden, the verandahs shaded by vines.

In this house the arrangements in every room are make-shift. All the light shades are made of paper. The kitchen table is too big, bought for another room. Each object my gaze falls on – a vase, a cushion, a lamp – seems to belong to someone else. I have lived in this city as a stranger.

From next door, where an extension to a dilapidated Victorian mansion is being demolished, I can hear the intermit-tent pounding of jackhammers. Until the Health Department closed it down it was a nursing home. Once an old man in a dressing-gown knocked on the front door. When I opened it he begged me to call a taxi to take him home to Ashburton, but, guilty and sad, I took him back to the institution next door. For the rest of that day I felt his displacement: his grief.

Where the stripped brick walls have been prised away they are exposed to the weather, and jagged doorways open onto air. The building has been turned inside out.

When I open the back door to go to the laundry, I notice the dust that shrouds the brick paving and the leaves of the peach tree. I see everything differently now that Delia is here: it is as though everything familiar and solid behind me, as I stand on the step looking down, is being demolished too.

❖

Delia leaves the next morning. I think how strange and yet normal it felt to be sleeping under the same roof, as we did at school for six years. I think how just as on our last day together there – I don't remember saying goodbye before her mother scooped her up, it seemed, into her car and away – our parting feels like an interruption to a long and intense conversation which might never be resumed.

We hug, and Delia shoves her bags into the back of the taxi and says something to the driver, who laughs. She slides into the passenger seat, and is gone.

I stand shivering in the doorway. I'm aware of the blandness of the sky above the tops of the trees and of the backdrop of the buildings opposite, of the now meaningless spaces between the trees in the park at the end of our street. From where I stand, the familiar streets and paths wind away in a maze.

❖

That winter, I lie in bed in the grip of the flu. Delia's visit has shattered my defence against the memories of what happened when I was seventeen, and afterwards. When the noise of the jackhammers stops in the afternoon, the house is quiet except for the sound of the wind, which threatens to shake the house out of its socket. In the pictures of the world framed by the two long windows, I can see the people bend under its weight, the cars plough into it; the trees are acrobatic. The turbulence inside me, and in the city outside, are seamless. Then the rain falls. It plummets. It beats and beats the earth. The gutters overflow.

In the sea of rain, the house is an island. The world I drift in is fluid, the world outside – buildings, trees, trams – is blurred. This house becomes another one that in my mind is always dark. Once, in a feverish dream, I walk in daylight along the path from the gate to the verandah of the house in Abernant. An unseen force propels me to the front door, which opens at my approach into the darkness of night, and I awake in a long forgotten terror.

By the middle of the afternoon it is as dim as twilight, and the darkness and the cold seep through the bricks and mortar; they glide, ghost-like, through the shuddering windowpanes. The room I lie in becomes all the cold, dark rooms where I once lay with Lloyd. Time shifts like water, and I sink further and further into an inward world.

CUMBERLAND

No king or emperor on this earth has
the power of the priest of God.

JAMES JOYCE,
A Portrait of the Artist as a Young Man

On the day I met Lloyd, in the autumn of 1967, I studied in the garden for an hour as usual before the other boarders were awake. I was dressed for mass in my dark green tunic and blazer, and the pixie hood we boarders wore in the colder months. On my left hand was a worn brown glove; my right hand was bare so I could turn the pages of my Latin grammar. I'd won a scholarship to board at the convent, and I was determined to win one to go to university. As I walked the paths of the garden between childhood and adulthood, I could feel myself *being* young, at one with the pure light and air of the new day.

At school, I felt at home: I felt safe. I relished the peacefulness in the early morning, and in the late afternoon when the day pupils had gone home. The antique silence in the chapel. The nuns still wore medieval garments. They sang the Gregorian chant at matins, lauds and vespers: the simple, soothing phrases permeated the chapel walls and faded into fragments in the garden.

The beauty of the place still overwhelmed me: at sunset the row of black camphor laurels at the bottom of the grounds cut out of a red sky; the horizontal seams of slate roofs and violet air at early evening; the architecture of the trees. The cloistered buildings had been there a hundred years and might have been transported whole from Europe. Apart from the gardener, who also milked the cow, the only man we saw was the priest who came to say mass. The chapel bell rang for this at seven o'clock each morning, for the angelus three times a day, and for benediction every Sunday afternoon.

On mornings like this I loved the gauze curtain of mist that softened the light; the red of berries and the copper and gold of leaves; the scent of autumn roses and damp earth; the sting against my skin of an inland autumn morning. In rhythm with my steps, their soft crushing of gravel, I repeated the declensions and conjugations under my breath until I heard the bell ring for mass. At the bottom of the stairs which led to the dormitories, I slipped into place beside Delia in the line of girls on their way to prayers in the hall.

After mass and breakfast, I lingered in the senior library, my favourite place inside the school, where there were books with coloured plates of paintings by van Gogh, Matisse, Manet. When I first saw van Gogh's picture of the stars above the lamplit street I was stunned: struck by a desire, almost physical, to paint everything as I saw it, as I had been compelled to write, when I'd first read *Jane Eyre* and the poems of T.S. Eliot and Gerard Manley Hopkins.

On this morning, I was sitting at a library table drawing the view framed by the nearest window of the town hall clock tower, screened by jacaranda foliage. I had to turn my head to the left to see the view. When I looked in front of me I could see my reflection among the books in the glass door of the bookcase opposite, my fair fringe flopping onto the rims of the heavy black men's glasses I'd picked because they were different. Whenever I put them on to read or draw, I imagined I was the sophisticated, scholarly person I intended to grow into.

The next time I turned my head I saw a priest had stopped beside me, blocking the view. I recognised him as Father Nihill, the new curate, who had said mass in the chapel that morning. He was carrying an LP record under his arm.

I stood up. 'Good morning, Father.'

'G'day. Sit down, no need to stand on ceremony. I've come to give the English lesson.' He showed me the cover of the record. 'Sister Theresa's letting me take over for today. D'you like Simon and Garfunkel?'

'Yes, Father.'

'What's your name, anyway?'

'Maggie, Father. Maggie Reed.'

'Maggie Reed . . . Weren't you the girl they made dux of the school?'

'Yes, Father.'

'I must have seen you at the concert and speech night, that was just after I got here. I thought you looked familiar.'

His smile showed the whitest, most perfect teeth I'd ever seen. His face was the kind that was easy to draw: high forehead, and the bones of cheek and jaw parallel and sharp. It occurred to me for the first time that a priest could be handsome. He wasn't tall, but he seemed to take up more than his share of space in the room.

He looked at me – did I imagine this? – the way an ordinary man might, his gaze travelling slowly from my legs up to my face. I was confused and shy and flattered all at once. I felt self-conscious in my bulky green tunic, thick brown stockings and green jumper, all second-hand: the tunic shiny with wear, the stockings mended many times. The jumper was too big but I liked it that way; it was so long it almost covered my bottom and if I bunched them up over my belt, the pleats of my tunic sticking out below looked like a mini skirt.

The bell had rung for class, how long ago? It seemed that the priest and I had been alone in the library for a long time, but it had been only a few minutes.

Sister Theresa strode in from the landing, habit swishing, rosary beads rattling.

'Morning, Sister,' Father Nihill smiled at her.

I stood up. 'Good morning, Sister.'

'Maggie, why aren't you in class? It's not like you to be late. Good morning, Father.' She nodded at the priest. She didn't smile back. I could tell she didn't want to give up her class.

'My fault, Sister. Maggie and I were just having a bit of a chinwag.'

I felt guilty, although it wasn't my fault.

In the classroom, Sister Theresa sat on the rostrum behind Father Nihill, her hands folded into the sleeves of her habit, her head slightly bowed inside the black veil. Nobody fidgeted or opened her desk lid. We all looked up at the priest. His masculinity and his authority – superior even to Mother Borgia's – altered the atmosphere in the room. He looked up from the record player, one hand lifted in command: 'Listen to this!' Hand still raised, he swayed to the music for a moment, fluttered his fingers to the rhythm of the opening notes, in a parody of how we danced. Some of the girls giggled, they leaned back and stuck out their feet. Rested elbows on desks, chins on hands. His dance movements were cartoon-like. I could tell Sister Theresa wanted to roll her eyes, and I was embarrassed for him.

Simon and Garfunkel; The Beatles; Peter, Paul and Mary; The Rolling Stones: the music of the sixties was new, it was different, and it belonged to us. It chimed with the optimism I felt that I could alter the course of my family's history, with its roots in rigid class and religious conventions, its colonial and working-class lack of confidence, its provincialism, its violent legacy of war. We boarders didn't watch TV or read the newspapers, but music brought us news of the changing world, and it told us we could write our own futures.

'I bet you girls've all heard these songs before.' Father Nihill grinned then glanced behind him. 'Maybe Sister Theresa has too.'

Sister Theresa stared at the wall.

'But I bet none of you knew they were poetry. Hands up anyone who thought they were poetry?'

I put up my hand.

'Maggie? Can you tell us why?'

'Like poetry, I thought they were, because of the alliteration and the assonance.'

Some girls shone in the light of the smile he beamed around the room, others turned away. His arms now spread, now clasped behind his head, he bounded from one side of the rostrum to the other.

'Anything else? What about "I Am a Rock, I Am an Island"?' He spun on his heel, selected an upraised hand. 'Delia, isn't it?'

'It's got metaphors.'

'What are they for? What's the song about? Maggie?'

'It's about alienation.'

'Alienation! That's something we all know about, isn't it, in this modern world? Don't all of us feel alienated a lot of the time?'

I nodded back at him. He kept me in the corner of his gaze.

He turned to another girl. 'Colleen – your name's Colleen, isn't it? – Colleen's shaking her head. Did you want to say something, Colleen?'

'I don't feel alienated.' She sat back with folded arms.

But his grin didn't falter. 'Well, you're a very lucky young lady. I bet all the rest of us do sometimes, don't we? Even some of us in Holy Orders. Of course, I don't know about Sister Theresa here.' He turned to her, laughing as if he'd made a joke, but Sister Theresa cleared her throat – or pretended to, it was hard to tell.

He turned back to his audience. 'Some of us in the church are trying to change that, make it more relevant to you young-sters. They sing folk songs in some churches, did you know that? 'Specially in America. Even play their guitars. I don't think God'd mind.' He tapped a finger on the cover of the record. 'Some of this stuff is real profound.'

When he'd gone, Sister Theresa clapped the record player shut. Her face was red, her frown almost joined her eyebrows together. There was a lightening of air, a lifting of pressure. Girls stretched, they yawned and sighed, as if they'd just woken up. Some laughed.

Colleen Doherty sneered. 'My mother doesn't like his sermons. Some people are going to complain to the bishop.'

'Why?' I said.

Colleen looked at Sister Theresa – who acted as if she hadn't heard – then opened her desk lid, her ruddy face flushing darker. 'Never mind.'

'He looks like Marlon Brando,' someone said.

'No he doesn't.'

'Charlton Heston.'

'Not with that goofy crew-cut.'

'D'you think so?'

'They call them radicals, the ones like him,' someone else said.

'The pill,' another girl whispered behind her hand. 'It's because of what he said in that sermon about the pill.'

'Essay.' Sister Theresa rapped her desk. 'T.S. Eliot, "Prufrock". "What makes this a poem?" Two pages, by Friday. Hurry up, the bell's gone. We've wasted enough time this morning.'

Groans from around the room. Feet shuffled, desk lids dropped.

Delia left for her maths class at the Christian Brothers' school. I followed Sister Theresa to Latin. Whenever I opened the pale blue cover of Virgil's *Georgics*, I entered a place filled with a mellow Mediterranean light, with the buzzing of bees and the rustling of olive leaves and the scent of ripening fruit; but now I was distracted by the memory of a shadow, in the shape of a black suit, falling on the sunlit page, across the ancient landscape.

❖

After school, I bit into the apple I'd picked from one of the big baskets outside the refectory, scuffed my shoe on the gravel. At last Delia broke away from the swarm of girls on the cloister.

'Tomorrow lunchtime,' Colleen called out after her. 'Make sure we're on the same team.'

Delia waved without looking back and fell into step beside me. We followed the path past the hall, the bunches of girls lounging on the steps and leaning over the iron verandah rail. Some of them called out to Delia, who grinned and waved. No one tried to follow us. We walked on out of earshot, past the chapel, the garden, the new science block, the old junior school building.

'Colleen Doherty was so rude to that priest this morning, I don't know how you can like her,' I said.

'She was just giving her opinion.'

'I can't stand her sometimes.'

Delia laughed. 'You said you couldn't stand me once.'

'No I didn't. I said I hated you – and Colleen.'

'We were only teasing you, to bring you out of your shell. You were such a shy, skinny little kid in those days. You looked as if the wind would blow you over. I didn't mean to hurt your feelings, though.'

I remembered how I used to follow the group of girls around the grounds. Delia was always at the centre. I did whatever they dared me to, even if it meant I got into trouble. I'd felt that belonging was a privilege I had to earn. Then, in time, Delia had chosen me. She respected me because I worked hard and was smart. So was she. She could have come first in the class every year, but she didn't need to; she seemed happy to come second after me.

I said, 'Do you remember how you used to correct me every time I said, "you was"? Funny thing is, I didn't mind. Anyone else, I'd have been mortified.'

We reached the bottom paddock, stood in its wide sea of space, of calm air. High above, the plovers wheeled and piped. The sound dissolved like fading chords in the immense quiet that seeped out of the sky. A muted sound of shunting: between the railyards and the row of trees along the fence was a tract of blond, wavy grass, as mysterious and wide as Russia. It reminded me of the film *Dr Zhivago*. Enchanted by the beauty of the landscape, by the romance, I'd seen it three times.

Delia said, 'What about that priest, Father Nihill? How did he know your name?'

'I met him in the library, before class.'

Delia spread her arms, addressed the empty paddock. '"Some of this stuff is real profound."' She hooted. 'I liked him, though. He's different.'

'I liked him too.' Something stopped me from telling her how he'd looked at me. I imagined how she'd laugh to know I'd been flattered by it.

Delia was fair and small, as I was, but with a tanned oval face and an athlete's frame. Delia and Maggie, people said: Maggie and Delia. We ate at the same table in the refectory, shared a desk at study and in class, slept side by side in narrow beds. We sat and talked on steps and stairs, in the basement as we stoked the furnace, in the bottom paddock after school, or on rainy afternoons in a dormer window of the attic, behind the damp stockings strung from wall to wall. We often sat up talking long after lights-out, sitting on the rim of a bath, a blanket hung to hide the light.

We'd never visited each other's homes, in different towns in the Grainger Valley. In the summer holidays, which I always dreaded, Delia swam and sailed with her family at their holiday house on the lake. All her clothes had name tags neatly sewn into them for the laundry. Her father had been to university, her mother played golf. Sister Theresa had once called her 'fortune's child'.

She said, 'Are you applying for university in Coalport?'

'Too close to home. If I get a scholarship, I'll go to Sydney.'

'If I get into Sydney University I'll live at the Catholic college for girls.'

'I can only get into Macquarie without Maths. I wish I could go to Sydney too. It'll be weird not seeing each other every day.'

'If one of us was a boy, we'd be girlfriend and boyfriend.'

I nodded. I couldn't speak.

We leaned on the fence and looked back at the dwindled clutch of steep roofs and mellow walls dominated by the upturned mop of the Cocos Island palm, the crenellated bell tower of the chapel, the statue of Our Lady perched above the first floor of the central cloisters. The shouts of the girls playing softball and tennis were like shouts heard across water.

'Maybe we could go to the same university overseas to do our PhDs,' I said. 'Cambridge. Or the Sorbonne.'

'It'd have to be Cambridge – you know I can't speak French.'

A plover shrieked, flying low. As it dived, we ducked and fled. Beneath the shelter of a willow we lay panting, laughing. The grass was cool and sprinkled with yellow leaves.

'I was chased by crows once, when I was little,' I said. 'It's the first time I remember Dad coming home drunk. I was so scared when they started fighting I ran away into next-door's backyard.'

I remembered standing among the cabbages – their swollen veins, the curling lips of their leaves – and how when the crows swooped down I couldn't move or call for help.

Delia gazed up into the dome, its warp and weft of leaves and sky. 'I still can't believe no one tried to stop it.'

It was a long time since I'd told Delia about my life at home, one rainy afternoon in the attic. We'd never talked about it since.

I said, 'You haven't told anyone else, have you?'

'Of course not.'

'The next-door neighbours used to call the police, but when they came he pulled himself together. One night we were standing behind him at the front door when they arrived. I was so relieved to see them, but Dad said, "Nothing to worry about here, mate – you know what women are like." And the police went away.'

'Did your mother ever try to escape?'

'Once, when I was little, she took us all to stay at Aunty Joan's. At night-time we used to stand in the hall with the lights off, listening to him try to kick the front door down. Aunty Joan swore at him. One day Grandma brought the parish priest to see Mum. He told her she had to go back because Catholics aren't allowed to get divorced. Of course, she had to do what the priest said. I don't know how she can believe all that stuff.'

Delia was frowning and chewing on a grass stalk.

'A couple of years ago I went to the phone box at dawn and rang the police. I told them I was scared my father was going to kill my mother. And the policeman said, "We don't interfere in domestic arguments, love."'

Delia shook her head. 'You going home this weekend?'

'Not unless Mother Borgia makes me.'

'I want to go sailing with Dad.' She sat up, chin on knees. 'I was just wondering what we'll be doing at' – she looked at her watch – 'twenty past four in the afternoon in exactly a year's time.'

'Ten years. Wonder who we'll be with?'

'Wonder what they're doing right now? What if it's our husbands?' Delia laughed. 'Imagine us being married.'

'I couldn't stand it. But you don't have to get married. Look at Simone de Beauvoir and Jean-Paul Sartre. Remember I told you about them when I read that book? When she saw me with it Sister Theresa said Simone de Beauvoir was Sartre's non-wife. He's a philosopher, too. I want to study philosophy at university.'

'I wonder what we'll be like?'

The two people I wanted most to be like were Picasso and Simone de Beauvoir. But Picasso was a man. To live like Simone de Beauvoir and those people whose photos I'd seen in books, working at their desks in their book-lined rooms with the shadows of the balcony railings scribbled on the long white curtains, or sitting together at cafe tables on the footpath – the *footpath* – in the afternoons, you just had to be good at work and work hard, didn't you? Sometimes I felt the power surge in me as sap must, secretly, in the veins of trees.

'It's getting late,' Delia said. 'We'd better go to study.'

We got up, and parted the curtain of branches and shook ourselves free of leaves.

'Wait,' I said. 'Just look a minute how the light's changed.'

As we watched, the sun began to slip behind the camphor laurels at the bottom fence. The high horizon there was gilded. Above us the sky paled, around us the shadows grew and overlapped. Its source invisible, the light was one with air, the earth was sky. We stood a moment longer, then turned and walked back, it seemed, along the floor of the universe.

❖

A few days later I heard Father Nihill's voice in the courtyard at recess. Through the classroom window I saw the knot of green tunics tighten around his black suit. When I joined them he caught my eye, but I shied away.

I glanced back and he said, 'G'day, Maggie,' as if he'd known me all my life.

'Good morning, Father.'

'How come it's always you who comes here?' Colleen Doherty stood with folded arms. 'None of the other priests ever do, except to say mass.'

'Don't you want to see me?' He tilted an eyebrow and circulated a crooked smile.

'Yes we do, Father!' A chorus. But I looked down at my shoes: one lace was short, the other long.

Delia said, 'Next you'll be asking us to call you by your first name, Father.'

'Lloyd. You can call me Lloyd.' Some girls giggled, others stood shocked into silence. Colleen shook her head.

He was looking at me again, sidelong, for such a long moment that it seemed he was speaking only to me. I thought I felt a disturbance in the air, as though he'd taken a step towards me, but then I realised it was inside me.

Delia laughed. 'I wasn't serious!' She and Colleen were on their way to physics class at the Brothers' school, in their hats and gloves. Delia waved and walked to the gate, Colleen stomped after her. Delia called out, 'See you, Father Lloyd.'

Only Delia would have dared to use his Christian name, but she still called him 'Father'. Nuns and priests were like people born into royalty, but they were even more superior, because they were supposed to have been personally called by God. When my mother spoke to a priest on the church steps after mass, she said 'Father' after practically every sentence and used the kind of smile and tone people do when talking to someone whose authority they respect and fear. I thought of myself as an atheist, but I still felt like my mother did – like a Catholic.

Father Nihill said, 'Matter of fact, apart from enjoying the pleasure of you young ladies' company,' – mock bow, giggling from the crowd – 'I thought I should get to know you all a bit, since I'm in charge of the Young Catholic Society this year. I hope you seniors are going to join, if you haven't already? You know about the dance every Saturday night at the Parish Hall – and I'm organising a group for the big folk concert we're putting on later in the year. Danny Armstrong and I are going to give guitar lessons, for anyone who wants to learn.'

He held an imaginary guitar and mimed strumming with a blur of fingers, and laughed. 'Anyone here play already?'

'Maggie Reed,' someone said.

Everyone turned to look at me.

'Maggie? Is that so?'

'A bit. I mean, I can play a few chords. Danny taught me some.'

'Did he just? Can you come to our practice sessions after school, up in the hall?'

'If I'm allowed to.'

'I'll have a word to Sister, if you like. What've you got next?'

I could hear the frenzied clanging of the bell. The crowd trickled away.

'English, Father.'

'You seem to know a lot about poetry.' I half turned away but his gaze kept me there, though Sister Theresa was probably already on her way upstairs to class.

'English is my favourite.' I took a step back.

'You ever read *The Catcher in the Rye*?'

The bell stopped ringing.

'No, Father.'

If I was late for class, I'd get into trouble. But I couldn't walk away from a priest. I didn't want to: the way he looked at me made me feel pretty, even without make-up and in my uniform.

'J.D. Salinger, American bloke. Terrific book – think you'd like it. See you later.'

The courtyard was empty. He waved as he turned and walked towards the gate.

'Morning, Father.' I turned and sped up the stairs, glimpsed the tail of Sister Theresa's veil flick out of sight on the landing above.

❖

The casement window, sill level with library table, opened wide on its hinges onto slate roofs, sky. The mild sky flowed into the room.

Opposite me, Delia frowned over some complicated maths problem. After fourth year, she had chosen maths and science subjects. I had chosen history, ancient and modern, and Latin and French. We sat together in class only for English, but after school we studied at this table, just big enough for two. I ran the pad of my thumb over the groove inside the third finger of my right hand, calloused from writing and drawing, and looked at Delia intently. I drew the tiny cleft between her brows, my biro tense between fingers and paper, moving of its own accord, cross-hatching rapidly, from eyes to cheekbones: their symmetry, their slant. I lifted the biro down to the mouth.

When I glanced up again to memorise its shape Delia was watching. 'Have you finished your homework?'

'Don't talk. Go back to how you were before. Turn your head this way . . . that's enough. Just got to finish an essay – I'll do it tonight.'

'Are you going to the dance next Saturday? Danny asked me if you were. I said we probably will.'

But I wasn't thinking about Danny, I was thinking how Father Nihill would have to be there, now he was in charge of the YCS.

I said, 'It's getting late, I'd better go to the library and change my book.'

But when I stood up and looked out of the window, the air was silky against my face and neck; it opened out above the roofs and I saw how, thousands of miles away, it deepened from lavender to purple. How come everyone didn't stop a hundred times a day and stare at things like this? I forced myself to move away.

On the landing, I looked up from pulling on my gloves and saw Father Nihill standing at the bottom of the stairs, one hand on the banister post, the other against the wall. He grinned up at me, his face like a face from a dream, his foreshortened figure black against the doorway onto the courtyard. I looked down and saw the crowns of his thigh muscles stretching the cloth of his trousers. When I met his eyes, my face and neck felt hot.

'Good afternoon, Father, you gave me a fright.' No one ever came inside the gate after school.

'G'day, Maggie. I thought all you girls were studying at this time of day?'

'I'm going up the street.'

'I thought you weren't allowed?'

'Sister Theresa lets me go to the library in the town. I've read all the books in ours.' I took another step down, but he didn't move.

He said, 'What's that book you've got?'

I held it up. '*Life with Picasso* by Françoise Gilot. She was his . . . she was his mistress.'

We stood looking at one another. My other hand was sweaty, it stuck to the banister.

'Was she, eh? That'd be interesting, I suppose.'

'Yes, it is.' I took a few more steps. I was close enough to touch him.

'You read *The Catcher in the Rye* yet?'

'They might have it in the library, I'll have a look.'

'Let me know what you think, when you read it.'

'All right, Father.'

I took another step, but still he stood clutching the knob of the banister post. I could see the pores in the back of his hand, the glistening ginger hairs, the swollen fingertips where he'd bitten his nails. These contradicted his manly bulk, his black suit, his stiff white collar. The emptiness of the stairs behind me and of the classrooms on either side of the hall seemed to connect us, as if we were the only two people alive in an empty world.

'Excuse me, please, Father.'

'Sure, Maggie.'

As he moved aside, the hem of my tunic brushed the cloth of his trousers. I felt a sensation like hackles rising, all along that side of my body.

Before I reached the door, I heard the clicking of rosary beads on a nun's belt, a familiar soft but purposeful tread. I turned to see Sister Theresa looking from me to Father Nihill.

'G'day, Sister.' He smiled widely.

'What are you doing down here, Maggie?' Sister Theresa turned from me to the priest. 'Good afternoon, Father. Is there something you wanted?'

'I was just on my way to the library, Sister.' I held up my book.

'Very well then. Make sure you're back before tea.'

'Yes, Sister.' I moved towards the door.

Father Nihill said, 'Matter of fact, there is, Sister, I thought you might be around and then I ran into Maggie here.'

Sister Theresa frowned at him.

'Maggie!' he said. 'Wait a minute, Maggie, I came over to ask Sister Theresa about letting some of you girls come to concert practice.'

Sister Theresa regarded him without blinking, her eyes narrowed beneath her dark eyebrows.

'This concert's going to be a big thing in the parish, especially for the young folks. We need ones like Maggie, who can play the guitar. And singers. I heard your choir at the speech night. I was really impressed.'

Sister Theresa lifted her chin. 'What kind of concert, Father?'

'Folk music. It'd be a good way to get young people to stay in the church. A lot of them are losing interest, there's too much else around these days to attract their attention. They don't think the church's relevant to them anymore.'

'Relevant.' Sister Theresa looked at me. 'The girls in sixth year don't even have time for the choir. You're still going for a scholarship, aren't you, Maggie?'

'Yes, Sister.' Stiff with tension, with suspense, I faced the gap between the nun and priest.

'What if Maggie gave up going to the library for the time being? Just on Tuesdays for now, so she could fit in a bit of practice and still get all her homework done. Later it'll probably be a bit more often.' As he spoke he looked at me.

'It's not just a question of homework, in sixth year,' Sister Theresa said. 'But knowing Maggie . . . Well, Maggie?'

'I'd make sure I finished all my homework, Sister. I could still study as well.' I imagined that the concert was an excuse, that what he really wanted was to see me. I felt the same euphoria as when I won an award.

'Just on Tuesdays, five till six, up in the hall.' Father Nihill rocked back on his heels.

Sister Theresa sighed. 'Make sure you get all your work done, Maggie.'

'Yes, Sister, thank you, Sister. Good afternoon, Father. Good afternoon, Sister.'

'Folk music.' Sister Theresa shook her head, she reached behind her for her back scapular, snapped it like shutting a fan, turned and ascended the stairs with her precise steps.

'See you, Maggie,' Father Nihill called. 'See you soon.' But I was already halfway to the gate. I slipped through it and along onto Main Street. Before I crossed the road I had to wait and catch my breath, as though I'd been running. I looked across at the library, which reminded me of the smaller one in Abernant they'd demolished years ago, the first one I ever entered, to find a place of sanctuary and enchantment. I remembered it as it had been on winter afternoons: its white bulk beside the green mass of the pines, its two long windows lit so it shone like a lantern in the dreary town. Inside it the block of calm.

I stepped off the kerb. I couldn't wait to dawdle in the hushed, narrow aisles between the dusty shelves, each book a passage through other people's minds to other worlds.

❖

Although officially I was a weekly boarder, I stayed at school as often as I could get away with it – until Easter, when everyone had to go home. Even the girls from New Guinea and Thailand and Hong Kong went to stay with families in the Valley.

The afternoon school broke up, I lingered over my homework in the empty library. I could hear the excited voices in the courtyard below – *Hooray! See you after Easter! Have a good holiday!* By the time I walked out of the gate the place was empty. Even the nuns had vanished behind the cloisters.

The eighteen-mile bus trip home to Abernant always seemed quicker than the one to school. On the other side of Stirling Heights Cumberland disappeared, and the blue-grey eucalypts enveloped the bus. But on the edges of the small and even smaller towns, the trees had been cleared for mines.

I got off at the depot in Quarry Street and dawdled into Blacket Road. Passing St Paul's primary school, I remembered the smell of bananas ripening in the satchels hanging from the hooks on the verandah and the milk turning sour in the crates before playtime on hot summer mornings: the smells of boredom, and fear of the St Joseph nuns, with their cutting canes and tongues.

I'd been frightened to go to school in the morning, frightened to go home in the afternoon. Johnny and Billy at St Paul's, Anne at the St Joseph nuns' high school, Luke at the Christian Brothers' in Cumberland – still felt this fear every day: its cold, mineral taste; the lump in your chest, as if you'd swallowed a stone. I was lucky, but the relief of my escape was complicated by guilt. Now, on my way home, I felt only dread.

As usual, I could hear my father bellowing before I reached the house. When I shut the door behind me, I saw everyone bunched together in the hall. They turned and stared.

'Where've you been?' My mother seemed shrunken barefoot; her face was crumpled. 'I was getting worried.'

'Oh, look who's here!' my father shouted. 'Lady bloody Muck. Thought you was too good for us, you stuck-up bitch?'

I stood apart holding my port, embarrassed by the formality of my blazer and hat and gloves. 'I had to do some homework first. I needed to use the library.'

'When're you gonna do the decent thing and get a job, instead of usin' up all my money to go to boardin' bloody school? You're turning into a lazy slut, just like your bloody mother.'

'She doesn't cost you a cent,' my mother said. 'She pays her own way with her scholarship. Leave her alone, she just got in the door.' In the wall beside my mother's head there was a hole in the plaster where he'd tried to punch her years

33

ago, but she'd ducked just in time. I noticed the bruises, yellow and purple like pansies, on her soft white arms.

My father jabbed a finger into my shoulder. 'High time you left school and got a decent job. No use winning prizes if they don't bring in any dough.'

I felt the pressure of tears behind my eyes. Often he spent all his wages on gambling and grog. Our grandmother had sometimes brought us food. One time I'd had to stay away from school because I had no shoes. Since Billy had started school my mother supported us on her shop assistant's pay, she'd even bought me a cheap guitar on lay-by the Christmas before, but there were still many things we went without.

'Don't cry,' my mother said to me. 'You're no use to me if you're going to cry.'

'What did you have to come home for?' Luke hissed. 'It only makes it worse when you come home.'

'Oh, for gawd's sake.' My father groaned, he threw up his arms and rolled his eyes theatrically. 'The things a man has to put up with. You wouldn't bloody credit it, if you wasn't here. You can all go and get fucked, the bloody lot of you.'

He swung away from me and pushed the others aside. They shifted apart. Here the hall widened into the lounge room, and he tottered as on a tilting floor towards his chair.

I lifted Billy and kissed him.

'Put him down,' my mother said. 'He's too big to be picked up now.'

'He's still my boy, aren't you, Billy?' I said.

He looked uncertain, but yielded his small, warm body. His hair was fragrant, his breath brushed my cheek. Fortified, I put him down, propping him on his coltish legs.

I changed out of my uniform and went into the kitchen. I could hear my father shouting again, reciting his litany of my mother's faults and the faults of all her family, of us children: we were all the same, we were hopeless, we were no good. Nobody understood him, nobody cared whether he lived or died.

'That's for sure,' my mother muttered.

She sat at the table, and Luke poured her a cup of tea. I ate the stew she had kept warm for me. Anne was giving Johnny and Billy their bath. When my father was drunk, we hovered around to keep watch, ready to defend my mother in the next attack, or make her cups of tea, or stop the little boys from upsetting her.

Years ago, when I was little, in the late afternoons while we were waiting for him to come home drunk, she used to sing – there must have been other songs, but 'Somewhere Over the Rainbow' was the one I remembered. I could still see the smiling mask of her face, hear the extraordinary sound fill the kitchen as if the radio were on. The singing had made me feel lonely and sad. Now my mother never sang, not even in the choir at church, where she had been a soloist.

I finished eating, and I took Billy and Johnny into their bedroom and tucked them in and closed the door. When there was a lull in my father's shouting I took their fingers out of their ears. 'Once upon a time, two little boys used to live inside the hollow trunk of an old tree, in the middle of the bush . . .'

Billy was soon asleep. In the light from the streetlamp that came under the blind, I saw that he still slept as he had in his cot, his feet tangled in the blankets, his arms flung up beside his head in an attitude of surrender. He looked so defenceless I blinked away tears. Johnny nodded off, and I closed the door and crept out into the hall.

When I was passing the lounge room, my father called out to me: 'Come and light us a smoke, Mags.'

I was the only one he had a nickname for, and it embarrassed me. I was glad he hardly ever used it now.

'In a minute, Dad.' If I went in to him he'd make me stay and listen to his shouting, belittling my mother, and worse: I'd be trapped.

I slipped into the kitchen where the others were sitting around the table.

'Better do what he says,' Luke said.

Anne nodded.

'I don't want to go in there,' I said.

But he was suddenly behind me. 'I knew it,' he yelled. 'I knew you'd come crawling to your mother. You're just like the rest of them.'

He went for my mother but Luke blocked him off, arms upheld and crossed in front of his face. Anne and I bundled my mother away into our room. Luke sneaked in after us, and the four of us hid behind the door.

Through the crack between door and jamb I watched my father prowl. 'When I find her I'll fuckin' murder her,' he bellowed. He turned and seemed to look right into my eyes. When he was drunk he looked shorter, he was all muscle and bulk, his body a weapon. He lurched towards the room.

'He's coming in here,' I whispered. 'He's got the poker.'

It was hard not to scream. In my mind, I walked in the garden behind the chapel, and I heard the soft chanting of the nuns singing matins in the chancel. But my heartbeat was so loud I couldn't concentrate.

My father burst into the room and turned on the light. He lunged at my mother. Luke tried to wrestle the poker from him. Anne and I tugged at his belt and his arms. He swiped us off. My mother pummelled his chest. We tried to squeeze between them, we begged him to leave her alone. Everyone was yelling. Then, as if in slow motion, I saw blood oozing out of the tear in my mother's forehead, trickling down and dripping onto the black hairs of an eyebrow. The poker wafted, it seemed, onto the carpet, and time resumed its normal speed.

My mother was wailing in outrage and pain. I could hear Billy and Johnny crying in their room. My father kicked the poker against the wall. He staggered into the lounge room where in between attacks he camped in his chair, beside the little coffee table with his bottles and glasses, his cigarettes and ashtray, set out on the rings of dried beer.

Luke and I held my mother up while Anne blotted the blood with a hanky. I was stricken at the sight of my mother's blood. It was my fault, because I hadn't obeyed him.

In the kitchen, Anne washed the wound and taped a wad of gauze to it. I put the kettle on. We made tea at times like this, as though it were time to relax and have a break. I dropped two Aspros into a glass of water and tilted it to my mother's lips.

Soon we heard the scrabbling sound of my father getting out of his chair, and the menacing drop in the volume of his voice. This time we hid my mother in the yard. One hour might have passed, or four, or three. I was bored, I was tired, I was scared. Was this what he had felt like, creeping through the jungle in New Guinea, the Japanese snipers hiding in the trees?

'I don't know what I've done to deserve this,' my mother said.

'You haven't done anything to deserve it,' Anne said.

'At least you children'll be able to get away one day.'

Anne said, 'We wouldn't want to leave you here.'

'You don't have to worry about us,' I said.

'You make sure you keep on studying hard, Maggie.' My mother sighed. 'I never had a chance like you've got. If you children can make something of yourselves, it might've all been worthwhile.'

'Dad said I had to leave school and get a job.'

'Over my dead body.'

But I had already made up my mind that if he tried to make me stay at home, I'd run away to school.

My eyes burned, my body ached. A craving for sleep over-whelmed me, like thirst. At last the darkness paled, and in the east, between cloud and horizon, a sliver of sky glowed gold.

'Listen,' Anne said, after it'd been quiet for a long time.

I tiptoed in through the back door. When I was home it was my turn. I found my father in the bedroom, sprawled in his clothes inside the hollow on his side of the kapok mattress, the blankets flung aside. He lay on his back, his eyes closed, his mouth open. A lit cigarette dangled from his fingers. I glided forward, stepping over the boards that always creaked beneath the carpet.

My hand shook as I reached over to take the cigarette from between his tobacco-stained fingers. But I had to put it out: once he had gone to sleep with a lit one and the mattress had caught fire. Just in time we smelt the smoke, pushed him off the bed and rushed with the mattress down the hall. When we flung it out into the yard it had exploded.

His head rolled towards me. I froze, but his eyes stayed shut. I eased the cigarette out from his grip as if it were a live grenade. When it was safe my mother would be able to go to bed. Every night my parents slept side by side in this bed. But they never smiled at one another, or kissed, or spoke except in anger.

Tied to the bed by the slender threads of sleep, my father snored. I stabbed the cigarette into the stinking, overflowing ashtray on the bedside table. Hardly game to breathe, I crept out of the room.

❖

Every morning at home I woke to the nausea, to the questions – what did anything matter? why were we here? – that surfaced in the cloudy space between sleeping and waking. But today, as I reached beneath the pillow for my book, I remembered it was Sunday and the pubs were shut.

I was the only one who went to early mass. My grandfather waited outside in his car, the engine running. I got in beside him and kissed him on the cheek.

'How's school?' my grandfather said.

'Good thanks, Granddad.'

We drove in silence. My grandfather's presence was like the presence of the statues inside the church, which, now it was Easter Sunday, were divested of the purple cloths that had hidden them during Lent. The windows in the low, modern vault let in the sun, which lit the clouds of incense and the gilded chasuble of the priest. The altar was ablaze with flowers and candle-flames among the branches of dazzling brass. The stone was rolled away from the cave.

My grandfather drove me home afterwards, stopping off at the newsagent's so I could buy the papers for my father. My grandmother was waiting outside in her big yellow Dodge to drive the others to the later mass. Even if they went to the same mass, my grandparents drove in separate cars and sat in separate pews. Like the violence at home, this was never talked about, as if it were normal. My grandmother looked straight ahead through the windscreen and not at the house because my father was inside. I kissed her hollow cheek through the car window. I had never seen her smile.

'G'day, Grandma.'

'G'day, Maggie. I hope you're learning how to be a refined young lady, at the convent.'

'I don't know, Grandma. I suppose so.'

My grandparents had made money managing pubs. They'd paid for my mother to board at St Dominic's before me, so she'd learn to be a lady and marry a good Catholic. My father had been born a Protestant. He'd become a Catholic to marry my mother, but he wasn't practising. I knew my grandparents didn't approve of him because of this, and because he got drunk.

My mother lowered herself into the front seat while the others scrambled into the back. She was wearing a long-sleeved cardigan – too warm for the mild autumn day – to hide her bruised arms, a hat that hid the gauze dressing on her forehead, and lipstick and rouge to hide her pallor.

In the lounge room my father was sitting in his chair, reading a murder mystery from the library. He also liked to borrow the *Reader's Digest* and the *Saturday Evening Post*. When he was sober, he read all the time: in his chair even while he ate, or at the table, where he sat only for breakfast. If he didn't have a book, he read the labels on the sauce bottles – anything in print.

When he and my mother had been engaged and separated by the war, he'd written her long romantic poems: my mother said he was brilliant. Now, a long way from his family who were in Sydney, he worked in menial jobs for the council, collecting garbage, cleaning public toilets, mending the roads. I thought this must be the reason he got drunk. But I didn't understand how he could hurt the people he was supposed to love.

I'd given up hoping that my success at school would make him happy or proud. When my mother made me tell him – always on a Sunday – I'd come first in the class, he just nodded and kept reading. I felt guilty for being at school, and deflated, because he didn't value my hard work, which everyone else praised and even rewarded me for.

Now I handed him the newspapers and he took them without looking up. His clothes were clean, his hair was washed and combed. The feather of smoke from his cigarette rose up into the air above his head, circled it, and dispersed into a blue mist that filled the room. Mixed with the smell of the smoke was the smell of stale beer that lingered, even though he'd taken the empty bottles outside, building a pyramid of them against the garage wall.

I could see the dust clogging the rigging of the wooden sailing ship he had carved before I'd been born. Next to it on the sideboard was a framed photo of him and my mother on their wedding day, outside the old church on the edge of the town: my father in his army uniform, my mother in her satin dress. The shadow of the pine trees in the cemetery darkened the church. The hot February wind lifted my mother's veil and the corner of her train. The dust it carried mingled with the dust on the glass of the frame.

In the house was the silence that follows a storm. After breakfast, I went into my room and did some Latin exercises. Before I'd left for St Dominic's, my father would take the comics out of the newspapers for me every Sunday. Sometimes in those days, if he came home from work sober before going out again to the pub, he would ask me to dig out of his hand the splinters he'd got from the handles of the pick and shovel he used when working on the roads. He said I had the gentlest touch. He would stand patiently while I dipped the needle in a flame then probed at the calloused skin of his blistered palm. He'd always called me 'Mags'. Once, with a brief and mysterious enthusiasm, he grew strawberries in the overgrown garden down the side, and when they ripened he picked the largest one and held it out to me where I stood beside him, full of wonder and hope.

But when I'd become a teenager he'd turned against me, and I was ashamed of my swelling breasts, of the hair that grew in private places, and the blood that flowed out of me each month.

Now I left him sitting in his chair reading the *Sydney Morning Herald* and went into the kitchen to peel the potatoes. The others were always late, because my mother, wearing her red-painted smile, would stand talking on the church steps after mass. But none of the people she talked to ever came to our house, and no one came to see my father, either.

At home, my mother took off the smile with her good shoes and hat and dress. She cooked and carved the roast. On the table, she set aside the plate with the largest helping.

'Take that in to your father,' she said to me. 'Take it in to Dr Jekyll.' She wore the dignity and the righteousness of her moral victory.

When I crossed the invisible line between the hall and the lounge room, I felt like a collaborator.

'Here you are, Dad.' I handed him the plate.

He took it, mumbling, 'Ta.'

Did he remember what he'd done? Was he sorry? Maybe this different person would apologise: explain. But it was a long time since I'd hoped for this. All day he sat alone in his distant, silent world. On Sunday, it was my father who was beaten.

I couldn't wait to go back to school, to work hard. If I didn't win a scholarship, I'd never escape.

❖

One afternoon in the Cumberland library, as I scanned the titles in a fiction aisle, I felt a presence close behind me.

'Maggie.' A man's voice whispered my name.

Startled, I turned around.

It was Father Nihill. I'd never seen him here before. He grinned at me.

'Good afternoon, Father.'

I had found one of the books I'd been looking for but now I forgot the title of the other; his proximity seemed to displace everything else in my mind.

'You find *The Catcher in the Rye* yet?'

'Someone else's borrowed it, Father. I asked if I could have it next.'

'I borrowed it myself from a mate, otherwise I'd lend it to you.'

I looked around, worried that someone might hear us. Talking in the library, even whispering, wasn't allowed. But of course no one would remind a priest.

He'd made himself comfortable, one elbow leaning on a shelf, facing me and taking up all the space in the aisle. He stood so close to me it felt exciting and dangerous, like standing on the edge of the high diving board at the baths.

'Are you looking for a book, Father?'

He shook his head. 'Thought I might find you here, this time of day. Can you come outside? There's something I've been wanting to ask you.'

I took my book to the desk and Father Nihill went out into the street. What could he want?

Outside, I caught up with him half a block away where he'd parked his old green car.

'Anyone teaching you how to drive?'

'We haven't got a car, Father.'

'Would you like to learn?'

'You mean you teach me? I don't know, Father, I've never thought about it. I don't think I'd be allowed.'

'Nobody has to know – it can be just between us, for now. You could meet me sometimes after school when you go to the library. You've got a bit of time left, haven't you, before you have to be back? Why don't we start now?'

He opened the passenger-side door and I got in. I felt the sharp thrill of breaking a rule, as when Delia and I used to sneak out to buy fish and chips after lights-out. But surely I wasn't doing anything wrong now?

'Better to start you off where there's no traffic.'

He drove away, the two of us sitting side by side in the enclosed space as though it were the most ordinary thing in the world to do. At the town's edge, where the farmland began, Father Nihill turned onto a narrow, deserted road and stopped. On either side, lucerne grew higher than the car, as though to hide us. He motioned for me to slide closer to him on the bench seat so I could watch him demonstrate how to use the pedals and the gears. We were almost touching. The atmosphere was complicated, like the atmosphere between girls and boys at a dance. I could barely concentrate.

Finally he opened the door and got out. 'Okay, now you have a go.'

I slid behind the wheel and he swung himself into the other side. He sat so close to me that our sleeves touched.

'Turn it on, like I showed you.'

The engine rumbled and vibrated. I drove off slowly as he instructed and changed into second.

I let out the clutch too quickly and the engine stalled. He laughed.

I started the car again, and he watched my legs while I worked the pedals. The movement made my tunic ride up, exposing my thighs. He looked at my legs and smiled: I was relieved he didn't make eye contact. I was so self-conscious I failed to coordinate accelerator and clutch. The car moved and bucked and stopped.

'Sorry, Father, I just have to get used to it.'

'You'll soon get the hang of it. One more try.'

This time the car moved slowly along the road. I laughed, delighted.

'Good girl! Just go down to that turn-off, see? I'll back in there and turn around . . . That's good. Now pull over here. Gently on the brake.'

What if someone came out onto the road? I pushed the brake too hard, and the car jerked to a stop. He reached across and turned off the engine. I felt a sensation as if he'd actually touched me and imprinted my body with the shape of his arm.

'I have to get back,' I said. Although the window was open and cool air flowed into the car, I felt hot and I was sure my face was bright pink.

He drove us back into town. He leaned an elbow on the frame of the open window and steered with one hand, his easy confidence in contrast with my clumsy efforts. We reached the library as it was closing.

'Might as well drop you off here. You'll make a good driver, Maggie. You just need more lessons and a lot of practice. Could you get away Thursday afternoons, say, and meet me in the car park behind the cathedral?'

'Yes, Father.' I couldn't wait to be alone with him again. Not since my piano lessons in earlier years had an adult paid me such concentrated regard.

Every week after that I drove through the back streets, and once we went onto the highway. On Thursdays I woke up as excited as I did on my birthday. I hadn't felt like this since my piano lessons with Sister Bonaventure. She used to lean back and close her eyes and let me play by ear. When she rang the chapel bell for mass she'd beckon me from the line on the cloister into the belfry, and let go the heavy rope when I took hold. One spring morning, while I rang the bell, she picked a jasmine flower and held it out to me. I pressed it in my missal; its fragrance reminded me of her. Colleen Doherty had teased me for having a crush on Sister Bonaventure, but I didn't care. Then, when I came back to school at the beginning of fifth year, she was gone, transferred to Coalport. I'd grieved, and recovered, and was happy again. Now Father Nihill's presence became a gravitational force as Sister Bonaventure's had been. I was aware of him when he wasn't there, attuned to his possible movements, rushing to driving lessons and concert practice as though falling involuntarily through space.

❖

On a sunny Saturday morning in winter, Delia and I stripped our beds and remade them, our freshly washed hair wrapped in towels, the dormitory filled with the flapping and snapping of sheets and the buzz of voices freed from weekday silence.

My hair still wet, I swung open the gate and stepped before Delia down onto the street. I could hear a Beatles song – 'Penny Lane' – spilling out of open windows from people's radios. How lucky I was to be young now, to be different from my parents, whose youth was frozen in black and white, shadowed by the Depression and war that still seemed to dim the house, its rooms never fully opened to the light. There'd never be a photo of me on a sideboard in a wedding dress and veil.

On the cracked tessellated tiles of Danny's verandah, we pulled off our hats and gloves. Mrs Armstrong opened the door. She was always happy to see us. She was white-haired but not old, and so small we both looked down on her. Music poured from the lounge room into the hall.

'Michael's here already,' she said. 'You can go and get changed in Danny's room. He's gone to pick up his new record. He even cleaned up in there for you this morning, Maggie.'

Since we were sixteen, girls from the convent and boys from the Christian Brothers' had been allowed to go to the Young Catholic Society dances, because they were supervised by the priests. There we'd somehow formed pairs, Danny and me, and Delia and Michael Cullen. Tonight I'd sleep in Danny's bed while he slept on the hard old couch. Tomorrow I'd go home, and my father would be sober.

In the summer holidays the four of us caught the train to Coalport beach. Sometimes in winter Danny took me to see a film. On our way home from a dance at the end of fifth year, I was puzzled as to why he was leading me off the street into the lane behind his house. He stopped beside a pole in a cone of light and I saw the serious look on his face and I understood. He turned to face me and leaned across the cobblestones in the space between us, holding both my hands. His lips were soft and moist and he opened them slightly and poked the tip of his tongue between mine. I struggled to suppress a nervous laugh.

Now in Danny's room I changed into another oversized jumper and a miniskirt. Delia put on her skirt – knee-length; she didn't care about fashion – and a checked shirt under a crew-necked jumper. She rolled her eyes while I put on my blue eyeshadow, and my eyeliner and lipstick.

The front door banged, and Danny plunged into the hall. 'Had this on order.' He held up the record album. He was breathless. On the cover was a photo of The Beatles dressed in shiny uniforms, among a brightly coloured crowd. 'It just came in.' He smiled and looked away.

'You've got the new one!' Delia said.

Danny's face was round; he had no sharp edges to him anywhere. When he walked, he carried his head and shoulders slightly ahead of the rest of him, as though he couldn't wait to get to where he was going. If you called out to him he ducked before he turned around. I remembered the sound of his breathing in the picture theatre and the warmth of his sweaty hand. He liked watching James Bond films. He wanted to own an E-type Jag. Sometimes, on my way back to school from the library, I sat in the cathedral and listened to him practising the organ. I never told him this. He loved to play Bach. He created shimmering sculptures of sound that balanced in the air beneath the vaulted ceiling after he had lifted his hands from the keys.

I said to him, 'Thanks for making your bed for me.'

Danny's gaze swerved past me, and he blinked. 'That's all right,' he muttered, as though overcome by the sight of us out of uniform.

All afternoon we sat crammed into the lounge room, on the floor in the space between the big old-fashioned armchairs and couch, listening to the new album. The music connected us. It was something we could share only with one another.

Danny jumped up to play 'Lucy in the Sky with Diamonds' again. 'Did you hear that?' he said. His face was pink, his eyes shone.

'Is it a synthesiser?' Michael said.

'No,' Danny said. 'That's a Mellotron.'

He worked out the chords of some songs on his guitar. He showed me how to play a bar chord, standing behind me and pressing my fingers beneath his against the strings. My happiness seemed to fill the room, to spill out into the bright afternoon.

❖

After tea, when the other two had gone to Michael's and I was ready for the dance, I found Danny waiting in the lounge room. From the kitchen I could hear the sound of running water and the clatter of cutlery, the clink of plates. I stood in front of the fat armchair Danny sat in next to the fireplace, his hands resting palms down on its arms, his legs crossed. I could tell that the chair was his father's, and that his father sat in it like that. I'd never seen his father, and nobody mentioned him, either. Michael had told Delia that sometimes Danny's father didn't come home at night.

'Aren't we going to go?' I said.

Danny lifted his hand and made a twirling gesture. 'Turn around. Slowly.'

I turned around while he watched.

He said gruffly, 'You look good in those kinds of dresses.' At that moment, he emitted a masculinity that charged the atmosphere in the room. I was wearing my favourite mini-dress, with a black bodice and orange skirt. It made me feel grown-up. I liked to dress as fashionably as I could in the few clothes my mother could afford on lay-by from the Co-op Store in Abernant.

The YCS dances were nothing like the ones the nuns held each term in the school hall. They taught us old-fashioned dances like the barn dance and the Pride of Erin, the kind that kept bodies mostly apart and partners changing. We girls giggled and blushed self-consciously at the touch of the sweaty, clumsy boys from the Christian Brothers', under the scrutiny of the brothers and the nuns. Before the dance we lined up in our dresses and skirts – we weren't allowed to wear mini-skirts – while Mother Borgia inspected the height of our necklines, the length of our hems. Sometimes a girl who failed the modesty test was forbidden to attend: we had a responsibility, Mother said, not to provoke the boys to impure thoughts or deeds, not to tempt them out of the State of Grace.

At the Parish Hall, Father Nihill and Father O'Rourke stood against the wall in their clerical suits and collars, hands in pockets, feet planted apart. While they spoke, they looked about them at the white and pastel shirts and the bright dresses of the dancers glimmering in the blinking, coloured light. The priests looked out of place. They looked lonely.

Danny sang in the band and played lead guitar. He looked down at me where I danced by myself in front of the stage, an expression on his face of rapt contentment.

Whenever Father Nihill's face came into view, between the shoulders of the other dancers, it seemed he was looking at me. I was careful not to look at him directly, because I was shy, and anxious that someone might notice, but I hoped he thought I looked nice. Danny had said I did. It was confusing knowing he thought this, and hoping that Father Nihill did too. I felt as if I were two people, and didn't know which one was really me.

The band was playing 'L'il Red Riding Hood'. Danny was on keyboard, and he sang to me. He threw his head back and howled, and everyone laughed. When the band stopped for a break he put on a record, jumped down off the stage and loped towards the group where I danced. He jigged round till he faced me.

'I like watching you dance,' he said.

'I like dancing, Danny boy.' The music was inside me, and my body felt like an instrument made to express it. We smiled at one another and my happiness was uncomplicated, not like the fraught exhilaration in Father Nihill's car. Dancing with Danny I felt normal, as though I wasn't having secret driving lessons with Father Nihill and my home wasn't a war zone.

When the track was finished, Father Nihill walked a zigzag route through the crowd, shaking his hands on either side of him and calling out, 'Mingle, mingle, mingle!' Everyone laughed.

He stopped beside me. 'How did you girls manage to get away for the night?'

'I'm supposed to go home on weekends, but tonight I'm staying at Danny's place.'

'How about that?' He arched his eyebrows and pursed his mouth in a pantomime of scandalised astonishment. 'The nuns let you do that, do they?'

'Our parents do, on the weekend.'

'Well, I hope all you young people are having a good time. But don't just stick to the one partner – mix around a bit, get to know each other.' He moved off into the crowd.

'How old d'you think he'd be?' I said.

Danny shrugged. 'Hard to say. About thirty, I suppose.'

'D'you think he'd be that old?'

When the music started again, a slow track, Danny moved into the gap between us and took one of my hands in his damp one. I could smell his sweat. His other hand burned against my back, but he kept a column of air between us, out of shyness, or because of the priests.

I caught sight of Father Nihill talking to Father O'Rourke in a corner and saw his glance slip sidelong, seeking me out. His gaze seemed to move in slow circles, following the ones I danced in with Danny. Danny's shoulder, though broad for a boy's, felt round and soft beneath my palm. I had an uncomfortable feeling, as though Danny and I were children playing at being girlfriend and boyfriend while the adults looked on. But I was glad Father Nihill noticed me.

Afterwards, Delia and Michael and I waited for Danny to pack up his equipment. Delia and Michael were talking about some science experiment that had gone wrong. Delia was showing him the small scar on her face from when she'd mixed the wrong chemicals out of curiosity in third form. While they talked, Father Nihill sidled up beside me.

'Did you get that book from the library yet?'

'I've started reading it.'

'I got a real kick out of it. It's different from other books I've read, the way it's written and everything. That Holden Caulfield's a funny character, isn't he?'

'From what I've read so far.'

'It's like he's talking to you and telling you things he can't tell anyone else.'

'A bit like Huckleberry Finn. I mean, because you can practically hear his voice.'

Talking to Father Nihill about the book linked me with him and separated us from the others as the only people who'd travelled to that other place and met the people there. It was more intimate, too, because we'd spent so much time together in the car.

He said, 'It makes it easier to identify with him. Like when he feels alienated from everyone and runs away, and Phoebe is the only person he can talk to.'

'I haven't read that bit yet. But I feel sorry for him because his brother died, and he's so lonely.' I understood the kind of loneliness Holden Caulfield felt, and it seemed that Father Nihill did too.

The other thing about the book was the strangeness of the non-Catholic world: it seemed unruly and superficial and seductive – but I didn't know how to say these things to Father Nihill. If I tried, I'd make a fool of myself. I said, 'I'm only up to the part where he goes and dances with those girls in the hotel.'

'What girls?' Danny was suddenly in front of us.

'Not any you're ever likely to meet, mate.' Father Nihill smiled at him. 'We're just talking about a book.'

Danny looked at me then back at Father Nihill.

'What tickles me,' Father Nihill said, 'is the way Holden goes on all the time about phoneys.'

'Phoneys?' Danny tapped one foot and frowned, looking across at the groups of people trickling outside. He glanced over at Delia and Michael. They were waiting for my conversation with Father Nihill to finish, too.

'I think I know what he means,' I said, 'but I never would've called them that.'

'What would you've called them?'

'I don't know.'

'Come on, Maggie.' Danny took my hand. 'See ya later, Father.'

'Before you go' – Father Nihill held up his palm – 'some of us from the YCS are going down the coast in a few weeks' time. I've got a shack at Lantic Bay, we can put up some tents. We could do with a bit of extra practice for the concert.

Everyone'll bring their guitars, who's got one. D'you reckon you youngsters might be able to come? You can tell your parents I'll be chaperone.'

We looked at one another.

'We'll all come,' Danny said.

'What about you, Maggie?' Father Nihill said.

'Yes, Father.' I was elated, that he'd singled me out.

'I'll be in touch then,' he said, with a gesture of dismissal. 'Off you go. Don't do anything I wouldn't do!'

'Give us a break, Father!' Danny said.

Father Nihill laughed. He followed us to the door.

In the street, the air was cold and damp, as though it had risen from the depths of the river a block away. Outside the hall some other young people were getting into the cars of parents and older brothers and sisters. Danny and I crossed Main Street with Michael and Delia. Danny held my hand and walked so slowly I had to dawdle too, and the others were soon half a block ahead.

I said, 'D'you still want to go to the Conservatorium next year?'

'I don't know. Me and the boys might see how we go with the band.'

'In Coalport?'

'Nah, Sydney.'

'That's where I want to go, too.'

'That'd be terrific, if we both went.' He squeezed my hand.

Delia turned, and I heard her laugh.

'We'd better hurry and catch up,' I said.

'Let's go this way.' Danny turned into the same lane as before and stopped under the same streetlight. He faced me and held both my hands in his.

I could hear his breath coming fast, as if he were frightened. He leaned towards me. He poked the tip of his tongue between my lips and moved it around, but I was too shy to open my mouth widely enough to let him in. If I turned away now, would it be enough? I didn't want to hurt his feelings.

I said finally, 'Don't you think we should catch up with the others?'

'Wait a minute. You're my girlfriend, aren't you? I mean, we've never talked about, we've never said . . .'

'Yes I am, Danny boy.' I wasn't passionately in love with him, as Cathy was with Heathcliff or Lara with Zhivago, but I liked him. I'd kissed him, and slept chastely in his bed, and let him put his arm around me while we watched a film. He beamed at me, and we walked on down the street holding hands.

Later, I passed close to him on my way to the bathroom, he on his way back towards the lounge room and his bed on the couch. In the narrow space of the hall we stepped at the same moment onto the cracked floorboard that always threatened to give way, so we hesitated, our bodies almost touching. The air between us seemed full of static, as it did when Father Nihill leaned across me in the car. Then we said goodnight and went our separate ways.

❖

'I'd better sit next to Maggie,' Father Nihill said, 'since she's going to drive.' We were standing next to the car.

'Maggie drive?' Danny said.

'Father's been giving me some lessons.'

'When?'

'Just after school sometimes, when I go to the library in Main Street.'

'I didn't know you went to the library. Why didn't you tell me? I'm supposed to be your boyfriend, aren't I?'

'I never thought about it. I just go and change my library books, that's all.'

'And have the odd driving lesson.' Danny frowned and crossed his arms.

I looked from him to Father Nihill.

Delia said, 'Why didn't you tell me too about the driving lessons?'

'She wanted to surprise you all, didn't you, Maggie?'

'Yes, Father.'

'Come on, you kids,' he said. 'We haven't got all day.'

Delia sat in front on the other side of Father Nihill, to make room in the back for Danny and Michael and the guitars. I drove slowly towards the Main Street corner. On the edge of my vision the presbytery, where the priests lived, slid past on one side, on the other the cathedral.

Father Nihill's shoulder and thigh were touching mine. Sometimes when I wrenched the gears he put his hand over mine and guided it into place. The day was unseasonably warm. The breeze that flowed through the window prickled my hot cheeks. I was wearing green stockings and a brown miniskirt. Father Nihill was watching my knees move up and down. He was smiling. Delia, her head turned towards the back seat and deep in a conversation with Michael, didn't notice. Danny gently strummed on his guitar. Sometimes he sang 'Rock My Soul' or 'We Shall Overcome' and everyone joined in except me. I was trying to control what felt like a huge beast.

On the highway I got stuck behind a slow truck.

'You can overtake him, if you want,' Father Nihill said. 'This is a pretty safe stretch, no bends or hills – that's what you have to watch out for. Nothing coming the other way?'

'Only a long way off. But I'm too scared.'

'You'll be all right. Go on, don't you trust me?'

I swung out past the truck and sped past. As I cut back into my lane an oncoming car swished by and swerved.

'Whoops!' I said. 'Where did they come from?'

'God, Maggie!' Delia said. 'That was a bit close, wasn't it?'

'Should've got Father to hear our confession first, before she got behind the wheel,' Michael said.

Father Nihill laughed. 'Good girl! Just watch very carefully for oncoming traffic. Don't hold back or you might miss your chance.'

'Were you really worried, Delia?' I said.

'Worried? I was terrified.'

Nobody laughed. Danny played a soft chord, each note separately vibrating.

'Come on, Delia. You're fearless, compared to me.'

'But not reckless.'

'Not to worry, I would've grabbed the wheel if necessary,' Father Nihill said.

I could feel the warmth where our thighs touched. On either side of the car the blue-green bush glided by in a soft blur. Sunlight slatted the road ahead. Surely the wheels weren't even touching the ground?

When I turned in off the road at Lantic Bay – a track scraped through the bush out of the sandy soil – the others were already there, putting up the boys' tent in a clearing among the sun-dappled gums. I drove in and braked and turned the engine off. The shack, a big box built of fibro and corrugated iron, seemed to stand in the middle of the forest. But there was a wire fence threaded among the trees.

'My little home away from home!' Father Nihill said, in the sudden silence.

'I thought priests weren't allowed to own anything, Father?' Michael said. 'I thought you were supposed to be poor?'

'So did I,' Danny said.

'Poverty, chastity and obedience,' Delia said. 'Didn't you have to take some kind of oath or something, Father?'

'This is in my old man's name, but he really bought it for me.'

We got out of the car and took our bags from the boot. The breeze was salty and fresh. Father Nihill waded through the sunny air towards the others with a measured, mesmerising gait, arms outstretched, hands spread. 'Welcome to paradise!' he said.

They all turned to him. Some laughed. Others beamed, as if they'd been blessed.

'Is the beach far from here, Father?' I was walking beside him.

'Just up the road. I'll show you later, if you like. I'll take you for another driving lesson if we've got time.'

'I'll come too,' Danny said. 'I'd like to have a go.'

'We probably won't have time,' Father Nihill said.

Danny frowned and sighed and rolled his eyes at me. I shrugged and looked away. I felt guilty even though it wasn't my fault.

Father Nihill dropped his bag, swerved in mid-step and bolted away towards a group of boys kicking a football about in a clearing near the fence. His legs a blur, his torso erect, he propelled himself into their midst among a quickening of movement and shouts. He butted them out of the way and grabbed the ball, shook off attackers, diverged and straightened and sidestepped and left them reeling, and with a violent thrust of his right leg kicked the ball high and clear between two distant trees. The semicircle that had gathered round the clearing roared. *'Go, Father!' 'On ya Father Nihill!'*

'What a show-off,' Danny said.

'Didn't he used to be a champion, in Sydney?' Michael said.

'Only in the seminary, I thought,' Danny said.

The crowd broke up, and Father Nihill walked towards us, grinning and flushed. His eyes were bright, his body quivered.

'Haven't lost me touch,' he said.

'Not bad for a clapped-out old coach,' Michael said, and ducked from Father Nihill's gentle fist.

'Did you used to be a champion, Father?' I walked beside him in the atmosphere of heat and confidence his body emanated.

'God protect me from the sin of pride' – he laughed – 'but I wasn't bad in my day.' We walked towards the shack. 'Tell you one thing, I'll make champions out of these YCS blokes if it's the last thing I do.'

'Reckon we'll win next week, Father?' Michael said. 'Against that Coalport mob?'

'Win? We'll wipe the bloody floor with them. What's the use if you don't intend to win?'

'I like winning too,' I said. 'I mean, not at sport.'

Delia hooted. 'Supposed to be fielding at softball and Maggie disappears up the nearest tree with a book.'

'Softball's boring,' I said. 'Sport's boring,'

'Well, you're good at other things,' Father Nihill said.

I felt myself blush with pleasure.

Inside the shack it was cavernous and dark. There was one big room where the girls spread their sleeping bags on the folding stretchers placed in rows along the walls; opening off it were Father Nihill's bedroom and a tiny kitchen.

'Not much in the way of luxury, I'm afraid,' Father Nihill said. 'Toilet's outside, and a bucket shower. There's a tap round the back. We have to heat water and wash up in a dish.'

'It's nice,' I said.

'You reckon? Not a bad old place, I suppose.' He carried his airline bag into the bedroom. Through the doorway I could sec the double bed under the window. I looked away. I had never seen the nuns' bedrooms – they called them cells, and I imagined bare walls, small, high windows, narrow beds. Did they sleep on mattresses? Or on bare boards for penance? The lives of nuns and priests were mysterious, filled with privation and demanding rituals and rules.

Father Nihill's bed was made with blankets and sheets. As he put his bag on it he saw me watching, and he smiled. In his white T-shirt and jumper, in the ordinary bedroom, he looked ordinary too – more human than the other priests.

'Come in and have a look if you like,' he called out.

An upturned packing case served as a bedside table: on its surface were a candle stuck to a saucer, a box of matches, a torch, an old alarm clock. A pair of swimming trunks hung from a nail on the wall, from others a threadbare towel, a faded dressing-gown with a grubby cord. He watched me look at each object in turn.

'My boodwah.' He laughed. 'This is where I come and relax when the bishop's giving me a hard time. I hope you'll be comfortable enough out there?'

'Yes, Father.'

He was still standing beside the bed. I looked out of the window, because it was impossible otherwise to avert my gaze from it: I felt impolite looking at such a personal piece of furniture, especially a priest's.

I could see the others outside: I knew the older members of the YCS by sight, but only a few by name. The boys' tent was up, and they were building a fire for the barbecue. I could hear them chattering and calling to one another and laughing, and I could hear the bellbirds, but the sounds were faint, as though Father Nihill and I were the only living creatures within miles.

'Glad you could come down with us,' he said.

'So am I.' When I looked him in the face I felt shy and overwrought. The room had an enclosed, private atmosphere at odds with the clamour outside.

'Better go and see how that fire's going,' he said.

'Yes, Father.'

'Lloyd. Call me Lloyd when no one else is around.'

'All right, Father.'

'All right, *Lloyd*.'

'All right, Lloyd.' I hurried from the room, overcome, and he followed me.

People were wandering about beneath the trees or gazing into the fire. 'We need some barbecue tools, Father,' one of the young men said, watching the flame ignite the kindling.

'Sure, Dave, they're in the shed. Can you go and get them, Maggie?'

'Yes, Father.'

'Much obliged to you.' He bowed to me and smiled. 'It's round the back.'

I found it among the trees. It was no bigger than the outhouse in the opposite corner of the yard. Paint tins and tools hindered the opening of the door. I shoved it hard, but I had to grope about inside to clear a space for it to swing. I was scrabbling among the clutter when Father Nihill came in and closed the door behind him.

'Wondered if you'd got lost,' he said. 'I thought I'd better give you a hand – it's a bit of a mess in here.'

I turned towards him. 'I can't find them.'

The only light, already faded, entered through cracks between the boards in the walls. We stood peering at one another. He stepped into the tiny space between us and encircled me with his arms. Instinctively I put my arms around him. His hand beneath my chin, he lifted my face to his. He opened my mouth with his tongue and kissed me with such violent intensity it felt as though he wanted to eat me. My own tongue surprised me, it seemed to know the inside of his mouth by heart. A current of pleasure surged through my body like a mild electric shock. I'd felt this once before, the day after Danny had first kissed me – when I thought about it on my way home on the bus.

We stood a moment holding one another. The musty smell of the shed mingled with the scent of his skin. The dimness after the light outside was a different element, like water in which we'd learned to breathe.

'You're shaking!' He unclasped my hands from behind his back and held them up in front of him, as Sister Bernadette did when she inspected our nails.

I looked down at them, then up at him. I was breathing fast and my legs felt weak. 'What are we going to do?'

He laughed. 'Can't we just love one another for a little while?'

What could he mean? We'd broken a sacred law. If anyone found out we'd be punished – banished. 'Isn't it wrong, for us?'

'Not if we love each other. But you mustn't tell anyone.'

Who could I tell? Not even Delia. 'We'd better go back.' It seemed like hours since I'd left the others. I was terrified someone would come looking for us.

'You go first. Tell them I'm still looking for the tools. Wait . . .'

I paused, my hand on the door.

'Next time I say mass at the convent, d'you think you could bring me my breakfast afterwards? Would you do that for me?'

'I'll try.'

I opened the door. The sun setting above the trees blinded me: for a moment I was lost.

Danny and Delia and Michael were sitting in the circle around the fire, singing with the others. Danny was playing his guitar. He smiled and jerked his head towards the space beside him, where he'd put mine. So I sat with them – with them and apart – and tried to think of the words.

❖

To stop the trembling of my hands, I clasped them tightly as if in prayer. I tried not to look at Lloyd, especially at the altar rail when he gave me communion.

I no longer believed, but the guilt was automatic: I hadn't gone to confession. How could I tell another priest that I'd kissed Lloyd? What if Lloyd was on the other side of the screen? No one had ever missed communion: that would mean you'd committed a mortal sin. So I knelt before Lloyd and opened my mouth.

At breakfast in the refectory after mass, his black suit caught my eye, rippling among the blades of the palms beyond the cloister. From behind the window I watched him cross the garden on his way from the sacristy to the parlour. I felt so animated, I couldn't sit still. I swallowed a mouthful of tea, put down my cup and stood up in one swift movement so that the cup rattled against the saucer. Everyone at the table stared at me.

'Where are you going?' Delia said.

'Father Nihill wanted to talk to me about something.'

'She's got a crush on him,' Colleen Doherty said in a loud voice.

Delia chuckled and looked at me with raised eyebrows.

My ears and neck felt hot. 'Shut up, Colleen.'

Sister Bernadette nodded her permission. I went into the scullery and knocked on the kitchen door. Sister Matthew came out, wiping her big, red hands on her apron, her sleeves and veil pinned up out of the way.

'Good morning, Sister. Sister Bernadette said I could take Father his breakfast.'

In the oldest building I thought of as a manor house, Lloyd was sitting at the small mahogany table in the corner of the parlour. When I entered the room, he looked up and smiled delightedly.

'Good morning, Father.'

'Lloyd!'

'Lloyd.'

I set down on the table the tray with its covered dishes of bacon and eggs and toast, its silver teapot and starched napkin. Lloyd pushed the plate towards me but I hadn't been able to eat even my own breakfast. In this room the nuns received the bishop, missionary priests, parents, the mayor. I shook my head and pushed the plate back.

'Close the door, Maggie.'

I closed it and sat down in a chair of tapestry cloth and wooden feet like paws. I couldn't believe this priest and I had kissed, and now I'd boldly followed him into the nuns' parlour where he sat eating as though nothing had happened.

I was embarrassed watching him eat and looked around the room. In its gilt frame on one side of the marble mantelpiece hung the print that Sister Theresa had brought me in to look at – how many years ago? – when it'd been new. While Lloyd chewed his bacon, his eyes upon me, I studied the picture, its serenity of light and domesticity, remembering how Sister Theresa had pointed out the concentration on the woman's face as she poured the milk from the jug into the bowl; the light from the window gilding her cap, her face and hands, the curves of sleeve, bodice, skirt. The room in the painting reminded me of the parlour, which faced south: it seemed that the window in the painting let in the only true light.

I said, 'Do you like that painting?'

Lloyd glanced across at it. 'Yeah, that's a nice picture, isn't it?'

'It's a Vermeer. A print of Vermeer. He was Dutch.'

'Is that so?'

'Did you know all this was under water, in the flood?'

'The flood of '45, eh? Yeah, I suppose it would've been, wouldn't it?'

'One of the nuns restored everything in this building after the water receded. She made it exactly like it was before. I don't know how she did it.' I wished I could stop talking, but at the same time I was worried about running out of things to say.

I followed Lloyd's rapid glance around the room, at the marble mantelpiece, the intricate skirting boards and architraves. The walls were white and silky, the floorboards shone, the nap was thick on upholstery and rug, and milky lights gleamed in the smooth legs of the chairs, on the surface of the table behind which he suddenly stood up, the napkin clinging to the waistband of his trousers like an apron.

He brushed it off and said in a hoarse voice, 'Come here.'

'But someone might come.'

'No one ever does.'

I couldn't move. He walked over to where I sat between the windows that overlooked the street. He took my hands and raised me to my feet, kissed me with open mouth, and pushed me down onto the floor.

I could hear the voices of the girls now swarming on the cloister and the garden paths beyond the closed doors of the parlour and the hall. Delia might already be carrying her books through the passageway behind the refectory, almost right alongside this room.

How could such a clean floor smell of dust? My tunic was bunched beneath my thighs, the pleats were twisted. I could hear Lloyd's breathing and smell the sweat in his hair. A bulge in his trousers moved against my groin, like something separately alive. How long would it have to go on?

Beyond Lloyd's head the woman in the white cap looked away and calmly poured the milk into the bowl. I tried not to panic. What if they came looking for me? Lloyd ground and ground himself against me, against cloth and flesh and bone. Then he shuddered, he groaned, he sighed. From the hall outside I heard the faint clattering of rosary beads, the giant ones the nuns wore hanging from their belts, the tapping of shoes on the marble tiles, the rustling of voluminous garments, louder, louder.

'Quick!' I pushed Lloyd off and stood up, straightening the pleats of my tunic as best I could without unbuckling my belt. The footsteps were almost deafening. I was stiff with the kind of paralysis you feel in a nightmare, when you're running and running without covering any ground. My mouth was dry, my hands were clammy. Almost at the same instant as Lloyd slid into his place at the table and I perched back on the edge of my chair, the door flung open and Sister Theresa strode into the room, followed by Sister Bernadette.

'Sister, come in, come in!' Lloyd boomed. He was leaning back in his chair, his hands clasped behind his head, as if he might at any moment swing his legs up onto the table beside the dishes.

'Good morning, Sister.' I looked from one to the other. 'Good morning, Sister.'

There was a void between my back and the back of the chair. Where the upholstery ended the timber frame of the seat dug into my thighs. I was using all my leg muscles to stay seated.

'Good morning, Father.' Sister Theresa regarded Lloyd. She was small and slight but the force of her intelligence, of the integrity expressed in her upright person, made her seem tall.

They turned to me, Sister Bernadette smiling behind Sister Theresa, Sister Theresa not smiling. Sister Theresa said, 'Isn't it time you were getting ready for class, Maggie?'

'Yes, Sister.' I stood up. Beyond the door, this building opened at the other end of the hall onto the cloister, onto the wide courtyard where the palm fronds glinted in the sun and you could smell the rubbish in the bins stacked in the rotunda outside the kitchen and hear the clatter of saucepans, and at the other end of the cloister outside the study hall the shrill voices calling and laughing, and now Colleen Doherty ringing the bell.

'Maggie's helping me organise the folk concert, aren't you, Maggie?' Lloyd said.

'Yes, Father.'

'Didn't mean to keep her late for class, but.' His smile turned sheepish. 'It's my fault. See you later, Maggie.'

I turned away. In the corner of my eye I saw the fluttering movement of his hand. 'Good morning, Father.'

As I opened the door, he said in a bright voice, 'Well, what can I do you for, Sister? And Sister?'

I left the room and fled down the passage and out onto the cloister where I halted to catch my breath. My heart was quivering. On the other side of the garden, as on every sunny morning, wedges of slate on the chapel roof gleamed pewter above the shadowed walls. The stark, rounded clarity of the gardenias and the camellias, and the spaces connecting one to the other across gravel and grass, seemed sinister, turning the emptiness of the garden into a kind of devastation. Everything was familiar, yet completely changed, as though since I'd last looked at it the floodwaters had arisen and filled the place to the brim of sky. I stood staring, shocked, until the vision receded, and the cataclysm took up again its proper place inside me.

If Sister Theresa had opened the parlour door a minute earlier, she'd have seen a vision she might have had of hell, in medieval colours: human figures grappling in illicit, helpless lust among the flames, among the gloating faces of the demons.

I grabbed my books from my desk in the hall, hurried back along the cloister and entered the refectory. The path between the tables, the crooked passage beyond the back door which connected it with the senior school, seemed a maze I would never find my way through to the classroom where my empty desk waited among the ignorant, innocent others.

❖

On a Tuesday afternoon, I walked with Delia to the bottom paddock.

She said, 'I've been meaning to ask you: why did Father Nihill want to see you at breakfast that day? Sister Theresa asked me where you'd gone so I told her.'

'What did you do that for? It wasn't any of her business.'

Delia stared. 'What's got into you, Maggie?'

'He wanted to talk to me about the songs for the concert.'

Had I ever lied to her before? We stood on opposite sides of a chasm. Delia nodded. 'First chance I've had to ask you since then. We don't see much of each other, lately.'

'I've got so much to do after school – I've got to go to concert practice now, in fact.' The truth was I couldn't wait to see Lloyd, and this made my deception even worse.

'Already?'

'I have to get there early to learn something on the guitar.'

We walked back in a fraught, unfamiliar silence.

When I entered the Parish Hall, Lloyd and Danny were working out harmonies and chords. Danny was still wearing his grey uniform. Beside the square-shouldered man he looked rounded and unfinished, not yet chiselled into his adult shape. He was so happy to see me, it was hard to look him in the eye. I sat down and tried to concentrate on tuning my guitar.

'Let's play Maggie the new song,' Lloyd said. 'Bet you already know the words, Maggie – join in if you want to.'

He sang to me with exaggerated enthusiasm, jerking his head from side to side to the beat, and I couldn't help laughing. I followed the simple pattern of the chords in 'The Times They Are a–Changin'. Danny harmonised and smiled at me sidelong, his face flushed with pleasure.

In the middle of a chorus Lloyd's eyes widened and he clapped his hand to his mouth. 'I nearly forgot. I promised Kevin Flaherty I'd pick him up.'

Danny and I followed him out to the car. He opened the driver's side and motioned for me to get in, then he slid in next to me. Danny stood frowning for a moment, then he swung himself in beside Lloyd.

'Why can't you teach me how to drive too, Father?' Danny said.

'Your old man's got a car, hasn't he? He can teach you. Maggie's got no one else.'

'He never has time. He's always out.'

Lloyd lounged with his arm on the back of the seat, almost touching my shoulder. With the two of them alongside me, I was unnerved. I drove now jerkily, now smoothly, and turned and crossed the bridge to Argyll. The house was separated from the river only by a dirt road, in the lowest ground where the floodwater spilled first.

Kevin ran up to us when I parked the car on the unpaved kerb. 'Mum and Dad said you've got to come in for a cuppa.'

Lloyd said, 'We'll just say a quick hello.'

We got out and picked our way through a swarm of younger Flahertys to the house. Walking down the hall I wondered what was unusual about the rooms on either side, then saw it was the bareness: lengths of skirting board were exposed where normally furniture would stand. In the lounge room a pair of vinyl armchairs was afloat on the expanse of floor.

'Father! Come in!' Mr Flaherty waved us into the kitchen.

'Hello, hello!' Lloyd grinned.

Mrs Flaherty looked up at him from the wood stove, nodding and smiling. 'Got the kettle on, Father.'

'Only got a minute, Eileen, but if it's on the go. You know Danny. And this is Maggie. Come and sit down here, Maggie.' He sat at the table and patted the space beside him on the wooden bench.

Mrs Flaherty turned to open the door of the stove onto the fire, and stoked it. On either side of the chimney the blue-grey oblongs of dusk paled inside their frames.

The fire was raw, like living tissue, like something that wasn't supposed to be seen. Lloyd pressed his thigh against mine beneath the table. Danny sat on the other side of me. I felt the heat creep over my skin, from the rim of my collar to the roots of my hair. It was as though Mrs Flaherty had opened a door onto what we were hiding. I knew Danny was smiling – he looked so happy – because he was sitting next to me. Lloyd was talking and laughing as though we were sitting separately rather than joined together, sharing the heat of our bodies through our clothes, but my awareness of Danny was a pressure that made it hard to act normally. I made up my mind to tell him that afternoon that I couldn't be his girlfriend anymore.

Then Mrs Flaherty closed the iron door. The room was lit again with fading light, spilling from the quiet evening streets. I could smell the damp seeping from the river and into the house. Mr Flaherty got up and turned on the light. He clapped Lloyd on the back and sat back down opposite him. I was warmed by the pleasure these people took in Lloyd's presence in their house. Like Delia, he had the gift for quickening the atmosphere of a room, enlivening everyone in it: shifting them out of the everyday and relieving for a moment the loneliness of solitary destiny.

I was struck by the likeness of husband to wife, both plump and short and dark with identical round shoulders, and a deep, calm contentment in their eyes at odds with the chaos of the kitchen, where shabby garments dried on the backs of chairs, a drifting, useless clutter covered almost every surface, and children darted in and out, now climbing up to the table, now wrestling amiably beneath it, filling the doorway with their coming and going. Mr Flaherty scooped up a chubby baby who crawled towards the stove and sat her on the edge of the table.

'Which one are you again?' Lloyd reached out a hand and tickled her awkwardly on the stomach. 'Number nine or number ten?'

'Nine.' Mrs Flaherty set out cups without saucers on the bare table and filled them with red, smoking tea. 'There isn't going to be a ten.'

'Thanks to your sermons, Father,' Mr Flaherty said, 'we believe it's all right to follow our conscience on that one.'

'Joe,' Mrs Flaherty said.

'It's all right.' Lloyd nodded towards Danny and me. 'These kids are all right.'

'Bishop still giving you a hard time over that one last Sunday?' Mr Flaherty said.

'You mean about the pill?' Danny spoke gruffly to hide his embarrassment, and to sound grown-up.

Lloyd said, 'I got carpeted again last night – warned off about the next one.'

'Pity he wouldn't spend his time finding out what it's like for us ordinary married people.'

'Joe . . .'

'If there were more of them like Father Nihill, the church'd be a more popular place.'

Lloyd glowed in the warmth of their praise.

The wife sat down beside the husband and they each put an arm around the other and briefly nestled dark head against dark head. They loved each other, I realised with a small shock. They were old, not pretty or handsome, they had no money and too many children to look after. Some married people loved each other. But the thought of living the life Eileen did was horrible.

'Things are changing,' Lloyd was saying. 'There's a lot of us in the church trying to bring in a more humane approach. More in line with modern times.' He looked at me and grinned. 'What do you reckon, Maggie? Do you think there's a need for change?'

'I suppose so, Father.' I didn't think the church, which had failed to protect my mother, should tell people what to do. But I wasn't used to giving my opinion among adults.

What they were talking about had something to do with my determination to live however I wanted: with the move-ment of my life away from home, the slow unloosing of the painful bonds that tied me to my family. Sometimes when I sat alone on the old red bus, the slippery seat shuddering with the labour of the engine, the flow of landscape in the window matching the flow of freed, uninterrupted thought, physical motion merged with the forward, upward motion of my life. I'd always live like this, as separate and free as when I left Abernant on the bus. But now I'd lost track of the talk.

'Father?' Danny said. 'Don't you think we'd better get back to the hall? The others'll be there by now.'

❖

They were waiting, the boys from the Christian Brothers' and day pupils from the convent, and the ones who'd left school. But they laughed at Lloyd's dramatisation, with bended knee and beaten breast, of his remorse. They dragged into the circle more chairs from around the walls.

'Danny and me've been teaching Maggie to play the new song.' Lloyd handed the sheets of music around the room. 'Danny, you can start playing and I'll help Maggie learn the chords.'

He stood behind me and positioned my fingers on the guitar strings to play each chord, while I strummed in tune with Danny. When Danny had touched me this way I hadn't felt breathless.

We practised the Dylan song until six o'clock, when the harmony broke up into a loud discordant babble, and everyone began drifting towards the door. I was planning to wait for Danny outside.

'Before you go . . .' Lloyd held up his arms. 'Nobody think about being late. We're first on the program.' He gave me a secret, sidelong wink.

'Maggie?' Danny caught up with me in the doorway. 'I thought you might want to go to the pictures one weekend. Haven't seen you for a while. You never even come to the dances. Mum's been asking me when you're going to come and stay again.' He leaned towards me in his eager way.

'I don't know. I mean, I'd like to, but I never get away much on weekends, I've got so much studying to do.' Since the weekend in Lantic Bay, I'd felt too guilty to go out with him.

'So when am I going to see you again? Just us?'

Whenever Danny was excited or shy his gaze slipped sideways and back again, as though he couldn't bear to keep looking at me. I saw this now, and my throat hurt with unshed tears.

'Danny boy, I can't be your girlfriend anymore.'

He reared back as though I'd hit him. 'Don't you still like me?'

'It's not that. I have to work extra hard to get a scholarship.'

'You can't study twenty-four hours a day.'

'Danny, I'm sorry. I wish . . .' What? It was too late to wish anything. While I spoke I could hear Lloyd laughing with Kevin, their voices becoming louder as they approached us. I couldn't see Lloyd but I felt him looking at me: the whole side of my body nearest him felt the force of his attention. It was an effort not to turn towards him.

Danny's eyes looked moist. We stood there in our separate states of misery.

'I have to go,' I said, 'or I'll be late for tea. I'll see you around. I still want us to be friends.'

I started to walk away, but I heard Danny call my name and I turned back to face him.

'Don't ever call me Danny boy again.' His voice was shaky, but his gaze was level. I managed to hold it, and I waited until he broke eye contact and turned and walked away from me. I felt deceitful and cruel. All I could do was respect his dignity.

I watched him for a moment, his familiar, forward-leaning gait. He was moving more quickly than I'd seen him move before. Then, before Lloyd could reach me, I walked out into the street against a sinking of the heart and an impulse to turn back as strong as if I'd left something valuable behind.

In the dusk the facades of the shops formed on either side of the road a single dim mass against the sky. Sometimes in this place the buildings, their classical symmetry, their reflective roofs of slate and iron, seemed to have been made to show off the beauty of the sky. Now this was lavender, in its final luminosity before the dark. Its lightness lifted me against the weight of the darkening earth, of my distress.

I reminded myself that Lloyd loved me – *Can't we just love one another for a little while?* I carried the secret inside me, through the convent gate, to the line the girls had already formed on the cloister, ready for Sister Bernadette to give the signal to walk along to the refectory. I stood holding it beside Delia, who always kept my place, and wondered how there was enough room inside me to hide something so enormous.

'Maggie Reed.' Mother Borgia was behind me. I turned to her and the others went on without me. She stood with her hands folded beneath her cream scapular. She was tall and stout, as though her authority had increased her stature. My legs shook. How could she have found out?

'Yes, Mother?'

'When was the last time you wrote home?'

I almost cried with relief. 'My parents don't really expect me to, Mother.'

'When was the last time you went home for the weekend?'

'I don't know, Mother.'

'How many times do I have to remind you you're supposed to be a weekly boarder?'

'I need to stay at school to study, Mother.'

'You have plenty of time to do your homework during the week. I've seen you studying in the garden before mass, too.'

'Yes, Mother. I'll go next weekend.'

'Write and tell them.'

'Yes, Mother.'

She turned with a sweeping gesture, her capacious robes swirling in line with her movement, down the steps, along the path to the nuns' private cloister. I almost ran to the refectory.

❖

The next Friday afternoon I stayed in the town library until it closed, then I bought fish and chips and ate as I walked along the towpath beside the narrow backyards of the shops, looking across the Grainger River and the sandy flats to where, beyond the town, the landscape rolled away to the horizon, the river landscape of soft greens, of grasses and rushes and willows.

When it was dark I followed Lloyd's directions. The street was unfamiliar. In the small house the windows were unlit. I saw the green car parked a block away. From the verandah I watched Lloyd get out of it and walk towards me, looking about him.

He unlocked the door furtively and we felt our way along the hall. Lloyd tripped on a toy, something with wheels. 'Shit!' He whispered it, although no one else was there. In the quiet it made a loud hissing sound.

'Come on,' he said. 'This must be the kids' room.'

He was disembodied except for the hand I clutched. We bumped into furniture misshapen by darkness, with unexpected corners and edges. We shuffled in circles. When we came out again into the hall, I couldn't tell if I was walking towards the front of the house or the back. The rooms smelt of strangers, their food odours, their different soap.

'Are you sure they won't come home?' I whispered. 'Are you sure they wouldn't mind?'

'I told you, they've gone to Carlyon Bay. I offered to look after the place and they gave me the key.'

In another room our shins rammed into a horizontal rim of metal or wood; it was like walking into the side of a sunken boat hidden beneath the water. Beyond it our groping hands met a soft, chilled surface, patted it until we learnt its breadth, its width.

'Take off your clothes,' Lloyd said.

'It's too cold.'

'I'll soon warm you up.'

I took off my blazer and jumper, my tunic and blouse. But I was frozen, and shy in spite of the dark, and I left my pants and bra and spencer on. No one had seen me naked since I was a small child. In the dormitory we had to get dressed facing our lockers, our dressing-gowns draped over us like capes so we didn't see each other even in our underwear. I crawled into the bed where Lloyd was waiting. Naked, he felt smaller, and soft: a creature without its shell. He peeled my spencer off and unhooked my bra. Between the marble sheets we clung together.

'What did you tell the nuns?'

'Mother Borgia said I had to go home, anyway.'

'What did you tell them at home?' He pressed himself against me.

'I said I'll be there tomorrow.'

'Good girl.'

Lloyd writhed and moaned. From the time he'd kissed me at Lantic Bay, he'd taken me by surprise. Now we were naked together in these parishioners' bed. Wherever he wasn't touching me I ached with cold. I was relieved that he didn't try to push himself inside me. I wasn't prepared for it yet.

I couldn't stop thinking about the family who lived here. In the dark room I felt their presence, as though they were watching us, and might tell everyone in the town what they had seen.

'What's the matter?' he said afterwards.

'Nothing. I feel funny in someone else's house when they're not here.'

'Can't you just think about me?'

'I wish I didn't have to go home tomorrow.'

'Well, it's only a couple of days.'

'Dad gets drunk, especially on the weekends. He goes berserk. He yells all the time and he hits Mum.'

'Gee, that's no good, is it?' He sounded sympathetic but not shocked, or even as though I'd told him something serious.

'What about your dad?' I had never imagined Lloyd's parents. He seemed powerful enough to have created himself: completely unconnected from the mundane world families come from.

'He never got drunk. I didn't see that much of him except on holidays from boarding school. Then he was always working.'

'What about your mother?'

'She died when I was little.'

'Oh, you poor thing. That's terrible.'

'I don't even remember her.' He looked at the luminous dial of his watch and separated himself from me. 'I'd better go before the shit hits the fan.'

I reared up. 'But you said you could stay here with me the night!'

'Steady on! I'll be back soon. If I don't put in another appearance, His Grace'll get pretty toey, just to put it mildly. He keeps pretty close tabs on me these days.'

'But I can't stay here by myself – I'll be too scared.' I felt suddenly very small in the double bed.

Lloyd laughed. 'Scared of what? There's nobody around. The place is all locked up.'

But my terror was of the dark, its bottomless depths, the predators I imagined inside it.

'Can't I come with you?'

'Don't be silly, you'd freeze in the car. You just stay here and keep warm; I'll be back before you know it.'

I watched his deft, shadowy movements as he dressed, and then he melted into the darkness.

For a long time I lay rigid, curled up in the middle of the bed. In this house I had never seen the reassuring signs of domesticity, the harmless acts of eating, washing, sleeping; the human scale of rooms. I lay still, barely breathing, listening for the tread of a murderer, the rustle of a ghost.

Then I must have dozed. I woke to the sound of footsteps. Inside or out? I strained to hear above the hurricane of my breath. I hadn't heard Lloyd's car. Someone was opening the front door. I could cover my head with the blankets, but the waiting would be worse. I strode out of the bedroom and into the hall. At the other end I saw silhouetted in the doorway, against the streetlight, Lloyd.

'It's you!'

'Who did you think?'

'I don't know, I didn't hear the car.'

'Didn't bring it, I didn't want them to hear me going out.'

We got back into bed. I was warm, and I wasn't alone. Lloyd had again what he called a climax. It was enough for me to feel wanted: that I mattered to him. I was afraid, too. It was like not being game to swim out past the breakers at the beach, for fear of being swept away.

Sometimes we slept a while, but at dawn I woke cleanly and the bed was huge. Standing beside it Lloyd was normal size – no longer, as in bed, the centre of the world. He smiled at me with such self-satisfaction that I felt like an accomplishment of his, as though he'd made me himself. The daylight revealed the room's ordinary dimensions: it contained a heavy ward-robe, a wood-veneer dressing table with curved drawers and a round bevelled mirror, and a gilt-framed picture of waves.

He said, 'Anyone asks you what you're doing here, tell them I asked you to check up on the place.'

'I'll stay till it's time to catch the bus.'

'Why not go to the dance tonight?'

'I told you: Mother said I had to go home.'

Lloyd started to get dressed. 'I haven't seen you at a dance for ages.'

'I've got no one to go with, Danny and I broke up. I broke up with him. I wouldn't want to go by myself, and anyway he'd be there. It'd be awful.'

'What did you do that for?' Lloyd froze, his head buried in his T-shirt. He sounded alarmed.

'It wasn't fair to keep on being his girlfriend. Don't worry, I didn't tell him about you.'

'You didn't have to break up with him. As long as no one knows about us, it doesn't matter.'

'It matters to me.'

'You're a funny one, aren't you?' Lloyd sounded disappointed in me. He shrugged his T-shirt on over his shoulders and shook his head. He looked put out.

'Am I?' I was disconcerted. I thought I'd done the right thing.

'It would've made it easier if you just acted as normal. If anyone found out about us I'd be finished. I'd be kicked out of the priesthood with no work and no place to live. I've got a real vocation, there's a lot of good things I can do for people here. If the bishop got wind of it, he'd do his best to ruin my life. You wouldn't want that to happen, would you?'

'Of course not. Lloyd?'

'What?'

'I know you've got a vocation, but you love me, don't you?'

He finished getting dressed. 'Of course I do.'

'I love you too.'

He stood smiling at me. 'That's what makes it all right. But only as long as we keep it between us.' He looked at his watch. 'I have to go and say mass at the convent. Make sure nobody sees you leave.' He leaned over and kissed me swiftly and was gone.

I dressed quickly and went out the back door and scurried along the sideway. For a moment I was lost. Which way was the bus stop? I felt a panic out of proportion to my confusion. What was I doing going home, instead of to Danny's with Delia, and later to the dance? When I calmed down and got my bearings, I slipped out into the sunny street, the light pouring down from the sky into all the crevices of the world.

❖

On Saturdays, while he was still sober enough, my father cooked sausages for dinner. I could smell them before I entered the house. In the kitchen, he stood at the frypan. He looked up at me. I could tell from his jaunty stance, his cheerful expression, the glint in his eyes in which there was a stubborn defiance, a ruthless anticipation, that he was not completely sober from the night before, not completely drunk, and that he was planning as usual on Saturday to go to the pub straight after dinner to get blind. I picked Billy up and held him.

'Mags! Just in time. Guess what your old man's got cooking?'

I put Billy down. Anne and Luke were watching. They all waited for me to speak. If I smiled at my father as he demanded, I'd be a traitor. If I didn't his good mood would break and it'd be my fault.

'Sausages and onion gravy.' I sniffed the air, peering from a distance into the pan.

'It's ready,' he said. 'Sit down and get it into you.'

My mother came in wearing her black-and-white work clothes, her faded make-up. She didn't speak but sat down sideways at the table and leaned an elbow on it, head bowed, and prised off her shoes.

'Look at that.' My father served my mother and thrust a plate of sausages before me so that the gravy slopped onto the rim. I looked down at my plate not to seem disloyal to my mother, who even as she ate regarded the food with contempt. In a corner of my vision, as he turned back to the pan and served himself, I could see the look in my father's eyes.

It occurred to me that the loneliness you brought upon yourself might be worse than any other kind. I should have smiled at him. Would it have made any difference? In his grudging enthusiasm, his awkward pride in his work, I almost saw what he might have been like if he didn't get drunk.

In the silence, I could hear the frantic crescendo of the race call on the wireless from the pub behind the house. This sound from the alien, unruly world of drinking and gambling my father would soon go out into, combined with the smell of sausages and onion gravy, meant that the longest day of the week had begun.

I summoned a memory of Lloyd, of his solid warmth against me. In front of everyone, in the familiar kitchen with its cluttered lino benchtops and its stack of unpaid bills behind the clock on the corner shelf, this was shocking. But I clung to it, my head above water, my lungs filled with air.

My mother said to my father, 'Did you show Maggie what you made?'

'Give a man a chance,' he whined.

But he got up from the table and went over to the bench near the sink, beckoning me with jerks of his head. 'Come over here, Mags.'

I looked at my mother. She nodded. I went and stood beside him. I could smell coconut. There were two trays: in one a white confection, in the other a pink, inside the frilled collars of their greaseproof lining. He'd never made anything like this before.

'That one's marshmallow,' my father pointed with a nicotine-stained finger, 'and that one's coconut ice.'

I glanced behind me and saw the little boys straining to see, my mother hovering. But behind them Luke sat frowning at the window; Anne leaned against the table, arms folded.

'He made them for you.' My mother got up from the table. From her emphatic tone, the way she paced, I could tell she'd put him up to it, to make up for the way he'd yelled at me the last time I'd come home, and the insulting names he'd called me which had hurt so much I'd been unable to hold in the crying. I couldn't imagine my parents in private conversation about me, about anything. And in what life had he learnt to make such things? Not in the war. Not from my mother, who made only stews and roasts, packet cakes on birthdays. I could feel them all waiting.

'Thanks, Dad.' I tried to sound enthusiastic. When I had to pretend like this I felt a tightness in my heart, and in my whole body. But if I didn't he'd blame my mother as well as me and use it as an excuse to hurt her physically, later, when he was properly drunk.

With a knife he levered out a square of the pink marshmallow, and handed it to me. My stomach clenched against it, but I bit and swallowed. 'Thanks Dad. It's nice. Here, why don't you all have some?' Now I could smile, passing it round, seeing Billy's face. Lollies were a luxury. My mother nodded and sniffed. My father stood watching, hands on hips.

'I'm off now. I feel lucky today – think I'm gonna back a winner.'

The atmosphere turned like the weather. He looked disgusted. 'What's the matter with you miserable bastards? Can't you wish a man luck?'

When he was gone I said to my mother, 'I didn't know he could make things like that.' I felt shy saying it. We never talked about what was happening, as if there were no room for ordinary conversation, or because we wanted to pretend it wasn't real.

My mother shook her head and sighed, and she started to talk. Often at night, while waiting for my father to come home, she told us children long, involved stories about her carefree life before we were born: before her wedding and the war. In these stories she was either a heroine, or a victim of malice or fate. But now she was telling a story about our father in which he, too, was helpless and wronged.

'I blame the war for a lot of it,' she said. 'He wouldn't talk about it much when he came back, but what I did find out . . .' She shuddered. 'Once he was walking through the jungle, beside his best mate, the Japs were hiding in the trees, they were snipers – they never knew when they were going to shoot – and your father's mate, I forget his name, anyway, he was shot right beside him, just like that, just fell down dead beside him.'

She said: 'His mother's that selfish, if it wasn't for her, he wouldn't've put his age up and gone to the war so young, he was only seventeen, she made him leave school when he was fifteen, your father was brilliant, his teachers begged her to let him stay, but she said he had to start bringing in some money, she made him go and work as a labourer in a pottery, he hated it . . .'

Later in the afternoon my father came home drunk.

'What are you doing here?' he said to me. 'Thought you didn't live here anymore. Thought you was too good for us. Thought I told you to leave that stuck-up school and bring in some dough? Who do you think you are?'

I didn't care. Last night, Lloyd had told me he loved me.

❖

On the day of the concert, Delia and I circled the room beneath the spindly rafters of a willow in the bottom paddock, outstripping the cold.

'Better get back soon,' Delia said. 'It's going to rain. Got to hand in my English essay, anyway.'

'I haven't done mine yet.'

Delia stopped and blinked. Then she laughed. 'You're joking.'

'I'll start it in study. I can finish it tomorrow morning. It's only due in today.'

More than once I'd settled down to face the whiteness of the page, to sift *King Lear* for the smallest seed of a beginning. But these days when I sat quietly to work, to think, my mind slipped gear and slid into daydreaming about Lloyd.

'But you never hand anything in late. Sister Theresa will kill you.'

'I don't care. It'll only be one day.'

Delia snapped off a twig and chewed it, frowning at me the same way she did at her algebra homework. I tucked the scarf ends of my pixie hood into the upturned collar of my blazer and sidled out through a gap in the branches. Above the open paddock the sky was grey as water under cloud. The black plovers swam in it. Their piping, melancholy in this light, was still the anthem of peace.

Delia followed me. 'It's not like you. And I saw Danny today, first chance we've had to talk for a while. Why didn't you tell me you'd broken up with him? I thought you couldn't go to dances because Mother said you had to go home on weekends. Is it because of Danny?'

'We'd better get a move on – it's going to rain any minute.'

'Is it something about home?'

'Nothing new there.'

'I don't get it, Maggie. You like him, don't you?'

'Not like that.'

'You could still go out. You don't have to be serious about him. I'm not about Michael either. They know we're planning to go away to university next year.'

A slow wave of colder air swelled and broke. Beyond the camphor laurels a train clanked and chugged, picked up speed and slid invisibly towards Sydney.

Delia said, 'And not finishing your essay. You want to win a scholarship, don't you?'

'What else would I do?'

'You're not making sense, Maggie.'

'Come on, it's starting to spit.'

'And you're always late for tea, when you come back from the library. We hardly ever talk, I can never find you after school.'

'I'm only late to get in the line, not for tea.'

I knew Delia was hurt, sensing that I was shutting her out. I felt a lump in my throat as big as a marble. We walked on inside the silence, and, as we always did at this time on rainy afternoons, climbed the stairs all the way to the attic. Here the juniors washed in the mornings at the double row of basins set on long benches, and kept their clothes in lockers. Delia and I walked into the private space of a dormer window.

We looked down onto the blurred crown of the old mulberry tree far below and the roofs of the houses beyond the school wall. The rain slid down the windowpanes, and the wet under-clothes drying on the makeshift lines behind us seemed to bring the cold and damp inside.

'I've been wanting to tell you. I didn't know how. I still don't know how. I'm not supposed to. Father Nihill . . . he's in love with me. I'm in love with him too.' I blurted it out before I could stop myself.

Delia stared at me, speechless, stricken. Facing her, with the secret in the open between us, I realised how much I missed the simple, happy world I'd left behind.

'You have to stop.'

'I can't.'

'But Maggie!'

'I don't know how. I don't want to.' I wanted to and I didn't want to. How could I explain this? I didn't understand it myself.

'But where can it lead to? It can't lead anywhere. It'll only get you into trouble.'

'I can't help it.' I fell and fell through galaxies of rushing air. 'You won't tell anyone, will you?'

'Not if you don't want me to.' Delia's voice was flat. 'But I think you should.'

'Who? There's no one I could tell. I'd get expelled. Lloyd'd get excommunicated or something. Mum'd die – after she'd killed me.' I tried to smile, to bring the conversation onto some kind of normal ground.

Delia didn't smile. 'Well the nuns then. They might be able to help you. Or just Sister Theresa. I'm sure they'd still let you do the exams at this stage.'

But this was unthinkable, and it was too late. I stood outside the walls, the doors behind me bolted shut, the drawbridge up. 'Lloyd said he'd be kicked out of the priesthood, if anyone found out. He'd have nowhere to go. He said he's got a real vocation, but he loves me too.'

'But what's going to happen to you? He can't have both. How can that work?'

'You don't understand.'

'Okay, maybe you can't help how you feel. But if you go on seeing him in secret, someone's sure to find out.'

'What's it got to do with anyone else? I don't believe in mortal sin, or hell. Neither do you.'

'What about him?'

'We don't talk about religion. But he says it's not wrong if we love each other.'

Delia stood up. 'I wish I didn't know about this.' She shook her head.

I saw the look on her face. I hadn't thought that telling her would cause her pain – not that I'd stopped to think. 'I haven't got any choice.'

'Yes you have.' Delia sighed. 'You've always got a choice.'

'We'd better go to study. And I can't be late for the concert.'

'Who cares about the concert?'

I looked out on the sodden, dimming world. I could no longer look at Delia. She let out a breath, as though she'd been holding it a long time, and, ducking under the stockings and underclothes on the lines, walked out into the attic and down the stairs. I felt marooned, unable to find my way forwards or back. Then I followed her.

In the library I joined her at our usual table beside the casement window, now closed against the rain which struck the glass aslant. She didn't look up. I loved to work on afternoons like this, inside the warm, golden room of wooden floor and wooden ceiling beamed and vaulted, the rows of books glowing behind glass: to look up from my homework and out at the cold, blurred world outside. Now the rain made me feel drowsy and dull.

'Did you hand your essay in?' I said.

Delia nodded.

I opened the play and got out the essay question. Again the sweet lethargy took hold. I'd have to write it sooner or later. But all I cared about was that tonight I'd be in the same room as Lloyd. He was the only person I could be close to now.

'Margaret. Margaret Reed, I want to talk to you.'

I turned my head. Sister Theresa stood behind me.

I jumped up. 'Good afternoon, Sister.'

She called me Margaret only on formal occasions, like speech night.

'You haven't handed in your essay.'

'No, Sister.'

'Why not?'

'I haven't done it yet, Sister.'

'Why haven't you done it?'

'I couldn't think of anything to write, Sister.'

'You've had two weeks. We read the play in class. And discussed it. Well? I suppose you were intending to go to this concert tonight?'

'Yes, Sister – I'm in it. Everyone's going.'

'Until you've written this essay, you'll stay here.'

'But, Sister, I'm *in* the concert.'

'After tea, you'll come back here, and you'll stay here until it's finished.'

'Yes, Sister.'

Delia was looking at me. She tilted her chair back so that it balanced on two legs, and steadied herself with her fingertips on the table. I could see she was hoping I'd say something to Sister Theresa, at least tell her that I had a problem. But I stayed silent, to keep the room, the world, intact.

Sister Theresa clasped to her scapular the pile of essays she'd collected from the teacher's desk in the classroom next door. With a flourish of her veil she turned and vanished onto the landing outside, where Lloyd had entered the library on that autumn morning, it seemed years ago.

The bell rang. Delia said, 'Coming to tea?'

I shook my head. 'Not until I get this finished.'

She left with the girls who got up from the other tables; they whispered and stared.

Now the windows framed darkness. I tried to concentrate on the book in front of me, and turned the pages. The words looked foreign. The poetry usually excited me, but now it seemed deliberately to slow me down. I looked at the question although I knew it by heart, forced myself to think. I picked a scene, wrote notes in pencil in the margins, made myself write down quotes. The small effort – spent against the weight of my indifference, my desire to be elsewhere – exhausted me.

I got up from the table and paced out to the landing halfway down the stairs, at the bottom of which I'd seen Lloyd that other afternoon, on my way to the library in the town. Despite the rain I could hear the clatter of cutlery and crockery, and the voices from the refectory: I wanted to run down the stairs, along the covered passage and into the big, cheerful room. But instead I went back to my work.

Delia came back after tea. 'How're you going?' She took from behind her pinafore a sandwich of bread and butter. 'It's all I could carry without Bernie noticing.'

'I'm not hungry. But thanks anyway. I've started making notes.'

'You'll be here till midnight.'

'Delia? Do me a favour?'

'What is it?'

'Tell Lloyd – Father Nihill – what's happened. Tell him I'm sorry I won't get there on time. Don't know if I'll make it at all.'

She hesitated, then nodded and left.

The empty room seemed huge. I examined my notes, traced a pattern of ideas. As I started to write, I heard in the street, beyond the nearest gate, the voices heightened like the voices at a party, and the footsteps of the seniors on their way to the town hall. Sister Theresa glided into the room, and I jumped.

'Well?'

'I've started it, Sister.'

She stood a moment without speaking. Then she said, 'It's not like you to be lazy. You were always a self-starter.'

I rolled my pen between two fingers.

'Is there something the matter, Maggie?'

I blinked away the sudden tears. 'No, Sister.'

'Are you sure?'

'Yes, Sister.'

'You could be a scholar – if you work hard.'

I glanced up at her. I'd never told her the extent of my ambitions, beyond winning a scholarship and going to university. Now she was encouraging me, as if she'd guessed.

'I'll leave you to get on with it.' She moved away. 'I'll be in the hall, when you've finished.'

I set to work again. The desire to give up, to stop at every hurdle and turn back, was almost physical. I pushed against it. In three-quarters of an hour I'd finished the rough copy. Why hadn't I done this before?

Sister Theresa rustled back into the room, set down a cup of tea, and went away. Looking up, I sensed a lifting of pressure, a gap in the atmosphere. The rain had stopped. Back at work I lost consciousness of everything except the old king, blind and mad in the storm on the heath, the wars splitting up family and country, the threads of the argument I wove on the page.

When I finished it was quiet outside except for the splashing of drops into a puddle. Only now did I look at my watch. It had been hours since I'd started. Would the concert be over? But if I hurried I'd still see Lloyd.

At the teacher's desk in the hall, where the juniors sat doing their homework, Sister Theresa accepted the essay. She looked at me with a quizzical frown, and nodded.

A shiny darkness coated the streets. Behind the shifting gauze of cloud were stars, a milky moon. I registered the cold but didn't feel it. Only the slipperiness underfoot stopped me from sprinting.

As I opened the heavy door into the hall, I heard Lloyd's voice, his laugh. Inside they were all on the stage, spotlit, Lloyd and Danny and the others, still tuning their guitars. I couldn't hear what Lloyd was saying, only the sound of his voice, the waves of laughter from the audience. We were supposed to go on first. He must have changed the program for me. But I'd forgotten my guitar. Then I saw it resting against the empty chair between Danny and Lloyd. Delia must have brought it. The sight of it filled me with remorse, as if I'd betrayed her as well as Danny. Then I could think only about sitting next to Lloyd. I floated, it seemed, towards the stage, where I climbed into the light.

'Ah!' Lloyd said. 'Here she is. The one we've all been waiting for. Now let's get this show on the road.'

❖

Lloyd was good at getting people to give him their keys: they trusted him. On a late afternoon, when Brendan Rigby, the parish caretaker, was in Sydney visiting his family, I walked quickly past the cathedral and the presbytery, around the back of the Parish Hall and across the yard to Brendan's flat in the converted stables. The back windows of the hall and the shops that fronted Main Street reflected the clouds. I imagined faces looking down.

Lloyd had slipped out of the cathedral and unlocked the door between confessions. In the tiny kitchen I took off my hat and gloves. I kept my blazer on, but still shivered. There was one small window which looked out at the ridge of the levee bank at the end of the yard. I pictured the bend of the river, imagining how in times of flood a torrent of muddy water would overflow the bank and force its way inside, as if a beast that lived beneath the surface had awakened.

I had never felt such cold in a Cumberland winter before. I usually loved the long term in the middle of the year, bracketed by shorter holidays than the Christmas one. Even though there was no heating, the proximity of other bodies in class, in study, in chapel, at table, seemed to warm the rooms. We boarders kept our blazers on over our pinafores and wore our pixie hoods out of doors. Delia and I walked; we stoked the furnace in the basement, toasting on a fork the bread we'd smuggled out of the refectory. Now wherever I waited for Lloyd, and when we were together in unhospitable places, my flesh bared for him to touch, I froze. The heat of his body seemed soon to dissipate in contact with mine, with the frigid air.

I sat waiting for him at the table, which was gritty with crumbs, and set aside a cup, half filled with cold tea, and a stained newspaper opened at the form guide. From the library books I'd borrowed on the way I selected *Ravages* and began to read.

The light dimmed, the words faded on the page. I wasn't game to turn on the light. I listened for the sound of Lloyd's furtive footsteps in the yard. A light mist rose from the river, and the stillness and the quiet spread.

I was supposed to be in the town library. Soon it would close. It would be time to line up on the cloister to go to tea. I became agitated. All day I'd been looking forward to seeing Lloyd. To miss him would be unbearable.

The door opened and he appeared, his soutane flapping and settling about his legs beneath his black overcoat. 'I hope you haven't been waiting too long.'

'Not really.'

He went over to the window and stood staring out of it. Then he turned and walked to the bottom of the ladder leading to the loft bedroom and stood looking up. His expression was startled and blank. He didn't look at me or speak. He sighed and rubbed his eyes with the heels of his hands.

'What's the matter? Has somebody found out?' I felt hollow and weak.

'A dreadful thing's just happened, that's why I'm so late. O'Rourke told me about it when he took over in the confessional. Brendan's been killed on his way back here. In a car crash.'

I stood up and the black wings of his arms enfolded me. I clung to him. I loved to press my cheek into the prickly folds of his maroon scarf and breathe in the smell of the wool. This time it was no comfort. On a white plate on the table the butter had congealed in a half-eaten pile of baked beans on toast. Across a chair-back lay a limp brown jumper, its limbs and torso still twisted from the force of the haste in which it had been flung.

'That's terrible.' I was ashamed: appalled at my relief. Then I saw the mangled body in the crumpled metal, amid the splintered glass.

'Yeah. The poor bastard. He was a good mate.' I'd never seen Lloyd's face drained of colour, of animation. I felt sorry for him.

'What can we do?'

'All we can do is try and console one another.'

'I have to get back. Study'll be over soon.'

'Come upstairs, just for a little while.'

'But it's so late, and somebody might come. I mean, now that . . .'

'Not today they won't.'

'But what about Brendan? It feels wrong to stay here now.'

'Brendan wouldn't mind. He knew I was going to bring you here.'

'You told him about me?' I was mortified to think that the big, gentle man had known what I did with a priest: what a priest did to me. I looked up at him.

'I told O'Rourke, too. Sometimes I have to swap confessions with him so I can get away.'

'Father O'Rourke?'

'We play golf together. He's a good cobber.'

'What did he say?'

'Sam? Oh, he said, "You lucky bugger."' Lloyd smiled. 'He said, "It's a lonely life, mate."'

I was too shocked to speak.

'What's the matter?' Lloyd said. 'It's all right, Brendan wouldn't have . . . O'Rourke would never let on. But you mustn't ever tell anyone – you know that, don't you?'

'I just told Delia.'

'You what?' Lloyd's face reddened with anger, the veins stood out on his temples.

'You told people too.'

'They're my best mates. Brendan was, anyway. What did Delia say?'

'She said I should stop. She said I should tell someone.'

'Jesus Christ. Why didn't you just do what I said?' Lloyd unclasped my hands from his back and stepped away from me.

He'd never raised his voice to me before. The terror and the impulse to placate him were reflexes as strong as though he'd physically tapped a nerve. 'I'm sorry. I know I shouldn't have told her. But Delia would never tell anyone – you don't have to worry.'

'What if she blabs to the nuns?'

'I trust her. She's my best friend.'

'She's still only a kid.' Lloyd sat down, his hands in his coat pockets. He sucked in a mouthful of air, puffing his cheeks, and expelled it noisily.

I was suddenly exhausted, as when I'd crammed my mind for too many hours with too many facts.

Lloyd looked at his watch. He sighed. 'We've still got a little while. Let's go upstairs.' He stood up and took off his overcoat.

The room seemed empty, even though Lloyd and I were standing in it. Death was this vacuum, it was the greyness of an early winter evening, the quiet in the abandoned flat, the numbing cold. It was fear of not being loved.

I couldn't believe that other men, one of them a priest, had known about us and thought it was all right. Delia didn't think it was. My hands were trembling violently, and I picked up my gloves from the table. Lloyd moved close to me and took the gloves from me and put them back. His expression had softened. He took both my hands in his and rubbed them warm. It was as though he'd lit a little fire in the room. Walking backwards, he guided me to the bottom of the ladder.

We climbed to the loft. The open doors of the lowboy were draped with a pair of trousers, a cardigan, a shirt. I stood looking at the dead man's bed. The blankets were flung aside, the sheets were twisted.

'Hurry up and get undressed,' Lloyd said. 'Who knows what's going to happen now you've blown our cover. This might be the last time we can be together, so let's make the most of it.'

'I don't want to get into his bed.'

'Come on, Maggie.'

I needed to feel that he wanted me; it was the only way I could know he really loved me. My fingers thick with cold, I unbuttoned my blazer, unbuckled my belt, took off my tunic and curled inside the empty hollow in the bed. I watched Lloyd take off his soutane. The black cloth that covered his chest, with the celluloid collar attached, wasn't a real garment;

it had no back or sides but only strings to tie behind. In his white T-shirt he looked vulnerable. Someone who could be smashed to pieces by the force of a speeding car.

'"No more but such a poor, bare, forked animal,"' I said.

'What?'

'Nothing. We did *King Lear* in English. Sister Theresa made us learn bits by heart.'

'You say some queer things sometimes. Let's forget about Shakespeare for the time being.'

Lloyd held me to him: he moved back and forth against me, he breathed loudly into my ear, he shuddered. But my flesh was stone, even where it joined with his. The sheets were clammy, and the blanket he drew up behind me as I lay on my side felt stiff, as if it'd been in a freezer.

Over his shoulder, I saw through the sloping window the thickening mist, the enveloping dusk. At home it would be quiet while they waited for my father. The children would soon leave off their games, the chirruping birds flee the yard, all sounds of cars and voices recede, and the house would become an island of silence, of dread calm. At school the nuns would be filing out of the chapel after vespers. In the senior library the other girls would be yawning and restless. The refectory would be bright with light, the tables laid. If I didn't get back in time my place would be empty. It was like looking back on the world after I'd died.

I disentangled myself from Lloyd and sat up on the edge of the bed.

'What's up?' he said.

'I can't stay here.' I pulled on my uniform.

'Because of Brendan?'

'Because of everything. We can't even come back here again. It's the only place we've been able to go for ages except the car.' Adrenaline seemed to pour into me invisibly from some inexhaustible source. I had an instinctive desire to run from the flat, from Lloyd, from our predicament. But I was riven; I was fighting against myself.

'You can come and see me at the presbytery.'

'I'd be too scared.'

'No need to be scared, if we're careful.'

'I don't like telling lies about where I've been. I don't like having to hide all the time.'

'We haven't got any choice about that.'

'It'll be the September holidays in a couple of weeks. Then the exams, then I'll have to leave school. What are we going to do after that?'

'Worry about that when it happens.' Lloyd looked annoyed. He sat up and searched for his clothes. I was already dressed. It was almost dark. I thought about Brendan not ever coming home to this room, his body already cold. Not to see Lloyd anymore would be a kind of dying, too.

I said, 'I have to go or they'll start looking for me.'

'Will you come and see me at the presbytery? Everyone visits me there. No one'll think anything of it.'

'I might.'

I moved to the trapdoor, sped down the ladder rungs and scooped up my books from the table. I ran along Main Street, around the corner and through the convent gate, onto the cloister where already they were walking to the refectory. The movement quickened my blood. I was warm. I smelt the food. Across the garden the chapel windows were brighter than the dimming sky, the faces around me luminous. And beside her, though she turned away when she saw me, Delia had kept my place.

❖

After the holidays, at the beginning of third term, wearing my short-sleeved blouse and straw boater, I entered the school through the gate in the high brick wall adjoining the chapel, which partly formed one side of the perimeter of the grounds. As soon as I shut the gate behind me I felt free from fear, from harm. The fragrance of the star jasmine festooning the chapel cloister was afloat on the warm air.

Every morning, before anyone else was awake, I breathed in this scent while I studied in the garden, and felt again the pure, clear happiness of earlier springs. I recited vocabulary under my breath, I memorised the causes of wars in modern Europe and Ancient Greece, and I learnt poetry by heart. The days, the weeks, rushed on. I had to work fast to catch up after the daydreaming about Lloyd in second term.

I'd thought about him enough during the holidays. I missed him, but I had to concentrate on work, on winning a scholarship.

Straight after school on weekdays, and after breakfast on weekends – with the exams so close, I had a good excuse not to go home – I went to the senior library to study. Delia joined me there: we smuggled in our pieces of fruit under our pinafores, in case Colleen saw and reported us, but we ate and studied opposite each other in silence. Since Delia took all her classes except English at the Brothers' school, and we rarely met to talk on our own, I felt almost estranged from her. We never spoke about Lloyd.

When he came to say mass I avoided looking at his face, and I closed my eyes at the communion rail until he'd moved on to the next girl. If I heard his voice in the courtyard I stayed inside. Then, one morning in late October, I was studying alone in the sun in the courtyard when the gate opened, and there he was. I closed my English textbook on one finger to keep my place.

'Hello, Maggie. I hoped I might find you round here. I've waited for you to ring the bell at the presbytery every afternoon, so I could beat the housekeeper to the door. Mrs Delaney is the only one who opens it – you don't have to worry about seeing anyone else.' He placed one hand on the wall beside the bench where I was sitting and leaned towards me.

'I'm sorry. I've been studying for the exams.'

'I miss you. Couldn't you come over and see me one afternoon?' One corner of his mouth was open crookedly, showing a slice of bottom teeth. It was what people looked like when they were scared, or unsure of themselves.

'I don't know.'

Lloyd sighed. His black suit stood out in the courtyard like a mournful flag. I was holding on to the book so tightly my finger hurt.

'What about driving practice?'

'I won't have time till after the exams. My grandfather took me out a few times in the holidays. I told Mum you were teaching me, and she asked him to. She said it was good of you to take the trouble.'

'So when will I see you by yourself?'

He leaned closer. I felt the inner turbulence, the quickening of heartbeat and breath. The impulse to feel connected to him was so strong, even here, that I had to sit on the hand that wasn't holding the book. Lloyd looked at me with a plaintive expression.

I said, 'I'll come to the presbytery the day after the exams.'

❖

I had only seen the bishop at ceremonies, or when he'd said a special mass in the cathedral. He was a large, tall man – taller when he wore his mitre. At speech nights on the town hall stage he had sat in a special chair like a throne, and I was too shy to look up at him directly when he congratulated me on my award and held out his hand for me to kiss his ring. Now I had to go to his house and ask to see Lloyd.

I was so nervous I walked past the gate and climbed the steep bank at the end of the street and looked out over the river.

Fat with clouds, shimmering in the heat of late afternoon, it slipped between its wide, sandy banks. I looked behind me and saw that the windows of Brendan Rigby's flat were boarded up, the kitchen one broken behind the planks. I remembered the cold inside the flat the last time I'd met Lloyd there. I thought of the other places I'd been alone with him: his car, hidden among the lucerne paddocks on a back road; parishioners' houses when they were away. The convent parlour had become too dangerous. Now it was the end of the year, the end of my schooldays, and the presbytery was the last place we were going to meet. It seemed incredible that we'd been meeting in private for most of the year without anyone noticing.

Exhausted from studying until late into the night for so many weeks, and from the intensity of the concentrated effort in the exams, I couldn't grasp the reality that I'd sleep in the sixth year dormitory for two more nights, and then I'd have to leave. I was dreading the longer holidays at home with no school to look forward to when they were over. I felt bereft at the thought of parting from Delia for good.

After the English exam, the last one, I'd felt elated. I was certain I'd done well enough to win a scholarship. Going to university in Sydney seemed inevitable but it was unimaginable, as being an adult is to a child. In the same way, I hadn't been able to imagine what it would be like not to see Lloyd. But I already had the detached feeling of someone on a journey, watching through the train window as the people left behind recede and vanish.

On the way back to the presbytery I could hear Danny practising the organ for Sunday mass in the cathedral across the narrow street. I flung open the iron gate and scurried up the path, hoping Danny would soon be finished and I wouldn't run into him on my way back.

Mrs Delaney answered the door.

'Is Father Nihill there? He asked me to come and see him.' My mouth was so dry it was hard to speak clearly.

The hall was wide, the stairs were grand: they led to the secret apartments above, where Lloyd and the other priests lived their mysterious lives. Mrs Delaney watched, frowning, as Lloyd hurried down the stairs without waiting for her to call him. At last she turned away.

Lloyd closed the parlour door behind us. In that room I felt smaller. The ceiling seemed two storeys high, the furniture too large for human frames. Lloyd looked at me with an intense, hungry expression and led me by the hand to the part of the room furthest away from the two windows that overlooked the verandah.

'She's suspicious,' I said.

Lloyd took off my hat and then each glove and threw them onto the floor. 'She always looks like that. Come here.' He put his arms around me. He put one hand around the back of my head and pulled my face towards his.

'Wait a minute. Don't you want to know how I went in the exams?'

'Of course I do.'

'I think I did well. Especially in English. French and Latin too. Ancient history was the hardest.'

'That's good. I knew you'd go all right. Now let me kiss you, for God's sake.'

It was a shock: the bulk of him, the heat; his hard teeth, his probing tongue. He guided me down onto the floor and lay on top of me next to the empty fireplace. Even on this warm afternoon the marble mantelpiece seemed to emanate cold and I could smell the winter smell of cold ash.

Lloyd lifted the hem of my tunic and ran his hand along my thigh almost to the top of my stocking. The organ music lapped at the curtained windows in swollen, breaking waves. I had a moment of panic at the thought of the bishop in a room upstairs, as though he might sense what was happening on the floor below, possibly right beneath him.

When Lloyd was finished I sat on his knee in a plush-covered chair. We were both disarranged. I combed my hair with my fingers, and then his. He was smiling at me with a contented, satiated expression.

He said, 'I bet you're looking forward to the holidays after all that studying.'

'I can't stand the holidays. I'd rather stay at school.'

'I was only six when I went to boarding school.'

'What was it like, going there when you were so little?' I imagined the lonely boy in his little uniform. Sometimes a lost expression passed across Lloyd's features, like a shadow. He'd look momentarily unsure, then seem to force the cheerfulness back into his tone and expression.

'I hated it.'

'I'll miss it when I leave. I'll miss you, too.'

He stiffened. 'But we'll still see each other, won't we?'

'I mean when I go to university, if I get a scholarship. When I go to Sydney.'

'Why couldn't you go to Coalport?'

'I told you before: it's not far enough away from home.'

'What about me?' His face was contorted. It was hard to tell if he was angry or upset, or both.

'If I didn't go to university in Sydney, I'd die.'

'I never heard anything so ridiculous.'

Sometimes his tone could make me feel childish, or silly, but now it reminded me of my inferiority. I saw how the shabbiness of my hat and gloves stood out on the floor against the immaculate rug. I was still a schoolgirl, and an intruder in the presbytery parlour. I felt the discomfort physically and got up off his lap. 'I'm leaving school. Nothing can be the same.'

'Don't you love me?' Now Lloyd looked piteous. He stood up and I leaned into him and felt the sharpness of his collar against the top of my head.

'Of course I do.'

Somewhere a clock chimed. I stepped away from him. 'I have to go, I'll be late for tea.' I hadn't heard the music for a while. Danny must have gone home.

'So you're going to make me go all the way to Sydney to see you?'

'You don't have to.' I hadn't thought beyond the effort of getting there.

'Wouldn't you want me to?'

I didn't know what I might want in that life I couldn't yet imagine. He still looked wounded. I didn't want to leave him, and I didn't want to stay any longer in the presbytery, which had the hush and the dimmed daylight and impenetrable coolness of a fortress. I had a horror of being caught there and unable to escape.

He looked at his watch and sighed. 'I have to go and hear confessions. But I'll see you when you come back for your driving test. We could go to Lantic Bay, if you can get away. We'll work it all out then.' He was recovering, and sounded like someone making normal arrangements.

'That'd be good. I'll have to mind the boys while Mum's at work, but I should be able to get away for a weekend.'

'Ring me up in the holidays. Make a person-to-person call.'

Outside the room the front door opened, and a heavy tread echoed in the hall. Lloyd opened the parlour door a crack. I straightened my tunic and put on my hat and gloves. When Lloyd nodded, I sped out of the hall and down the steps, my back exposed to the gaze of the housekeeper, of the bishop in an upstairs room. The mansion behind me grew in my imagination as huge as the Vatican, as the vast establishment of the church.

❖

The next day, I stood alone in the bottom paddock in the late afternoon, listening to the plovers' scolding cries and the slow shunting of trains, until the camphor laurels darkened to black shapes against the orange-pink sky. I walked back up through the garden and leaned on the verandah rail outside the hall where the younger girls sat in silence over their homework. Across the garden the western wall of the chapel glowed red. The nuns were singing vespers. I watched the sky of soft mauve above the slate roof turn to violet then to twilight blue. I waited for the stars to appear one by one – the first two forming the base of a triangle, the third the apex – as if lighted by an invisible hand.

'I suppose I'll miss this place.' It was Delia, at my elbow.

'I know I will.'

'I can't believe it's our last night.'

'If I wrote to you would you write back? We could even see each other sometimes, if we're both in Sydney.'

'We'll keep in touch somehow. I don't feel any different, you know, since you told me about you and Father . . . about Lloyd. I don't reckon anything'd ever make a difference. At first I was shocked. Well, stunned. And ever since I've been worried.'

I nodded, without taking my gaze from the sky. I didn't trust myself to look at her, and I couldn't think of any words.

Delia said, 'What'll happen now? With you and Lloyd?'

I shrugged. 'I don't know. He wants to see me in Sydney, if I go there.' So much was changing so fast. I felt overwhelmed standing beside Delia and looking up at the familiar view of the sky, which darkened and deepened, studded with burning stars.

'Wouldn't it be a good time to stop it?'

'I have to see him in the holidays when I have my driving test.'

Delia looked away and up at the sky.

After a while I said, 'It's hard to believe a lot of them are dead.' My throat ached. 'The stars. It's like looking at their ghosts.'

'Maybe they're not, if we can still see them. Their light, I mean. Maybe it's just a different kind of life.'

'Like memory?'

'I don't know. But they're still bright. It means something apart from them just being dead, doesn't it?'

The next day, while the younger girls were still in class, I walked to the bus stop carrying two ports, one filled with books, the other with clothes. All the other sixth year girls had left. Delia's mother had pulled up suddenly in her Morris Minor and then Delia was gone. I was dazed from the good-byes. My bed was stripped, my wardrobe, desk and locker bare. After dinner, the sixth year's table in the back corner of the refectory had not been set for tea.

❖

Every morning at home I woke to the monotonous calls of the doves that seemed to live outside the window, and to the nausea, which only abated when I opened my book. I had to read immediately so I could bear to get up.

At Christmas time in Abernant you walked around wrapped in a blanket of heat; you breathed heat instead of air. On the hottest days, if there was enough money, I took Johnny and Billy to the baths, where the children cavorted and shrieked in the electric blue rectangles of water set in the hot cement, and I made sure they didn't burn or drown. Or I sat at home in the cave of the mulberry tree, reading in my seat in the fork, while the boys built roadways in the dirt beneath for their Matchbox toys.

In the last year, Luke had grown into a tall stranger, with huge feet in flapping thongs, a rasping voice and an unfamiliar, elongated face. Relieved I was taking charge, he stayed out most of the day. When he came in he had the smell of sweat on him like a man, mixed with the smell of children who still play among dirt and grass and leaves. Anne was either working at the hospital as a trainee nurse, or sleeping before night shift.

In the afternoons I waited for the time to bring the washing in from the line and fold it, to peel the potatoes and shell the peas. When the light mellowed, soon after my mother came home from work, a hush descended. I imagined I could hear the sharp leaves of the oleanders scraping together, the rustling of insects in the grass.

When it was long past teatime and my father still wasn't home, the house seemed filled with random objects whose purpose was unclear. Nothing was solid: on the edge of my vision whole walls dissolved; I put out my hand to touch the back of a chair, and it seemed to crumble beneath my fingers.

Some things were detailed and clear: the bubbly texture of the tablecloth with the grains of spilled sugar and the stiff tea stains; a brittle flap of torn flywire sticking out of the screen door frame. The lounge room was empty: no one went in there or sat in my father's chair, as if it were haunted. When he came home, I waited for the long battle to finish, and to be able to go to sleep.

I waited for the exam and scholarship results to be published, and I waited to go to Lantic Bay with Lloyd.

One afternoon on my way to the shop I rang him from the phone box. I heard the operator tell Mrs Delaney it was a person-to-person call for Father Nihill. Lloyd took such a long time to come to the phone, I was sure he wasn't there. I stood looking out at the street, listening to the static. When he spoke I jumped.

'It's me,' I said.

'How are you? How are things going over there?' His tone was hearty.

'Everything's the same. How are you?'

'Good, real good. So, what can I do for you?'

'I miss you.'

'Good to hear. Always good to hear good news.'

'Do you miss me too?'

'I'm glad you brought that up. I couldn't agree more.'

Outside the hall where he was speaking was the street that led at one end to the river, at the other to Main Street and along to St Dominic's. How could the words reach me from so far away?

'Are you there?' Lloyd said.

'Yes, I'm here.'

'So I'd better confirm that date with you.'

'Are we going to Lantic Bay, too?'

'That's right. The first Saturday in February. I got us a special appointment – the copper owes me a favour. D'you think you'll be able to get away?'

'I'll tell Mum I'm going to stay with a friend.'

'Good, that's good. Well, I'd better go, mate, someone's waiting to use the blower. Take it easy, won't you? See you real soon.'

I felt lonely, hearing him talk to me as though I could have been anyone.

On Christmas Eve we went to midnight mass, leaving my father to bellow in the empty house. When we got home he was asleep. We put Billy and Johnny to bed, and opened the presents my mother had paid off on lay-by, leaving the little boys' in pillowcases at the ends of their beds. My mother had bought me some clothes for university; she was sure I'd get a scholarship.

On Christmas Day the pubs were shut, so my father was sober. It was so hot that the air smelt scorched, and it burned your nostrils as you breathed. After the roast chicken and tinned plum pudding and cream it was over – there was nothing to do but sit on the threadbare carpet in the hall waiting for a breath of air to be sucked between the two screen doors at either end.

On Boxing Day my father went to the pub and came home drunk, and he stayed drunk until after New Year's Day, when he went back to work. During that week the rain came. It filled the creeks with currents like writhing snakes; children waded in the unpaved gutters; muddy pools appeared in the dirt surfaces of the back streets; everywhere there were pools and runnels of warm, brown water, and the nights were filled with the zinging of mosquitoes and the belching of frogs.

The rain never drowned the sound of my father's shouting, half the day, most of the night. I tried to imagine I was walking in the convent garden, but it didn't work, because I was never going back. So I thought about Lloyd.

❖

My exam results arrived at last, and they were as good as I'd hoped they'd be. The morning the names of the scholarship winners were published was the first time I had ever seen my grandfather in our house.

'I got up early and bought the paper,' he said in the kitchen. 'But I haven't looked at it. I waited till I saw Maggie.'

His fingers trembled as he opened the newspaper on the kitchen bench beside the stove. I'd never seen him excited about anything. My mother, ready for work, looked over his shoulder.

My grandfather pointed out my name in the long lists. 'A Commonwealth one,' he said. 'And an education department one, too!'

I felt light, as if an invisible set of wings had sprouted and bore me hovering inches above the lino, ready for flight.

'Two! You've won two!' my mother said. She didn't hug anyone except babies, but I knew she was proud of me, and happy, because in her mind my escape was somehow linked with hers. The reason for her children's existence, we all knew, was to make her happy, and yet, unable to protect her from our father, we always failed. Now I had made her smile.

'Which one will you take?' my grandfather said.

'The Commonwealth. I don't want to be a teacher. I'd rather learn.'

'What do you want to be?'

'I don't know yet. I always wanted to be an artist, but I can't study that at university. Maybe a writer. Sister Theresa said I could be a scholar.'

'Can you earn money doing that?' my grandfather said.

'Plenty of time to decide,' my mother said.

❖

'Where do you think you're going all dolled up?' My father stood close to me, chin tilted, eyes narrowed.

'I'm going to a dance at the Parish Hall in Cumberland. Mum said I could. She said I could stay the weekend at a friend's.'

He put out his hand and ran his fingers over my face and neck. 'Not bad,' he said. 'Neck's a bit thick, though.'

I turned away. My mother frowned at him and shook her head.

'Don't you look at me like that,' he said to her.

'Who on earth would want to look at you?' my mother said.

My father clenched his fist into a hard ball.

'You,' Luke hissed at me.

'I didn't do anything.'

The front door opened. It distracted my father, and he dropped his fist. It was Anne, still dressed in her nurse's uniform. My father glared at her and the rest of us in disgust, and went into the lounge room. Anne and I led our mother into the kitchen. Luke took the little boys outside.

'I'll make you a cup of tea, Mum,' I said.

'Get me one of those Relaxa-tabs.'

'I have to go,' I whispered to Anne.

'Go on. I told you I'd take over.'

Our mother sat passively at the table, as if she couldn't hear us.

Luke came back in. 'Who do you think looks after her when you're not here?'

I went over to my mother and kissed her on the cheek. 'I have to go now, Mum. Hooray.'

'Hooray.' My mother didn't move or look at me.

I went out the back door. If I walked past the lounge room, he'd call out for me to pour him a beer or light him a smoke. I'd miss the bus. From the yard I could hear him winding himself up again, listing all my mother's faults, her imaginary betrayals.

In the street the houses flowed past, but I felt as if I were walking on the spot. I turned into Blacket Road. Behind the wire fence of the baths there was cheerful, ordinary life: the wet bodies flashed among the spray, the shrill voices bounced off the concrete and the tiles. I slowed down and took a deep breath. A part of me was still back there, trying to save my mother's life. The part that walked on towards the bus stop felt guilty that I was not. Maybe Luke was right to blame me for provoking my father's anger. I must have done something to cause it. When I went away for good it might be better for everyone.

❖

At the top of the hill above Hirst's Hollow, as the bus crossed the imaginary border, I looked down onto Cumberland. There the summer was different. The river water permeated the soil: grass and foliage were a deeper green. Somewhere there were cool gardens lit by golden lilies; wide verandahs floating on lawns; the fragrant shade of peppercorn trees at the bottoms of dusty yards.

Inside the locked gates of the convent it was as quiet as a graveyard. I walked on, past the cathedral and the presbytery.

Behind the boys' school Lloyd was waiting in the car, the engine running. I stopped thinking, finally, about what was happening at home.

'I've missed you,' he said. He looked injured, as though I'd stayed away from him on purpose.

'Me too. I've missed you too.'

'I don't know how you'll go in the test; it's been a long time. Better get a bit of practice in first.'

He got in the passenger side and I sat behind the wheel. He slid over close to me with his hand on my knee. I drove out into the farmland and around the lucerne paddocks. Back in the town I practised parking. When it was time to take the test Lloyd dropped me off at the courthouse. He greeted the police officer as if he were an old friend.

With the policeman sitting beside me, I drove around the town. There weren't many traffic lights. The man was about Lloyd's age. He was friendly and relaxed. He told me to drive, to park, to drive some more, then we went back to the courthouse and I parked under the spreading, summer-leaved trees. It had been easier than I'd expected. I had passed. I had no idea when I'd be able to drive again but it didn't matter: I was becoming independent, with my scholarship and soon a driver's licence, too.

Lloyd shook hands with the policeman. They exchanged a few words I couldn't hear and laughed. Then Lloyd got in the car and I drove off.

'You were lucky to get your licence first go,' he said.

'I had a good teacher.'

'The policeman said to me, "Have you got any more like that?"' Lloyd squeezed the top of my thigh.

'Fancy him saying that to a priest.'

He roared laughing and I turned to him, astonished.

Lloyd took over the driving when we got near the coast. The road to the shack was rutted and narrow. It cut through the forest of tall gums.

'Home sweet home!' He turned onto the track with a swaggering motion of the steering wheel. The sky was clear, and a salt breeze blew in from the Pacific.

In the bedroom Lloyd took off his black clothes and the stiff collar. Then he undressed me and we got into the bed. He soon groaned and lay still.

We lay side by side. Lloyd turned to me. 'You'll have to get some birth control, so I can make love to you properly.'

'It's all right like this.' Each time it still overwhelmed me, as it was.

'You can get some in Sydney. Will you live at the uni?'

'I don't think there's anywhere to live at Macquarie. Mum's boss's got an aunty who lives near there. Her husband died a long time ago and she gets lonely, so I'm going to board with her.'

'It's a bloody long way away. But I'll get down and see you when I can.'

Shadows of knotted leaves and sequins of sunlight rocked on the wall beside the bed. Outside it was quiet except for the melodies of the bellbirds. There were a few other shacks scattered nearby. No one in the world knew where I was except Lloyd.

He had brought bread rolls, and sausages which he cooked on the barbecue. While we ate it got dark, and the fire went out. We heated the water in the kettle and washed up in the plastic dish.

'Have to get up early in the morning,' Lloyd said. 'I'm saying both masses in Markethall. The old bloke's sick again – that's how I managed to get away.'

'But I don't have to, do I?'

'Didn't I tell you? Remember Ricky Farrugia and Sue Quinlan? They just got married. I promised them the shack for their honeymoon; they can't afford to go anywhere else. They'll be down here first thing tomorrow morning.'

'Where'll I go then?'

'I'll think of something.'

'I could go to the beach.'

'It'll be too early. Anyway, I don't know how long I'll be, I could get stuck.'

'No it won't.'

'I'll think about it in the morning.'

After Lloyd had fallen asleep I lay awake a long time, wondering what it'd be like to live in Sydney, to go to university. There was no moon. We seemed buried in the darkness, and I lay apart from Lloyd because it was too hot to lie against him. Lying on our backs, I thought we must look like figures on a tomb: the statues I'd seen in books.

In the morning neither of us heard the alarm, and we slept in. In the car, Lloyd, clumsy with panic, pulled at the choke and swore and twisted the keys in the ignition till I thought they'd snap off.

I said, 'Will you drop me off at the beach?'

'I've had a better idea. The Dohertys are down here for the holidays – they've got a place just up the road. You can wait for me there.'

'The Dohertys?'

'Colleen was a school friend of yours, wasn't she?'

'She wasn't a friend. She was in my class, that's all.'

'Frank and Vi won't mind doing me a favour.'

'But we can't just turn up on the doorstep so early in the morning. Don't they know about the shack? Won't they think . . .'

'I'll tell them we've just driven down this morning. They won't think anything. Not in a million years. Here it is, this is the turn-off.'

'I can't go there. Colleen used to tease me about having a crush on you.'

Lloyd was still tense, but he half smiled. 'Did she?'

'I'll come to Markethall with you; I'd rather go to Markethall.'

'You'd be hanging around waiting too long.' He made it sound like the final word.

But I said, 'I don't care.'

Lloyd ignored me and I shut up. I wasn't game to start an argument. I remembered how he'd sworn and banged the steering wheel with the heels of his hands. Now I bit my lip so hard I wondered if it had bled.

❖

Mrs Doherty opened the door in her dressing-gown. Colleen stood behind her. They were both startled.

'G'day, Vi. Colleen.' Lloyd showed all his white teeth.

When she had recovered, Mrs Doherty smiled faintly. 'Hello, Father,' she said, finishing on a high note of enquiry.

Colleen Doherty's mother was beautiful. She looked as if she should have been famous, like a film star. Colleen looked annoyed. Inside the cottage a baby cried. Colleen disappeared and came back carrying a tiny bundle in a shawl. She looked out at Lloyd and me from the distance of her private world.

'I'm giving Maggie here a lift to Sydney,' Lloyd was saying. 'She's starting at the university soon, aren't you, Maggie? She's got to make some arrangements and I've got some business there myself. But I've got to say both masses at Markethall this morning. I wonder if I could trouble you good people to look after her for a while, till I get back?'

They both looked at me. 'Yes, all right, Father.' Mrs Doherty nodded uncertainly.

'Where's Frank? Did he come down for the weekend?' Lloyd backed away towards the car.

'He's taken the boys fishing. They went early, to catch some for breakfast.'

'Good for him. Well, see you later then.'

Brows lifted, Colleen and her mother exchanged a glance: Colleen's was ironic and put out, her mother's intrigued. I wasn't pleased to see Colleen either. We didn't speak to one another. Now I followed the two of them into the house feeling as if I'd entered without knocking.

On the kitchen table were a baby's bath, a folded nappy, a set of tiny garments. Colleen lay the baby on the towel beside these and began to unwrap him, nodding and smiling and clucking. She dipped her elbow into the water. Mrs Doherty stood beside her and put her little finger inside the baby's fist. The mother and daughter stood with their shoulders touching, and the edges of their hair.

The baby's eyes were unfocused, and he moved his head from side to side, sucking at the air. I stood with my legs pressed together beneath my short dress breathing in the fragrance of the baby powder. The bed Lloyd and I had just left would still be warm from our naked bodies. I tried not to think about this.

'What's his name?'

'Francis.' Colleen gazed at him with an expression so soft I could barely recognise her. She held him in the water in the crook of her arm and sponged him. As I watched her tender gestures, I realised that I had never even tried to talk to her. She and Delia had been friends, they had sport in common, and science and maths.

Maybe Colleen thought I was aloof, rather than shy. What if I'd laughed when she'd teased me, instead of taking it seriously? She'd been right to tease me for having a crush on Sister Bonaventure, then Lloyd. This was the reason it had made me angry. Also, she didn't like Lloyd. I remembered how whenever she was near him she folded her arms and hardened her expression. We were opposites: she obeyed rules, I broke them; she was the captain of sports teams, I avoided them; she was popular, I was considered eccentric and left alone. But the true difference between us lay in the reasons we were here in this room, so early in the morning. I felt that Colleen understood this, too. I was ashamed, defiant, embarrassed, confused.

Colleen dried the baby and put his nappy on.

'Well, I'll go and get dressed then,' Mrs Doherty said.

Colleen picked up her brother and began to rock him, standing in front of the window, looking out onto the trees. There was a clean, fresh smell in the cottage. A white muslin curtain ballooned at the window. I looked away from a pile of neatly folded laundry on a chair. On the table the teacups and the plates were set out; a dish of butter, a jug of milk. Mrs Doherty came back.

'What are you going to do now?' I asked Colleen.

'I'm going nursing.'

'I got into Macquarie.'

'Good for you. Danny's going to the Conservatorium in Coalport. Did you know that?'

'Oh, that's great.' Of course Colleen knew I didn't. Everyone knew we'd broken up. Was she going out with Danny now? Unexpectedly my heart felt as tight as a fist. I had no right to be jealous but I was, and I felt a loss as though someone had died, but a long time ago. I said, 'I think I'll go for a walk, Mrs Doherty. To the beach.'

'I don't know.' Mrs Doherty frowned. She looked at Colleen. 'Father thinks you're staying here with us.'

'But it's such a nice day. He won't be back for a while yet.'

'It's a fair walk from here. We always drive.'

'I don't mind walking. Can you please tell Father I've gone down there when he gets back?'

'Well, all right.'

'Thank you for having me. Hooray, Colleen.'

'Hooray.' Colleen glanced at me sidelong, cradling the baby, still rocking back and forth from foot to foot.

I fled out the door and down the steps. When I was out of sight of the house I took off my sandals and ran down the track towards the road. Stones bit into the soles of my feet. The trees were a blue-grey blur. My chest and throat burned. When I reached the road I slowed down and walked beside it through the strip of bush from which the dirt tracks led to the scattered orchards and chicken farms and holiday shacks. The trees – smooth-trunked and white, or rough and brown – were slender and tall. Ribbons of sunlight fluttered among them. Magpies chortled in their branches.

Beneath my feet dry leaves crackled, twigs snapped. The stillness of the trees seeped into the air. I heard a car pass by along the road, saw the flash of metal. Maybe it was Mr Doherty and his children going home with the fish. I imagined the story that awaited them – the story they'd take back to Cumberland. I walked faster. After a while I stopped and leaned against a tree trunk, panting.

When I set out again I realised I'd lost sight of the road. Had I still been walking parallel? The pathways through the trees were random, circular, untrodden. Just spaces between trees. Was I heading towards the beach? Or back to the Dohertys'? I could imagine the cottage only from the outside: its fibro walls, its tin roof, its louvre windows, as if, at my approach, the doors would be locked, the curtains drawn. But I was sure I'd left it far behind, like all the other places I could never go back to. All I could do now was not panic, and try to find a way through the forest.

I followed the sound of a car and found the road. But it still took a long time to reach the main road that connected all the towns along that part of the coast. On the other side I found a sandy track winding uphill through the tangled tea-trees and melaleucas. At the top of the hill I looked down on the horseshoe bay, one of a chain stretching around to Crantock Beach, where a flotilla of board riders assembled early in the morning. But here the beach was almost deserted.

I slid down the sand hill, sinking almost up to my knees in the coarse, yellow sand which would soon be too hot to walk on barefoot. Under my dress I wore my old black swimmers. I lay on my dress for a towel until it grew hot, the sun melting my bones, then I waded into the water and swam against the shock of the cold. I swam and floated and swam in the empty bay. I felt clean.

When I got out I lay on the sand to dry myself, and then instinctively I sat up and turned around. Lloyd stood on top of the sand hill, a black silhouette against the sky. I waved for him to come down. He shook his head. I climbed up the hill. He was standing up to his shoelaces in sand, frowning behind his sunglasses, which were so dark and opaque I couldn't see his eyes.

'Have you been standing here long?'

'Why didn't you wait for me at the Dohertys'?' His lips were pale in his flushed face. 'I've been looking for you all over the bloody coast.'

'But I told them to tell you I'd be at the beach.'

'But you didn't say what beach you'd be at.' Lloyd spoke through gritted teeth. 'Anyway, I told you to wait for me there. How do you think I felt going back to pick you up and you were gone?' His jaw was rigid and the veins on his temples were swollen. 'Why didn't you just do what I said?'

'I'm sure they were suspicious. Colleen was, anyway. It was awful.'

'You should've waited for me.' He quivered with an anger that emanated so powerfully from him that I felt its heat inside the warmth of the sun. If I tried to argue I'd surely get burnt.

'Why don't you come in for a swim? You've got your swimmers in the car, haven't you?'

'Come on. We're going.'

I followed him to the car, which was parked in a clearing beside the road. Lloyd sat sideways on the front seat and tipped the sand out of his shoes and his trouser cuffs. He didn't speak.

'I have to go and get my dress and wash the sand off my back.'

While I swam I saw him appear over the crest of the sand hill in his swimmers. He hopped across the sand and into the water. When he reached me he twined his legs around me and locked them together.

'You won't get away from me this time,' he said.

I took a deep breath, wriggled out of his grip, and swam away under water.

❖

On my last morning at home my father went to work before I got up. At breakfast as usual no one spoke. Afterwards I found Luke in his room, knotting his school tie in front of the wardrobe mirror.

'I don't know when I'll be back,' I said. 'Might be the next holidays, I don't know.'

Luke nodded.

'I hope everything'll be all right,' I said.

'I'll look after Mum.' We were both whispering. He picked up his blazer and shrugged it on with a man's gesture.

'I know you will.'

I was leaving, Anne was going to live in the nurses' home, and he had years of it ahead. His willingness to take on the responsibility made it even harder to hand it over to him. I stepped aside to let him through into the hall. 'I just wanted to say hooray.' As he passed I kissed his fuzzy cheek, but he was already striding down the hall with his adolescent's loose, ungainly gait.

When I said goodbye to Johnny and Billy I felt as I had when I'd first gone away to St Dominic's, as if I were abandoning my own children. But the feeling of loss was so personal, so intense, that it was like leaving behind a part of myself, some lost child, to be forever trapped.

Anne ran into the house, calling for me. 'I thought I'd missed you,' she panted. 'I was late getting off my shift.'

She handed me a cardboard box. I untied the string and lifted the lid. 'I knew you needed a new pair of shoes. For university.'

The brown suede desert boots nestled together in tissue paper.

'They're lovely. You shouldn't have done that.'

We smiled at one another. Her face was red and damp. She said, 'Look after yourself.'

'You too.'

'Don't worry too much about Mum.' This was as close as we'd ever come to each other, and I was going away.

My grandfather brought me his big port. He waited in his car while I packed: I'd got everything folded and ready the night before. Then he drove my mother and me to Quarry Street. My mother got out first at the dress shop. I got out too and kissed her in the street.

'Write me a letter, won't you?' my mother said. 'So I know how you're getting on.'

'It's you I'm worried about.'

'Luke'll look after me; he's a real little man.'

I leaned towards her and put my arms around her. She put her hands on my arms and stood stiffly until I let her go. I felt sorry for her, and guilty, because she had to stay behind. I watched as she turned in the doorway and waved. I got back in the car and my grandfather drove on to the bus stop. I looked back, but my mother had vanished. Her disappearance seemed so final that the facades of the shops with their dusty windows and plain verandahs – their familiar outline against the empty sky – looked like a row of tombs.

But at Cumberland station, sitting in the shuddering, rumbling train, breathing in the smell of hot leather mixed with diesel fumes, I felt a surge of elation. The train rattled along the back of St Dominic's, past the bottom paddock. Between the trunks of the camphor laurels, I glimpsed the top of the Cocos Island palm, at one side of the hidden garden, and the slate roofs of the chapel and the convent, now gliding, now rushing out of sight.

SYDNEY

Who but a coward would pass his whole life
in hamlets, and forever abandon his faculties
to the eating rust of obscurity?

CHARLOTTE BRONTË,
Villette

Every morning in the house in Ryde, Mrs Simmons cooked me bacon or sausages or chops, and tomatoes and eggs and toast, and sat opposite me at the kitchen table drinking tea and nibbling toast while I worked on the breakfast. I ate as much as I could because I didn't want to hurt her feelings. After a fortnight I had to shift the buttons on the waistbands of my skirts.

With her neat person and white hair and small pink mouth, I thought of Mrs Simmons as a white mouse tiptoeing around on her hind legs with her paws crossed in front of her chest and her mouth pursed beneath the whiskers. While I studied in my room at the front of the house, at the desk inside the bay window, I could hear her scurrying about. Except at mealtimes I hardly saw her, as though she lived a secret life behind the skirting boards. But the house was filled with her quiet presence, and with the quieter absence of her dead husband and grown children.

After breakfast I caught the bus at the end of the street. The university of my imagination was one of generous lawns between old stone buildings rooted in the earth, of canopied spaces beneath trees and, shaping the interiors, massive volumes of air in which thoughts and dreams could bloom. Macquarie University was a vast building site, set in a clearing in the bush on the outer rim of the suburbs. It seemed often deserted, except for the workmen and their whining, hammering machines. Almost the only finished buildings were the student union and the arts faculty. In the middle of the empty space between them they were building the library. Sometimes on my way to a lecture I passed no one, and was surprised to find the lecture theatre half full when I arrived. There seemed to be only first-year arts students there. The cafeteria was often empty.

At a social gathering organised by the English department, I wondered where so many people had come from. I met a student called Prue, who pointed out to me a lecturer she said was a famous writer: the woman was dressed in slacks; she looked ordinary and middle-aged, and spoke in a loud drawl. I had never seen a person who had written a book before, and I couldn't stop turning to look at her.

I went to lectures with Prue and a few other girls, and in between we stood talking on the edge of the grounds of bare, dry earth, among the tall eucalypts. The others lived in Sydney with their families. I imagined big modern houses high on hills overlooking water or other houses whose windows reflected foliage and air in the glassy light. They talked about their lives there. 'Dad was sitting in the lounge room watching Shirley Bassey on TV; he wouldn't come and have dinner till it was over. Mum went mad on him.' I could never think of anything to say. Prue looked like someone in an advertisement, with her long, smooth brown hair and her slim body dressed in fashionable casual clothes. She lived in Turramurra with her mother, who was a doctor. She invited me to a party at her house one weekend, but I was too shy to go on my own.

Prue took me shopping for a pair of blue jeans. When I wore them instead of the skirts my mother had paid off on lay-by at the Co-op store, I felt as though I almost fitted in. I liked the confident way Prue strode past the men working on the buildings, and ignored their wolf-whistles. She always made sure I sat with her and the other girls in lectures.

When I wasn't with Prue I sat in the quiet cafeteria. I was so self-conscious I started smoking menthol cigarettes, to have something to do when I was alone at a table.

At night I sat at my desk reading and studying, and listening to the silence in the dark house. The books my grandmother had paid for, thick hardbacks and glossy paperbacks, were stacked neatly to one side. The work wasn't as hard as I'd expected, except for philosophy: I was never sure I'd understood the lectures, though I took pages of notes. It wasn't like anything I'd studied at school, but I loved to read it, to enter the new world of scholarship I'd dreamed about. I didn't ask many questions in tutorials because I was afraid of saying something silly or wrong. But I worked as hard as I could, and my marks in the first assignments in every subject were good enough. In time, when I'd got used to everything, I was determined to do better.

Mrs Simmons switched off all the lights except mine at half past seven, just before she went to bed. Outside in the quiet street the rows of purple-brick houses with white-framed bay windows, set among gum trees and shrubbery and lawns, had dematerialised. The peace here wasn't the same as at the convent, where even in the darkness you heard the reassuring sounds of other people sleeping, of their being alive.

❖

As I'd promised him, I sent Lloyd my address, and he wrote straight back to say that he'd be coming to see me the next weekend. He said he'd arranged to swap masses with Father O'Rourke, and that he'd find somewhere for us to stay the night. I hadn't expected to see him so soon. I was excited, and looking forward to feeling the warmth of his arms around me. I hadn't known anyone long enough yet not to be lonely.

The Saturday morning after his letter arrived I washed all my clothes by hand, even the cotton blouses and my new blue jeans, because I didn't know how to use the modern washing machine and I was too embarrassed to ask Mrs Simmons to show me how. It took a long time to wash and rinse and wring all the clothes by hand.

When I came in from the laundry Mrs Simmons made a cup of tea, and we sat on the window seat in the dining room. Wide casement windows overlooked the backyard and let in the breeze. I could hear the leaves rustling in the garden and in the gardens of the houses next door. The light lay in pools on the dark furniture as if it had been undisturbed for years. On the sideboard, in frames of brass and silver, stood the photographs of Mrs Simmons and her husband in their old-fashioned hairstyles and clothes, and of her children as babies, and as adults at their weddings.

'You look after your clothes well, Maggie,' Mrs Simmons said.

'Thank you, Mrs Simmons.'

'Your mother must be very pleased with you.'

'I don't know. I hope so.' I looked out of the window where the garden sparkled in the autumn sunlight. Because it was Saturday I'd woken up that morning with the automatic dread, and now I thought that the last thing my mother would be thinking about would be how I looked after my clothes. The dread had always cleared quickly at school, like morning fog, and it had today, too, at the thought of seeing Lloyd.

'Thanks for the cup of tea, Mrs Simmons. I'd better go and hang them on the line.'

'Are you going out today?'

'I'm going to see a friend later. From school. I'll probably stay at her place the night.'

'That's nice. I hope you have a good time.' Mrs Simmons nodded and smiled.

❖

When I reached the end of the street in the early afternoon, I saw the green car waiting near the bus stop. Lloyd was wearing a jumper over his white T-shirt. I got in the car and sat close to him. He looked delighted to see me. He put an arm around me and held me so tightly I could scarcely breathe.

'We'd better be careful,' I said.

'No one'd know us around here, would they?'

'I don't suppose so.' But I felt uneasy in the daylight in the front seat of the car, so close to Mrs Simmons's house.

Lloyd said, 'Let's go somewhere.'

'Where?'

'I saw a guesthouse on the way here, in Hornsby. It'd be cheaper than a motel.'

It was an old house at a crossroads. A row of tall pines cast a green shade onto the side verandah. The proprietor spoke without taking the cigarette out of her mouth.

'Jackson,' Lloyd said, smiling his wide smile. 'The name's Jackson.'

'Mr and Mrs?' The woman tilted back her head and looked at me over the stream of smoke, at the bare fourth finger of my left hand.

'Yes,' Lloyd said, and

'No,' I said.

'We're engaged,' Lloyd added, showing more of his teeth. He took some cash out of his wallet and slid it across the counter.

The woman pursed her lips and shook her head. 'This is a family establishment.' But she gave Lloyd a key and showed us to a room looking onto the side verandah and the pine trees.

Lloyd shut the door. 'What did you say we weren't married for?'

'Because we're not. Why should we have to pretend?'

'It makes life easier, if we don't go drawing attention to ourselves. We'll have to get you a ring.'

'I don't even want to pretend to be married.'

He threw back the thin bedspread and we undressed and lay together in the middle of the bed. There was a smell of dust and a sickly, stale smell – perfume, sweat – of the bodies of former occupants. Beyond the sound of Lloyd's breath in my ear I heard the roar of traffic on the highway.

'Did you get the pill yet?' he said. 'Like I told you in the letter?'

'I don't know where the doctor's is in Ryde.'

'Just look 'em up in the phone book.' He sighed. 'I want to make love to you.'

'But you do.'

'You know what I mean.'

But I was scared: of the doctor; of what Lloyd wanted to do. Beneath the blind was a strip of green light. I remembered how, waking up in my room at home where the sun shone through the green plastic blind, I'd feel under my pillow for my book and start reading before I was properly awake. Now I pressed closer to Lloyd, closing my eyes against a sudden image of us trapped together in an underwater cave. We kissed, I imagined, as though to breathe life into each other. Where we touched it was to bring each other piece by piece to life.

When we got up it was late afternoon.

'Let's go out.' Lloyd sat up with his back to me and put on his T-shirt.

'Where to?'

'I think we should buy you a wedding ring.'

❖

The doorways of Darlinghurst Road were neon-lit in the daylight. Inside them the staircases ascended or descended out of sight. In front of each one a man in a creased suit, or a younger one in tight pants and a leather jacket, lounged against the coloured photographs of naked girls, and some-times a woman paced up and down. The smell of rotting rubbish drifted from the lanes and mingled with the smells of food cooking in fat, roasting nuts, the salt air that blew in from the harbour. The footpath was crowded. Beside one of the doorways a young girl stood with folded arms. She looked younger than I was, she was dressed in tight jeans and a low-cut blouse and ordinary shoes. All the other women wore short, tight dresses and stiletto heels. The girl's eyes were swollen as if she'd been crying. I turned and looked at her and she looked back without any expression.

The pawnshop was in a side street beside a lingerie shop and a row of tiny cafes. Opposite these in a square, beneath the shade of peppercorn trees, some men sat on benches among the pigeons and their dirt, drinking out of bottles in paper bags. Lloyd and I examined the window display behind the black metal grille. There were a few pairs of binoculars;

a dismembered clarinet in a velvet-lined case. Watches and gold chains hung from hooks; ropes of pearls. The rings were laid out in trays, among the dusty waves of red and black velvet. There were a lot of wedding rings.

The shop smelled like the inside of an old wardrobe. We squeezed past the milk crates of records, the racks of leather jackets. The man behind the counter wore a grey cardigan and his face was grey with grey sideburns, as if he were covered in dust, too.

'What are you after?' he said.

'A ring,' Lloyd said.

'A weddin' ring?'

'We saw you've got some in the window.' Lloyd had his arm around me, and now he pulled me closer and grinned at the man. 'Can she try some on?'

'All right.'

I was embarrassed because it was obvious we wanted to pretend we were married.

The first one fitted.

'That's good,' Lloyd said. 'How much is that one?'

'Two dollars.'

Lloyd paid the man and we left.

When we got in the car Lloyd told me to put the ring on and I looked at my left hand: it reminded me of my mother's, except that she also wore on her fourth finger a thin engagement ring. I tugged the ring off.

'Leave it on, why don't you?' Lloyd said.

'I don't want to. Anyway, you told the lady we were engaged.'

Lloyd laughed. 'What have you got against marriage?'

'I don't want to get married, that's all. If you'd've wanted to get married, you wouldn't've become a priest.'

'D'you reckon it's that simple?'

It was too complicated to explain to Lloyd that with the ring on my finger I no longer felt like the university student who was free to do whatever she wanted. It was only an old ring, we were only pretending, but I felt a kind of panic. I felt trapped. And pretending to be married to a priest seemed absurd. So I said, 'Where are we going now?'

'Nowhere in particular. For a drive. Show you a bit of Sydney.'

We drove across the Harbour Bridge and then around the inlets of the Parramatta River, through the suburbs still dominated by the bush. It was dusk now, and in there it seemed to be already dark.

In a motel restaurant back on the highway we ate a T-bone each. I sat facing the door, and whenever anyone came in I looked up. I wasn't used to being alone in a public place with Lloyd. I imagined everyone who saw us could tell he was a priest. He had a jumper on over his T-shirt but still wore his black trousers. I was conscious of how much older he was than me.

Lloyd poured the last of the tea out of the aluminium pot. He said, 'You must have enjoyed that steak – you've hardly said a word.'

'It's a bit strange us being together in a place like this.'

'Let's go to the pictures. At least it's dark in there.'

I watched half of *Bonnie and Clyde* through the screen of my fingers, and when they shot them at the end I buried my face in Lloyd's shoulder. He laughed. 'It's just a film.'

Back at the guesthouse we made love again – love enough for me, if not for Lloyd.

'This is the kind of place they would've stayed,' I said.

'Who?'

'Bonnie and Clyde. They never lived in an ordinary house. They never lived anywhere.'

Lloyd shrugged.

'Why do you think they were like that?' I said.

'There are some things we'll never know.'

'At least we can think about it.'

Lloyd yawned noisily. 'Ooh,' he groaned. 'I'm buggered. Don't you ever get tired?' He turned over and I could tell from his breathing he'd closed his eyes.

I could hear the indifferent sound of the traffic on the highway, and someone snoring nearby: it sounded as if they were on the verandah outside the room. The wardrobe and chest of drawers were looming presences animated by the dark. I could smell the fluff that had gathered beneath them and the bed. I lay awake thinking about Bonnie and Clyde, how they were always running away and had no home, and how they could never go back to the homes they had had. How at the end their bodies jerked and twitched as bullet after bullet struck, and then they lay slumped and still.

'Lloyd?' I whispered. 'Lloyd, are you awake?' Not loudly enough to wake him, but just to hear the sound of my voice calling out to another living person in the dark.

❖

Lloyd had lived in Sydney; he knew his way around. The next time he drove down, he showed me the electrical goods shop in Leichhardt where he had worked for Mrs Rosenberg after he'd left school at fifteen, and before he had entered the priesthood. When he spoke about Mrs Rosenberg it was almost as a son might speak about a mother. Mrs Rosenberg no longer owned the shop. Lloyd hadn't seen her for years.

On a sunny Saturday afternoon we drove to Manly and he showed me the seminary high on the cliff above the ocean.

'You were lucky,' I said, 'being able to look out at the water. Could you hear the sound of the waves at night?'

Lloyd smiled. 'That's a funny thing to ask. I suppose so. I don't remember. I was so busy studying. It's the same as studying at university. Theology, we had to learn. Latin, philosophy . . .'

'Did you like it there?'

'I don't know if that's the word. It wasn't an easy life, not like at a real university: a lot of discipline. I liked playing on the football team.'

I tried to imagine Lloyd walking on the seminary lawns above the ocean, the wind blowing the skirt of his soutane about his legs, or in a football jumper and shorts with grass stains on his knees.

He stopped the car that night at the end of a street that ran down to the harbour, beside a park of Moreton Bay figs. We looked beyond the ghosts of yachts moored at the jetty, and across the gulf of the night harbour – the stars above, the ferries below, their bright skeletons floating through space – to the lights strung along the opposite shore.

'This is near where the Nihills lived when they first came out from England,' Lloyd said. 'They used to make a living building rowing boats. Some of them still live here, round in the next bay.'

'Do you ever see them?'

'It's been years. Dad and Mum moved up the coast, after they got married.'

We sat looking over the black water. Lloyd said, 'Why don't we drive round there, and I'll show you the place?'

The house was on the corner of another street that led to the harbour. Lights shone in the large windows and on the front porch as if visitors were expected.

'That's where my cousin lives,' Lloyd said. 'Looks like he's home. I wouldn't mind dropping in just to say g'day. Give him a surprise.'

'You mean now?'

'Yeah, since I'm right here. But I'd better not take you in there. What if I drop you off at a cafe or something, just for a little while? That be okay with you? I wouldn't be long.'

'All right.'

Lloyd ordered me a milkshake and sat opposite me at the Laminex table. He sat sideways on the chair without taking his hands out of his pockets.

'You sure you'll be all right?' He looked at me sidelong, one eyebrow raised.

'Of course I will.'

'It's a bit silly to be right here and not call in and say g'day, I suppose.'

'Yeah, go on. You go.'

The cafe was empty except for the tired Italian owner who brought over the milkshake. Once, I must have been seven or eight, my father had taken me to Coalport, where he sometimes saw the doctor about the malaria he still had from the war. My mother had wanted me to go so that, having to look after me, my father wouldn't go to the pub. But he left me in a cafe and went anyway. I finished my milkshake long before he came back, and tried not to notice the people staring at me and whispering and shaking their heads. When he came back he was drunk.

Now, after I finished the milkshake, the owner came and took away the container. I waited for a while longer and then asked him for a cappuccino so I could stay in the cafe. When he brought it I skimmed off the chocolate powder and slowly sipped the froth from the spoon, to make it last. A fresh breeze smelling of salt water and petrol fumes blew in through the open door. It was dark outside in contrast with the bright white light inside the cafe. I looked out where the lights of cars flashed by. Hardly anyone walked past now. I remembered how the streets across the road led down to the dark water, above which hung the faint city stars. How bright in comparison with these were the stars in the Milky Way above the bottom paddock at St Dominic's.

Once, in third year, I had run down there alone. I gazed up into the branches of the stars tossing about in the wind. If I looked into them for long enough, my head flung right back, I saw how far it was between each star, how far beyond. I saw how they depended on the space around them, how the space took its dimensions from the stars. After a time I felt weightless, as if I were up there too.

When I got back to the hall, Sister Theresa was sitting sewing at the desk, supervising recreation. I tried to explain to her about the stars.

'The spaces between the stars are like the spaces between notes. It's like listening to music.'

I'd forgotten what Sister Theresa had said. Something about God. About infinity. I remembered the coarse weave of the shapeless garment onto which she was sewing a button.

Later I told Delia about the stars. After everyone else had gone to sleep, we sat on the edge of a bath, a blanket draped over the window.

'You know how we don't believe in God anymore?' I said. 'Well, how do you think we can explain infinity?'

Delia shrugged. 'I think everything could be explained, if we knew enough about it. But it seems like a lot of it is still a mystery.'

'Maybe the mystery is so hard to live with for some people they call it God. It was funny tonight, looking up at the stars. After a while, it was like . . . it didn't matter how it all got there, or whether it had a beginning or end. It was like nothing else mattered, just that everything is. I don't know how to describe it. It didn't even matter whether it mattered or not. I felt different – like I was a part of it, infinity, or whatever it is. I felt lifted out of myself and up into it. Do you know what I mean?'

'I think so.'

It was a long time since I'd felt like that, and there was no one to talk to like this anymore. I missed Delia more than anyone, except my little brother Billy.

All the time I was thinking about these things, I was aware with a part of my mind of the man behind the counter, and of waiting for Lloyd. Now I heard the ring of the till, the chink of money. Then, beginning with the tables furthest from mine, the man began to place upon them the upside-down chairs, moving in slow circles.

Just before he reached me Lloyd rushed in. 'I hope you haven't been waiting too long. I tried to get away earlier. He was that pleased to see me.'

'It's all right.'

Lloyd paid the man. He said to me, 'I hope you weren't getting bored.'

'I'm never bored.'

'I kept trying to make excuses to get away. I couldn't tell him you were waiting for me.'

On the way to the motel I said, 'You believe in God, don't you?'

Lloyd laughed. 'Well, it'd be pretty funny if I didn't, wouldn't it?'

'But do you believe everything, I mean, like it says in the catechism, "Who made the world? God made the world,"' I chanted, 'and all that?'

'Well, I believe pretty much in the basics, I suppose, but I don't always agree with the church's teaching on everything – like birth control, celibacy . . .'

'But how do you really know? I mean, what made you so sure that you became a priest? Do you really believe when you give communion that you're giving people the body of Christ to eat?'

'Boy.' Lloyd widened his eyes and leaned forward over the steering wheel. 'If we get into this stuff, we'll be up all night. You should read the proofs for the existence of God.'

'How could anybody prove God existed?'

'It's a question of faith.'

'I used to think people knew things. But nobody really knows anything like that, do they?'

'You want to know too much.'

Back in the motel room he turned on a bedside lamp and took off his jacket and trousers. He paused, half-undressed, and regarded me in the way that made me feel I was already naked, and smiled. He took off the rest of his clothes and stood close to me. 'How about we just relax for a while?'

'So how do people know what to do?'

Lloyd unzipped my dress. 'Did you go and see the doctor like I told you?'

'He said I can't have it until I'm married.'

'Didn't you wear the ring?'

'Yes, but he still didn't believe I was married. He said I wasn't old enough. He asked me why I didn't have an engagement ring.'

'Didn't you try another one?'

'I was too embarrassed.'

'Maggie, there's a thousand doctors in Sydney. One of them will give it to you. For God's sake.' He looked annoyed, and I felt the flutter of anxiety in my chest.

I said, 'They'll only say the same thing. You should have seen the look on his face.'

The doctor had sat behind a huge desk. I owned up finally to not being married, and I told him my boyfriend said to ask for a prescription for the pill. The doctor asked how old I was. He looked angry. Then he said to tell my boyfriend to wait. I was mortified. I couldn't tell him that I didn't have a boyfriend, that the man who wanted me to get the pill was a priest.

And yet I was relieved. Lloyd finished undressing me and we lay together skin against skin. If he pushed in any further, the thread that connected me to my old self would break. Once in a film I'd seen a climber on a mountain, hanging by a rope over the abyss. There was no way back, and the only way down was to cut the rope.

I laid my head on Lloyd's chest, and heard inside his breast-bone the involuntary twitching of his heart. What power had set it in motion, would one day make it still? Nobody knew anything. I didn't know what to do.

So I held on to him to stop from falling. I remembered how beyond the darkness of the room there was another darkness lit from billions of years away. We became weightless then, touching one another with our human hands, with our mortal bodies made of extinguished stars.

❖

The next time, I waited for Lloyd near the bus stop at night. I could see through an uncurtained window of the nearest house a family sitting around a table, eating, talking, arguing, laughing. The modest drama of the scene absorbed me: Lloyd and I were so far outside this ordinary world, it seemed exotic. When Lloyd sounded the horn I jumped. He leaned over and opened the door and I got in. He kissed me, and we drove off. The breeze purling into the car chilled me and I wound up the window. I snuggled against him.

'What did you tell the old duck this time?' He put his arm around me, removing it each time he changed gear.

'She's not an old duck, she's a nice lady. Same as usual: I told her I was going to spend the night with my old school friend.'

'Well, that's true in a way.' Lloyd chuckled. 'Ever see much of Delia?'

'She plays sport on the weekends or she goes home some-times with her brother. I was supposed to meet her on Broadway a couple of weeks ago, but I went to the wrong place. I rang her up when I got back, and she said we were waiting on different corners.' I remembered how I'd waited until the hour when I could only imagine her, the Delia I knew, walking down to the bottom paddock in her green tunic and fawn pinafore. It hadn't seemed possible for her to travel such a distance, between that time and now, that place and here.

Lloyd turned off into another street of houses of dark brick and tiled roofs in shadowed gardens.

'Where are we going, anyway?' I said.

'You tell me.'

'"We ain't headed nowhere, we're just runnin' from."'

'What?'

'That's what Clyde said, remember? In *Bonnie and Clyde*?'

'I thought we'd go back to that motel in Burwood Heights. I'll drop you off there, I've got some business to do for the parish – that's how I got away. Have to go back first thing in the morning, too, in time to say ten o'clock mass.'

'I wish I would've brought a book or something.'

'You can watch TV.'

'I never watch TV. I wouldn't even know what was on. We didn't watch it at school.'

'What about at Mrs Simmons's? Doesn't she watch TV?'

'She goes to bed after tea, and I study in my room.'

After he'd gone, I looked at myself in the mirror before I'd taken off the wedding ring and the extra make-up Lloyd insisted I wear, and I was startled by the image of a stranger. I had a shower. I liked to use the new cakes of sweet-smelling soap. I drank two cups of coffee. I wanted to clean my shoes with the little pads, but you couldn't use them on suede. Wherever I walked in the room the bed got in the way, and I bumped into the corners. I could hear the traffic on the highway, and the wind. All around me the city stretched away in every direction, its bright, beaded arteries coiling through the darkness.

Every car that pulled up outside might have been Lloyd's. I turned off the bathroom light and pushed open the window. A man and a woman got out of a car in front of the unit below. The woman, who was waiting for the man to lift their port out of the boot, was middle-aged. She wore a miniskirt and high heels and her blonde hair was teased into stiff feathers. She was saying, 'That's what you always say, Bruce, but it's not good enough.' The man said nothing. He locked the boot and they walked out of sight.

I stood a while longer looking out at the car park and the reception area adjacent, its bright plate-glass window, to the cars passing along the road beyond the neon sign. But none of the cars turned into the drive.

I got into bed and dozed. I couldn't picture Lloyd: the room he was in, or who else was there. When he got into bed beside me I woke and fitted myself into him. 'I thought you mightn't come back.'

'Why would you think a thing like that?'

'I don't know.'

CATHERINE JOHNS

'You know I can't live without you.' It wasn't light enough to see his face. 'You know how much you make me excited. Here, feel that.'

'Do you love me?'

'Yeah, I'm crazy about you.'

'I love you too. But do you think we can just keep on going like this?'

'Did you start the pill yet?'

'I went to another doctor, but he wouldn't give it to me either.'

Lloyd was invisible. He was solid darkness weighing down on me.

'Why didn't you go to another one?' He was panting.

'I thought they'd all say the same thing.' I was so afraid I couldn't move. 'I don't want to get pregnant.'

He was trying to join us together, but it felt like he was tearing me apart.

❖

Mrs Simmons put the plate in front of me. I looked down at the glistening flanks of the chops and their curls of yellow fat, at the shiny membrane of the egg yolk, and the nausea welled up into my throat. Somehow I smiled at Mrs Simmons and, breathing shallowly to avoid inhaling the pungent odour of the meat, I cut into a chop. Its flesh was pale pink, the juice ran over the knife blade, and I took a piece into my mouth and chewed and swallowed it quickly. My wrists and

164

forehead were cold and sweaty. I got up from the table and went out the kitchen door, closing it behind me. I ran along the verandah to the toilet, and kicked the door shut and vomited into the bowl.

I sat down again at the table.

Mrs Simmons set her cup on her saucer, her kind, mild gaze concerned.

'Are you all right, Maggie?'

'Yes thanks, Mrs Simmons. But I'm not very hungry this morning. Do you mind if I don't eat any more? It's very nice, but I don't feel like eating such a big breakfast.'

'That's all right. I hope you're not sickening for something.'

As soon as I got off the bus at the university, I rushed into the toilets in the union and vomited again. Then I met Prue in the cafeteria as usual and we walked over to the arts building. Prue chattered about where she'd be going next weekend with her boyfriend. Whenever Prue suggested we all go out if my boyfriend could come to Sydney, I said we might one day, but he couldn't easily get away on weekends.

Now I knew that I wouldn't have to make excuses for much longer. I wondered as I half listened to Prue what I'd say to her. Already in the coolness and the soft light of autumn, with the breeze combing out the thin foliage of the tall gums, the place looked utterly changed: it had the quality of something remembered; it was no longer real.

❖

A few weeks later, I went to the doctor's for my test results – not the same doctor who'd refused to prescribe the pill. He said, 'What about the father?'

The question startled me. In my mind, Lloyd was in his connection with me imperceptible to everyone else. He didn't exist in the same world as the doctor.

'I haven't told him yet.'

'Well, surely he'll want to do the right thing and get married.'

'He won't. I mean, he won't be able to.'

The doctor frowned as though he was worried, although he didn't know me. 'So what will you do?'

My mind was blank. Then I lied: 'I'll go home to my mother, in the country.'

The doctor nodded and smiled a sad smile. He stood up then and showed me to the door.

Walking through the suburban streets I felt as if all my previous life – my self – had been erased, but there was not yet anything to take its place. The houses looked like fortresses behind the railings of fences and the tree trunks and palm fronds. On a verandah, a young woman with a baby on her hip put down her shopping bag, unlocked and opened the door, picked up the bag and went inside. I stood for a moment staring at the closed door, filled with a sudden longing for the ordinariness, the orderliness of the lives I imagined behind it.

'Do you want a cup of tea, Maggie? You look tired.' Mrs Simmons looked at me with her bright, dark eyes and emptied the kettle into the teapot with her pink paws.

I wanted to sit down at the table and say to her, Yes, Mrs Simmons, I'd love a cup of tea – I've just found out for sure I'm going to have a baby. She looked so fresh and innocent in her floral cotton frock and white cardigan, with her halo of white hair. How could I tell her that her studious boarder who hand-washed all her clothes was pregnant, to a priest?

'No thanks, Mrs Simmons. I think I'll just go and study for a while.'

I sat in the chair behind my desk. The bed was made, the desk was tidy. I got up and looked in the dressing-table mirror. My face was pale, with transparent shadows beneath my eyes. My body no longer seemed to belong to me.

❖

'Oh shit. Oh bloody hell. Are you sure?'

'I waited for the results before I rang you. I wanted to be certain.'

I pictured Lloyd at the telephone table in the hall of the presbytery. I could tell from his tone that he must look haggard. He dropped his voice: 'Did you tell anyone else?'

'Only you.'

I was standing in a phone box in Blaxland Road around the corner from Mrs Simmons's. I felt shaky and my stomach muscles were sore from so much vomiting.

'But it was only one time.' I heard the panic and anger in his voice and I felt guilty, and lonely, even though I was talking to him.

'I know.' I was still trying to hold on to the feeling I had before I got the news – the feeling I took for granted, that everything was normal – but I was starting to forget what that was like. I could tell that old feeling was starting to slip away from Lloyd, too. But it was different for me. Something was happening to me physically but not to him. I didn't just have a problem: I was a problem. Lloyd could still go about his business as if nothing in his life had changed. I didn't know how to explain to him what this was like. I didn't know if he'd want me to.

He said, 'Don't do anything rash. Just stay put for now. You're not thinking about telling your parents, are you?'

'Of course not, that's the last thing I'd do.'

Then he seemed to pull himself together. He was whispering now: 'I've got mates in Sydney, they'll help us work something out. I'll get down there as soon as I can. I'd better get off the blower now, sweetheart.'

He'd never called me that before. It made me feel better. For a moment I felt hopeful that he'd find some way to make it all right, though I couldn't see any possibilities that made practical sense.

I said, 'All right.' But he'd already hung up.

❖

It was hard for Lloyd to make up reasons to drive to Sydney: he said the bishop kept him on a tight leash. By the time he got away I was scared that Mrs Simmons, or someone at

Macquarie, might notice I was pregnant. My jeans were already too tight: I could zip them up, but not do up the button. I was studying as usual, handing in assignments, but my heart wasn't in it: before too long, I'd have to leave. It would have been shameful enough going to university pregnant, even if the baby's father wasn't a priest.

I packed a small bag and told Mrs Simmons I had to go home to see my family. Lloyd picked me up around the corner, for the last time. He booked us into the motel in Burwood Heights, then drove to a large red-brick house with white iron lace on the verandah and leadlight panels around the front door.

'A whole house just for him?'

'Not a bad perk, is it?'

A priest opened the door: a well-fed, silver-haired priest whose black suit looked freshly pressed. He stood a moment looking at me, his head on one side, his eyebrows raised, his lips pursed in a smile.

'This is Maggie,' Lloyd said, smiling. 'Maggie, this is Vince.'

'How are you? Come in!' He gestured smoothly and stood aside. To Lloyd he said, 'Good to see you, mate. Having a good rest?'

They both laughed. As Vince shut the door he winked at Lloyd and said in a low voice, 'Lucky dog.'

He led us into a room where a fat priest sat in an armchair holding a drink in one fist. When he smiled his eyes became two slits.

'G'day, Jack,' Lloyd said. 'This is Maggie.'

'Bun in the oven, eh?' Jack chuckled. How could he joke about this?

'Drink?' Vince lifted an eyebrow and stood poised over the bottles and decanters on the polished sideboard. In the light he was ruddy and portly.

'Whisky for me,' Lloyd said. 'I could do with something.'

'I bet you could.' Vince's eyes were the colour of shallow water; they twinkled. He seemed to be enjoying himself. Whenever he looked at me, he gave the impression that looking at anything else had been an interruption. This made me uncomfortably aware of the difference of my body, and I didn't know where to look. 'Whisky?' he said to me.

'A drop wouldn't hurt,' Jack boomed.

'No thanks, I think it'd make me sick.'

'Don't worry, mate.' Jack grinned at Lloyd. 'We'll arrange something. You're not the only one who's had to deal with this one. Eh, Vince?'

He winked at Vince who sat opposite sipping his drink, legs crossed, an arm draped over the back of his chair. Vince twirled his glass so that the liquid washed from side to side, then he raised it at Jack.

I stared from one of them to the other. 'D'you mean you've . . . there's been . . .'

Jack looked abruptly grave. 'Us blokes are only human. Accidents happen. We've all had our troubles. But it doesn't have to be the end of the world.'

I looked at Lloyd. He was smiling half-heartedly and looking down into his glass. The city outside might as well have turned into a desert, or the landscape of another planet. I focused on the rows of books in the shelves on the opposite wall. The sight of them was friendly and familiar. On the other walls there were prints in wooden frames.

'Lloyd said you're studying arts, Maggie?' Vince said.

'English and French and . . . I was, anyway.'

He got up from his chair. 'Come over and see what I've got. You can borrow something if you like.' I followed him across the room. He stood so close to me our sleeves touched. I felt disturbed and hemmed in, as though he'd taken up all the space around me so I couldn't move in any direction.

'Have you read the Russians? Dostoyevsky? Tolstoy?'

I shook my head. I could hear on the other side of the room the low murmuring. Out of the corner of my eye I saw Lloyd and Jack turn their heads from time to time and look in my direction.

'What about Flaubert?' Vince plucked a book from the shelf. '*Madame Bovary*?'

I shook my head again. 'We were doing *Manon Lescaut* in French.'

Vince held out the book, his eyes still skimming the shelves. 'It's a translation, I'm afraid. But I think you might enjoy it. There's a very famous episode in there that takes place in a taxi.'

'I might get it from the library one day.' Which library? There was no longer any library in my life.

I wandered over to the wall of prints. One of them was of a Vermeer: the one in which a woman sits sewing by the window in a pool of sunlight. I remembered the one in the parlour at the convent, which Sister Theresa had first shown me, in which a woman poured milk into a bowl in light of such purity that it had made me think of the first sunlight I remembered, in the yard in Abernant, flooding the world and gilding the petals of a rose on a bush that died later of neglect. Now I'd descended into a darker world.

'Do you like that one? It's one of my favourites.'

My face felt hot. Vince stood so close to me again, as we gazed at the picture, it seemed I could not stop my sleeve, or the hem of my dress, brushing against him. He didn't seem to notice, but I stood still, in case he thought I was touching him on purpose, or in case I hurt his feelings by seeming to shrink away.

Then I heard Lloyd calling me from across the room. Vince and I both turned to him.

'Jack wants to have a word with you.' Lloyd spoke to me but he was looking at Vince, as though to tell him something.

I went over and sat down beside Lloyd.

Vince said to him: 'Come and give me a hand out in the kitchen, will you, mate? I'm a bit peckish.'

When Lloyd and Vince had gone, Jack leaned forward as far as his paunch would allow and fixed his gaze on me. Deep inside their slits his eyes gleamed in tiny points of light. I couldn't see what colour they were.

'Now, Maggie,' he said. 'You love Lloyd, don't you?'

'Yes.'

'You realise what would happen to him if anyone found out about this?'

'He'd be excommunicated?'

Jack shook his head. 'You've got to understand: if the bishop got wind of it, Lloyd'd be kicked out of the priesthood, never allowed to say mass or give the sacraments again. It's not a question of being excommunicated; it'd be worse than that, for him.'

'I haven't told anyone.'

'Good girl, that's good. What about your parents?'

'I couldn't tell them.'

'Some girls get the idea in their heads a bloke can just resign, like resigning from a job. They think they can get married.'

'I don't want to get married.'

Jack beamed. 'You're a sensible sort of a girl,' he said.

'So can't a priest ever leave? Couldn't Lloyd stop being a priest, if he wanted to? I mean, not because of me.'

'He can leave, but what'd happen, he'd be out on a limb.' Jack waved a fat hand towards the corner of the room. 'He'd be the lowest of the low, in the church's eyes. Not mine, mind you, but . . . do you know what I'm saying?'

'I think so.'

'He does a good job,' Jack said. 'He does a lot of good work. I'm not saying he doesn't love you, but he loves his vocation, too.' He dropped his hands, palms down, on the arms of his chair. 'But all of a sudden, he'd have no job, and no home. He could get a dispensation, but it'd take years, and he'd have to prove he shouldn't have been a priest in the first place. He'd have to be able to prove he was crazy. It'd ruin him. Finish him off. You don't want that to happen, do you?'

'No.' It was like following someone down a passage so narrow that you couldn't see where you were going.

'And if he did get married after all that, he wouldn't be able to get married in the church. The church would never recognise the marriage. The child'd be illegitimate.' Jack sat back and looked at me. He had a loud voice and a large, authoritative presence. 'So what'll you do?'

I was trying to work out how all this information fitted together, and how it might help me, but the puzzle had missing pieces. A coldness in my chest spread throughout my body, I felt drained of energy and warmth. 'I don't know. I can't stay at Mrs Simmons's now. Mum'd find out. She's related to somebody Mum knows in Abernant.'

'So there's nowhere you can go.' Without taking his eyes off me, deftly, with one hand, Jack took a cigarette out of the packet on the arm of the chair, picked up his lighter, glanced swiftly at the cigarette while it ignited. He drew on the cigarette and raised his eyebrows. Then he offered one to me. My gorge rose, and I shook my head.

'What about the university?'

'I just wrote them a letter, I told them my mother needed me at home. I wrote one to the scholarship people and asked if I could defer for a year.' I felt the calm of waiting for the storm: the doors and windows shut, everything tied down.

I'd left Macquarie for good that day without telling anyone, even Prue.

Jack sat back in his chair and shook his head, setting his jowls aquiver. His eyes were closed. 'Not necessary. You can write to them all again. You don't have to give anything up.'

'What do you mean?'

'There's another solution. I've got this mate in Bondi: he's a doctor, see?'

He opened his eyes and saw my face, and sighed. He leaned forward again. 'It's not as bad as what you might think.' He waved his cigarette in the air. 'He's a good doctor; he's helped me out more than once. We just take you over to his place one afternoon, and next thing you know it's all over. Nobody ever gets into trouble – he knows how to be discreet. I had a girl, she went back to work the next day and nobody was ever the wiser, not even her mother had the faintest idea of what had happened, and she lives at home, too.'

It made me feel dirty, Jack talking about him and this girl he couldn't have loved, as if they were the same as Lloyd and me.

In a French book I'd borrowed from the Cumberland library, I'd read that a woman had died in a blood-soaked bed after she had an abortion, because she wouldn't let her friend call a doctor in case he told the police. It was illegal here too, I knew that much. Was it murder? What did the baby look like? I imagined a tightly furled bud of tissue, of blind, pink flesh. Was it a person yet?

I glanced towards the door. Where was Lloyd? I felt clammy and sick, but it wasn't morning sickness.

'I wouldn't want to do that.' I felt the pressure of Jack's gaze and looked away.

'The money's not a problem.' He paused. 'It's perfectly safe. And no one'd ever find out. What else are you going to do, if you don't want to tell anyone?'

'I don't know.'

I still felt afraid, but suddenly strong. Someone, or something that would become someone, was growing inside my body, in my care. I didn't want this priest in charge of it, or in charge of me. I sat upright and poised beneath the weight I had hoisted onto my shoulders.

Jack's eyes swam in their slits. I wondered if he thought the strings of hair he had trained across his scalp hid his baldness. He stabbed his cigarette into the ashtray on the table beside him.

'Well, you've still got time to change your mind,' he said. 'Just think about it, talk it over with Lloyd. We've arranged for him to have some time off, spend a few days with you here.'

He spread his hands widely and smiled, then slapped the chair arms and uncrossed his legs. He looked at the doorway where, as if at an inaudible signal, Vince appeared, smiling and carrying a plate of savouries. Vince glanced from Jack to me, and entered the room, Lloyd behind him.

I stood up. 'Lloyd? Do you mind if we go now? I'm a bit tired.'

Lloyd looked from Jack to Vince. Jack shrugged and shook his head. Vince looked disappointed.

Lloyd seemed uncertain. He was pale and he looked tired, too. To me he said, 'All right.' To Jack and Vince he said, 'I'll catch up with you blokes a bit later on.'

❖

'Did you know what Jack was going to talk to me about?'

We were sitting up in bed. It was so late now that the traffic on the highway sounded like drizzle.

'I had an idea.'

'Why did you leave me with him by myself?'

'I thought it was something you should decide.'

'Are you glad I'm going to have it?'

'I don't know. What are you going to do?'

'I'm trying to think.'

'You'll have to go somewhere until it's born. If you don't want anyone to know about it, you'll have to have it adopted out.'

'Adopted?'

Lloyd sighed and rubbed his eye sockets with clenched fists. 'If you keep it, everyone'll find out whose it is.'

'No they won't. I said I wouldn't tell anyone.'

'Who would you say the father was?'

'I'd tell them it was a secret.'

'But you said you couldn't tell your mother, anyway.'

'I can't. But I couldn't give it away, either.'

'We'll talk about it later. Jack and Vince are going to put their heads together. They'll think of something.'

❖

For the next few days, while we waited to hear from Vince and Jack, we lay together with the curtains drawn. The city, the world, had shrunk to a room, a double bed opposite the closed eye of the television set. Mrs Simmons, Prue, my mother, Delia were dim, distorted figures in my mind.

The days were shapeless. Sometimes in the late afternoon the room dimmed and the sound of the peak hour traffic, of the life of the invisible city, reached into the room where time had stopped. I felt hollow then, in spite of the kernel of flesh inside me, in spite of being with Lloyd.

What would I do when he went back to Cumberland, to his duties as a priest? He belonged to the church. I pictured this as a towering edifice carved out of solid rock. I saw its sheer walls, its battlements: at its heart, the Pope, sitting on a throne in his stiff vestments beneath the weight of his cleft mitre, one hand holding his staff, one raised in blessing. In the surrounding labyrinth of rooms and halls, the legions of cardinals and bishops and priests engaged in complex rituals; I heard them chanting in their archaic language, saw them in their swirling garments gliding in and out of the intricate passages, the secret chambers, the colonnaded cloisters . . . were there dungeons? Beside this ancient power I was puny.

When we made love it was consoling, a respite from anxiety. The child – in my mind it was already a child – related us. One afternoon we lay together afterwards thigh against thigh, our flesh welded together with heat and sweat, and I could not feel the seam where we were joined.

One night Lloyd went out and rang Vince from a phone box. The next day he went to see him and Jack. I sat on the bed. I drank cups of tea. I turned on the radio. The melodies, the harmonies and rhythms of the songs they played were linked in my mind with Cumberland and with a mood, a feeling I remembered, as if I had been cut loose from gravity and floated a few inches above the ground, as if I could have soared above the streets, freewheeled over the river and the lucerne paddocks and beyond. I turned the radio off. I imagined the river, only the rippling currents to show what slept beneath its surface, now rising up and turning the streets into torrents, the paddocks into lakes, the houses into underwater caves.

I waited for Lloyd without patience. I opened the book I'd picked up on my way out of my room in Ryde, but the words would not join together in my mind long enough to mean anything.

I paced up and down; I prowled. In the bathroom mirror I inspected my pallor, the blue shadows beneath my eyes, my thickened waist, my bloated breasts bulging beneath the jumper. I looked for some moments at this stranger, and then I turned away. I stood at the window and looked down past the white iron railing of the balcony into the bare, asphalt yard, the tiers of blank windows enclosing it, and the highway beyond the street: now a trickle, now a gush of traffic as the lights turned from red to green to red. In the yard a woman in a pink uniform hauled a mop and bucket, a man in a crumpled suit without a tie slipped out of a unit and lowered himself into his car. What made them keep going? Surely such lives were filled with bitter desolation. I wondered if the child was a boy or a girl. I was used to boy babies, their pink, boneless-seeming bodies, their tiny penises.

I turned away from the window. When I tried to think, to plan, my mind filled with fog. Where was Lloyd?

❖

Vince was in charge: with the manner of a master of ceremonies he ushered us all into the lounge room, poured the drinks and presented one to each of the men with a little flourish. His pale eyes twinkled, his small smile twitched. Jack regarded me with his tiny eyes; he winked and grinned. I wondered if the sharp rim of his collar, hidden by the thick folds of his neck and jowls, cut into his flesh. When he and Vince looked at me, I felt ashamed of the meaning of my condition, the reason for my presence in the room. I smoothed my dress over my knees.

'Well now, Maggie,' Vince said. 'We've been doing a lot of thinking, the last couple of days. And we've come up with an idea.'

Out of the corner of my eye I could see Lloyd beside me on the couch sitting with bowed head. I nodded and waited.

'What do you think about going to Melbourne till you have the baby,' Jack said. He wasn't asking me.

I turned to Lloyd. He didn't look at me. I turned back to Vince and Jack. 'Melbourne?' My mind was blank: in it no road, no thin, crooked line on a map connected Melbourne with the room.

'You have to get right away, if nobody's going to find out,' Jack said. 'Your mother wouldn't be able to get to Melbourne, would she? You don't know anybody down there?'

'I've never been there.'

I got up without thinking about it and walked across the room, and stood facing the wall of books. When I turned around they were all looking at me with upturned faces; the three black suits filled the room, they darkened it. Caught in their gaze my body felt not only different but provocative and perverse; an incitement to trouble, a betrayer of dangerous secrets.

'But I won't have my scholarship money anymore.' Was the sound of my voice able to travel to the other side of the room? I looked at Lloyd. He stood up and came over and put his arm around my shoulders.

He said, 'You'll have to get a job, sweetheart.'

I shrank inside his embrace. 'But what sort of job could I get, if I'm going to have a baby?'

'There's still things you can do. I don't see any other way out, sweetheart. I think it's the best thing for all of us.'

'Can you think of anything else?' Vince raised his eyebrows.

'Lloyd's got some mates down there, haven't you, Lloyd? They'll meet you and put you up somewhere till you find a place,' Jack said.

'What'll I tell Mum?'

181

'You'll think of something,' Jack said. 'But you'll be back to normal before you know it, once the baby's adopted out.'

'We've already booked your flight,' Vince said. 'It leaves the day after tomorrow, at eight p.m.'

❖

Vince drove me to Ryde the next morning. The street was quiet in the autumn sun, the crests of the gums gleaming in the blue air. The house looked closed and blank. Fitting my key into the lock, I felt like an intruder.

Vince followed me into the bedroom. He walked jauntily, smiling. He stood looking around the room. He took my grandfather's port down from the top of the wardrobe. I cleared the surface of the desk with one gesture of my arm, and stood listening to the books and folders thudding onto the floor. Vince shook his head and laid the port on the desk; he opened the clasps and flung back the lid. Then he sat on the bed; he leaned back, propped on his elbows, and crossed his legs, as if he were at home. He watched me. Before lifting them out of the drawers, I crushed the underwear into balls, to make sure he didn't see them. Then, unable to bear his scrutiny, I upended the rest of the drawers directly into the gaping mouth of the port. I threw the books in last; it was strange not to care that my clothes would get crushed.

'No need to hurry,' Vince said.

'I just want to get it over with now.'

At any moment, I expected the door to be flung open and someone to demand to know what I was doing there, although I knew Mrs Simmons would be visiting her sister.

'What about the wardrobe?' Vince got up and opened it. He stood a moment with his hands on the open doors, then lifted out a dress. He held it up and looked at it.

'This is a nice colour,' he murmured. 'Mm, I bet you look good in this.'

He folded it with caressing gestures and laid it in the port. Each time he plucked out a dress or skirt and handed it to me he smirked knowingly, as though we were about to get away with a crime.

He closed the port and watched me get down on my knees and lift the hem of the bedspread, and crawl over to the desk and peer beneath.

'What are you looking for?' he said.

'The key to that desk drawer.' I nodded at the one that was shut.

We searched behind the furniture and the curtains, in the wardrobe and all the empty drawers.

'What's in it?' Vince said finally. 'Is it important?'

'My letters from Lloyd.'

'Don't worry, he'll write you plenty more.'

'But what if Mrs Simmons finds them?'

'If we can't find the key, neither will she.'

I scribbled a note to Mrs Simmons, telling her I'd decided to study in Melbourne. I told her I had to start straight away, apologised for leaving in such a hurry without saying goodbye, and thanked her for her kindness. Then I propped the envelope on the table in the hall, and followed Vince out to the car.

'Well.' Vince patted my knee. 'That's that taken care of.' Now his smile was rakish, his face was flushed. I could see that this was an adventure to him, and that it excited him, and I was disgusted not only with him but with myself. I felt to blame, because I was the only person anything was happening to physically.

I couldn't stop thinking about the letters locked in the drawer. They tugged at my mind like a thread that wouldn't pull free. If anyone found them, they would ignite a scandal; I'd be permanently outcast. I put my head in my hands, buckling momentarily under the full weight of my situation: I was felled by fear, by grief. I sat up and saw Vince staring steadily ahead, as though he could see all the way to Melbourne.

When we turned into Blaxland Road, I looked behind me towards the university at the other end, but all I saw were the houses receding and the trees linking branches on the hump of the hill at the horizon.

❖

Delia frowned and shook her head. She opened her mouth and closed it. She walked to the window and stared through the diamond-shaped panes.

Sitting on her bed, feeling heavy and tired, I pictured the scene she looked down on: the curved gravel driveway bordered with bright flowers; the hedge dividing the lawn from the playing fields; beyond the fields, partly screened by tall trees, the university buildings. I imagined how, without taking any wrong turns, without asking anyone the way, Delia would find her way around.

She said, 'Leave university? But that's all you ever wanted to do.'

'I can't stand the thought of it.'

'There's no rule that says you can't have a baby while you're at university, is there?'

'I'd be too embarrassed. And everyone'd find out, if I stayed. About Lloyd.'

'But won't they have to find out anyway? I mean, sooner or later?' Delia turned and looked at me. Her eyes flicked down to my stomach and away.

I looked at the ridge in the polished brown lino where the seam of two floorboards jutted beneath. 'Not if I had it adopted out.'

'Is that what you want?'

'It's what they want – Lloyd and the other priests. But I don't know how I could do it.'

'I can't believe they offered you an abortion.'

'I'd be too scared. It feels wrong, anyway. I don't know if it's a human being yet, do you?'

'More like a collection of cells probably. But I know what you mean. Why doesn't Lloyd leave the priesthood so you can get married?'

'He can't leave just like that. Anyway, he wants to be a priest but he loves me too.' The confusion was exhausting.

'That hasn't worked out too well so far. Anyway, is that what you want? You always said you never wanted to get married.'

'I don't.' The brides in the back seats of big cars, in the white dresses with the white veils around their faces, looked as if they were wearing their shrouds.

'Well, you picked the right bloke.'

Our smiles – Delia's twisted – met and parted.

I could hear the voices of other students calling to one another in the corridor outside. At the sound of a name I saw Delia turn her head swiftly towards the door and then back. She stood, her hand on her chin in the familiar way she had when she was thinking. The afternoon light slanted through the leadlight windowpanes, laying out their pattern on the polished floor. She said, 'So if you've only deferred your scholarship and everything, that means you still might finish your degree?'

'I hope so.'

In my mind, I looked back at my desk in the bay window in Ryde, at the university with its fringe of gums, and the big brown box of the arts building – but these pictures were already faded, like old photos.

Delia hoisted herself onto the desk opposite the bed and drummed her fingers on its surface and bounced her heel against its bottom drawer. The life in her still set her in motion, it flowed from her extremities and charged all the world within her reach. Watching her, I was taken back to St Dominic's: but it had crumbled, like an antique city, into the stumps of walls, into the ruins of a garden. How many centuries ago had we lived together there?

I said, 'What would you do, if it happened to you?' The question sounded ridiculous.

'I'd go home and tell Mum and Dad. That's the first thing I'd do. And I'd definitely stay at university.'

'I couldn't tell Mum. Let alone Dad. I couldn't do it to her. It'd be bad enough even if it wasn't Lloyd. It'd kill her. She'd go crazy.' I imagined walking in the front door, pregnant. When my mother saw me, her eyes were wild, her face was ashen. If I put out my hand, her fragile white flesh might flake away beneath my fingers, the flakes crumble into dust.

Delia said, 'You might be surprised.'

'You don't know her. Anyway, she's got enough worries.'

Delia smoothed her brow with her fingers. She jumped off the desk and spread her hands in a relinquishing gesture.

'Well, when are you going then?'

'Tomorrow night. The plane's already booked.' I got up. 'I'd better get going. I have to meet Lloyd at Central. He might already be there. You won't tell anyone, will you?'

'Not if you don't want me to. I wish you would, though. I wish you'd told somebody before. But you know that.'

'I'll write to you.' I took a step backwards, towards the door.

'Wait, I'll come down with you.'

We walked along the dim corridor, down the stairs and out through the Gothic doorway into the fading light. At the top of the steps we stopped and looked at one another.

'Well, look after yourself,' Delia said. 'I hope everything works out all right.'

'Yeah, thanks. See you.'

Delia stepped into the gap between us. She opened her arms and we embraced and kissed awkwardly, missing each other's cheeks. I turned and stumbled down the steps. The image I glimpsed when I looked back, of Delia waving, was itself wavering. My smile was hurting. I turned the corner into the long drive and almost walked into one of the jacarandas that leaned across it, growing crookedly up above the dim tunnel, reaching into the light.

❖

Lloyd was pacing up and down beneath the station colonnades. Closer, I could see the anxiety in the set of his mouth and jaw, and the frown above the black sunglasses. The visible part of his face was the colour of milk. He saw me and stood dramatically still, and I hurried to him.

He said, 'I thought you mightn't come back. Thought you might have gone off somewhere.' His breath caught on the words.

'Don't be silly. Where would I go?'

'What did Delia say?'

'She said I should stay at uni. She said I should tell Mum. Don't worry, I'm not going to. She won't tell anyone, either.'

'I hope not.'

That night I hardly slept. At dawn I got up and went to the window and parted the curtains. I touched the glass with my fingertips and shivered. The room was still warm. Lloyd switched on his bedside lamp. The light in the room was oval-shaped, the darkness stuffed into the corners.

'It's tomorrow already.' I got back into bed. 'I wish you could stay with me a while longer.'

'You know I can't. Just make sure you're ready when Vince comes to pick you up tonight.'

'I won't be able to stand it, when you go.' I lay on top of him to keep him there.

Lloyd laughed softly. 'You're always so extreme.'

He shifted beneath me but I didn't move.

'Come on, sweetheart, I have to go soon.'

I rolled away. Lloyd threw the bedclothes aside and got up, and soon I heard the sound of the water gushing from the shower. Where Lloyd had lain the sheet was already cold. The air was cool now and stale, and the grey light had increased and entered the room and watered down the lamplight. Now the room was no longer ours, it was just a shabby box in a row of identical ones.

Lloyd came out of the bathroom in his underpants and T-shirt and switched on the radio. He looked at me. 'Aren't you getting up? I thought breakfast'd be here by now.'

'I don't ever want to get up again.'

He laughed. I watched him put on his priest's clothes. They made him look as though he was already somewhere else.

I felt paralysed. The music playing on the radio was so familiar, yet without meaning. I was cold, but I couldn't move to pull up the blankets.

There was a hollow knock. Lloyd opened the little trap-door and brought in the breakfast tray. He lifted the domed lids from the steaming plates and set everything out on the bench.

'Come on,' he said.

'No.'

'What about breakfast?'

'It might make me vomit.'

'Come on, Maggie. I have to go soon.'

'I'm not getting up. Ever.'

Lloyd replaced the lids and came and sat beside me.

I said, 'It's so far away. Melbourne.'

He leaned over me. 'I'll get down there and see you when I can. It's just until the baby's born.'

'I don't want to leave the baby there when I come back.'

'Maggie, it's too late now. I have to go today, or I'm in big trouble.'

I put my arms around him from behind and laid my head against his back.

He unlaced my fingers and lifted my arms and turned towards me. 'I'd better have something to eat,' he said.

I forced myself to get up and looked out of the window. The early morning cloud had cleared, the concrete of the yard was bright, the edges of the shadows sharp. People were climbing purposefully into their cars and driving away. Along the narrow balcony opposite a woman was wheeling a canvas laundry trolley overflowing with dirty sheets. Above the balcony rail bobbed the head of a skipping child.

I watched Lloyd wind the maroon scarf around his neck.

At the door I clung to him without shame. 'I love you. I want you to stay with me.' I rubbed my cheek against the lapel of his coat.

Lloyd was smiling but it was the hesitant, frowning smile of someone whose mind was already somewhere else. He said, 'I love you too. I'll be thinking about you all the time. Write to me as soon as you can.'

'Will you? Think about me all the time?'

'Of course I will. Now I have to go.'

He kissed me swiftly and deeply and took a step backwards onto the balcony. He looked almost fearful, as though my gaze might scorch him.

'See you later.' He smiled a small smile.

'Hooray.'

I watched him turn and gradually disappear into the stairwell. Then I closed the door.

I walked several times around the room, skirting the bed, my arms folded and pressed hard against my stomach, my head bent. I heard myself moan and make a sound like a dry sobbing. I got into the shower and under cover of the sound of rushing water I opened my mouth and I howled. Then I dried and dressed myself and sat on the bed. The room was paid for until the next morning, but before eight that night I'd have left. I packed the clothes I'd been wearing and the underclothes I'd washed in the bathroom the night before, and then there was nothing else to do.

I answered a knock on the door and opened it to the cleaner. Where was the skipping child? While the woman made the bed I stood hovering. I felt silly because I could have done it myself. So I picked up my purse and went out.

❖

I joined a queue and stepped onto the city bus. When I got off I let the tide of people carry me along the street, at the end of which the sky showed through the ribs of the Harbour Bridge.

At Circular Quay I leaned over the railing, the salt chill rising into my nostrils. At the same moment Lloyd was driving into the Grainger Valley in the green car. The air seemed squeezed out of me, as though I were dropping down into the deep. Melbourne was six hundred miles away.

I boarded a ferry and stood outside, at the bow. Opposite the bridge the Opera House was being put together, its sails like empty shells. I watched the houses and the boxes of flats on the north shore gliding past, perched on the shelves of rock; on the edge of the harbour I saw the trees growing into the light, and the trees growing upside down in the water. The ferry nosed in and out of the bays, where the masts tilted and chimed above the yachts in the sunny breeze. I loved to ride the ferries. Here in the beautiful, uninhabitable heart of the city, safely transported across lethal depths without effort, I had felt – in the steady labouring of the ferry's engine, the fluttering fabric of the breeze, the sliding landscape – the physical sensation of freedom. Now inside me was another passenger, almost weightless, but needing me to carry it, him, her, with degrees of strength I could only hope to find.

The ferry turned around, circling back towards the quay. I'd begun to feel I belonged in Sydney, though I'd lived here for barely three months. But I was already a foreigner: homeless and idle, travelling in circles.

On the quay I boarded a train that slid down into the tunnel. At St James I chose an exit at random and surfaced in Elizabeth Street. The energy had drained out of me, but I forced myself to walk between the airy green mass of Hyde Park and the solid block of the city. To wait in the empty motel room would be unbearable.

I caught a bus to Kings Cross because I'd been there with Lloyd. I saw cigarette butts and crumpled food wrappings all over the footpath; an old man with one arm in a sling carrying a plastic bag full of oranges; a woman beside a neon-lit doorway, rocking forwards on high heels, her arms folded over her short, tight dress, her eyes closed, her head dropping onto her chest as if she were asleep. Other people who'd fallen through the grid of ordinary life, their days shapeless, their nights lonely, their future a cloud. Beneath my feet the brown paper leaves of the plane trees crackled and split. I paused outside a cafe where chips hissed in a vat of oil, the hot smell drifting into the street. I was hungry and tired. But only the rhythm of one step, another step, kept my thoughts moving in any orderly sequence.

Maybe Lloyd was right and I should have it adopted. If I kept it the bishop would find out, and I'd have to tell my mother. This would be the worst suffering I could inflict on her. I could stay here and find a job somewhere. I had enough money left over from my scholarship to stay in the motel a few more days. I could hide here even from Lloyd so he wouldn't have to worry. After the baby was born I could go back to university.

Then I remembered Billy when my mother had brought him home from the hospital: his weary expression, his velvet skin, his furry, scented scalp. His helplessness. Now there was another life more vulnerable than my mother's, and I knew I had made a choice.

I walked past the fountain and down into the streets of blocks of flats with panelled halls set among jacarandas and Moreton Bay figs and the fronds of palms. On the downward slope of the hill were streets of grander buildings and houses sequestered behind fences and foliage: absurdly, I felt personally shut out.

The light lay in pieces among the masses of shadow. Windows were lit. In a park of Moreton Bay figs I listened to a bird call I had never heard in the Grainger Valley, and to the water lapping against the rocking boats beside the wharf. I stood behind the harbour wall and watched the windows catch alight on the opposite shore. If I stayed here long enough, the plane would leave without me. But I turned around.

I hurried back in the direction of the bus stop. In a tiny cafe – a golden lantern in the blue dusk – people sat eating and drinking on benches along the walls. As the people in Abernant had, when I'd passed them in the street on my way home, these people seemed unaware of their freedom. It was strange to feel frightened and trapped, away from home.

Soon Vince would arrive at the motel to drive me to the airport. Lloyd's friend would be getting ready to meet me. The one-way ticket was paid for.

Outside the bright doorways men stood in clumps on the footpath. Here even the sky was neon: electric blue. I could smell spilled beer, fish and chips frying and meat sizzling on a hot plate. I bought a hamburger, and ate it on the bus which seemed to speed, everything seemed suddenly speeded up, as in a silent film.

I saw his black figure standing in the car park, beside his car.

'Where on earth have you been?'

'Nowhere. I just went into the city.'

Vince followed me up the concrete stairs to the room. 'If we don't hurry you'll miss your plane.'

At the airport Vince put out his hand. I ignored it: he seemed already invisible. I saw him mouth something, but where we stood I heard no human sound. I hurried across the dim tarmac. My seat was in the back beside a window. As the plane soared I looked down and watched the skewed city dwindle and tilt, until it was a speckle of light on the floor of the darkness.

MELBOURNE

It is a very strange sensation to inexperienced youth to feel itself quite alone in the world, cut adrift from every connection, uncertain whether the port to which it is bound can be reached, and prevented by many impediments from returning to that it has quitted.

CHARLOTTE BRONTË,
JANE EYRE

To arrive by plane at an unfamiliar city in the dark, I thought, should have been exciting. Outside the terminal at Essendon a tall, bulky man was inspecting each of the passengers. As soon as he saw me he stepped forward. His smile was warm, it was reassuring.

'Maggie? Gerard.'

He had a soft, spreading Irish face and a lofty height packed with chunky bones and flesh. He wore an ordinary shirt under his jumper but to each lapel was attached a little gold cross like Lloyd sometimes wore.

When my port arrived he picked it up and I followed him to his car. Gerard's authority came not only from being a priest, but from something inside him. In this way he reminded me of Delia. And it had something to do with his air of belonging to this place: the impression that he could give you most of his attention and still make his way safely through the traffic to his destination. This made me more aware of my anxiety, and of the foreignness of the gliding city.

In a street of shabby terraced houses which had once been grand, the bony trees seemed to make way for the car.

'Where are we?'

'Parkville. Near the university. Here we are, Park Drive. Katrina's waiting for us.'

'Katrina?'

'She's the housekeeper at a presbytery near here, but she shares a house with some students. One's away at the moment; he said you could stay in his room.'

Katrina was setting a teapot and mugs on the scarred wooden table. From the back doorway I saw her dimpled reflection in the belly of the old kettle simmering on the green enamel stove. Gerard introduced us. Like Gerard, Katrina was about Lloyd's age, solid and calm in her movements and in the atmosphere she spread about her. Her hair was smoothed into a thick, heavy plait that reached almost to her waist; her open face was free of make-up. Without asking me, she put two heaped spoonfuls of sugar in my tea, stirred it and set it in front of me with a plate of biscuits. She and Gerard made conversation about people they knew, and the next issue of a magazine about current affairs they worked on – not to exclude me but to make me feel less of a stranger and, I sensed, to avoid mentioning why I was there.

'You look tired,' Katrina said, when I'd finished my tea. 'Come on upstairs and I'll show you your room.'

Each step on the frayed carpet of the narrow stairs took an enormous effort, as though I were stumbling in my sleep. As soon as Katrina closed the door, and without unpacking – what was the point? – I crept between the clean sheets she had put on the bed.

The next morning I woke to a feeling of dislocation as intense as if someone had transported me, unconscious, from one bed to another in the night. Before I got up I made myself write a letter to my mother, telling her that I had an opportunity to study a special course at the university in Melbourne, that for the time being I was living in a house with other students, and I'd send her an address when I had a more permanent one. I knew that as long as she thought I was studying, my mother wouldn't care where I was: she had too much else to worry about. It was a good excuse, as well, never to go home for the holidays.

Books and clothes were piled along the edges of the room where the student had put them to make room for me. On a wall was a life-size poster of Brigitte Bardot, pouting and almost naked, next to the words, *And God Created Woman*. I waited until the house was quiet, so I wouldn't meet any of the other occupants. The bathroom across the hall was musty with the smell of damp towels. I showered quickly in case someone else wanted to use it, and went downstairs. Katrina was in the kitchen. Her kind smile embarrassed me unintentionally because I needed kindness.

'Sleep all right? Ben does in there, he doesn't get up till noon sometimes.'

So his name was Ben, I had slept in Ben's bed.

Katrina poured tea while I made toast from the bread she'd put out. 'I'm off to work on the magazine now, but I thought I'd better tell you how to get to the Women's first.'

'The Women's?'

'Hospital. To book in to have the baby.'

'Oh, yes, thanks.' I couldn't tell her that I hadn't realised this was necessary.

❖

At the hospital clinic I waited among the women who sat with their dresses stretched over egg-shaped bellies speaking to one another in Italian or Greek. When my number was called I followed the yellow line to a cubicle behind a set of doors to get changed. In a room behind this I lay shivering on a high, narrow bed, my legs splayed under the thin gown.

I couldn't look at the doctor. He inserted the cold speculum into my vagina and pressed his warm hand against my abdomen, then the chilled coin of his stethoscope, his expression rapt, as though he were listening to music. I imagined a small lump of flesh resisting the pressure of the doctor's fingers beneath my skin. I wanted to ask what it'd look like, whether it had a nose and ears and fingernails, or if it still looked like a blind fish, but I was embarrassed to show my ignorance.

'Everything's all right.' The doctor nodded at the nurse beside him. 'So, a Christmas present for some lucky couple.'

He wasn't talking to me, I felt invisible. Then he was gone, in a flurry of white coat-tails.

With its long rows of chairs back to back and lining the walls, the waiting room was like a ferry. I wished I were riding on a Sydney ferry, up front to watch the bow butt the waves, my belly empty, my mind free. The room was crowded. Whole families waited together: the weary, ungainly mothers and the restless children and the chain-smoking fathers. Listening to the unfamiliar languages I imagined that Melbourne had disappeared, and that outside the hospital there was another foreign city.

I followed a line of a different colour, as I'd been instructed at the reception desk when I gave my name as Miss Margaret Reed. I'd have been even more ashamed to pretend I was married, and I felt defiant, too. Inside her tiny office the social worker, Miss Hart, sat under a small, high window. She glanced at the bare fourth finger on my left hand.

'So you're here to talk about having your baby adopted.' Her stomach was flat, she wore a suit with a short skirt and a white frilled collar sticking out of the neck of the jacket. She spoke kindly.

'I'm going to keep it. The baby's father might . . . he might be able to come down here.'

Miss Hart tilted her head as if to see me from another angle. I looked down. The two black points of her shoes showed under her desk.

'So you think he might change his mind?'

'I don't know.'

'And if he doesn't?'

'I'll still keep it.'

'Have you got family support?'

'They don't live here.'

Miss Hart raised her eyebrows. 'There's a lot of good people waiting to adopt – the baby would have a proper family, a stable home.' She touched a folder at the other end of her desk. 'I could start . . .'

I shook my head.

'You have to think about the child.'

'I am. I don't want it to grow up without me.'

Miss Hart sighed. 'We'll talk about it again next time. You know there are places you can go, until you have the baby? There's a home, run by the St Joseph nuns.'

I pictured a row of big-bellied girls lined up in the morning to wash their faces in basins of cold water; Joey nuns like a row of crows in their black habits and veils, looking on with pious disapproval; windows with bars; padlocked gates.

'I've got somewhere to stay.'

Miss Hart nodded and closed the folder. 'We'll talk about it again the next time I see you.'

❖

The houses I saw on the way back were much like some in Cumberland, but in the unfamiliar streets they looked like houses in a dream. The sunlight that struck weakly, briefly, through the clouds and lit the few yellow leaves on the spectral black elms and the thick grass on the plantations was the wrong colour: watery lemon, not the honey-coloured light I remembered from Sydney. The cramped houses, the rocking trams tunnelling through the avenues of winter trees, the damp, grey air seemed sinister, as though changed by some catastrophe: an invasion, or a war.

Since I'd arrived, I'd felt as though I was weeping without sound, without tears. Everything I saw made me sad. The closest feeling I'd had to this before was the dread when going home from school.

Gerard was waiting for me. 'I thought you might want to come and meet some friends.'

He drove us to Fitzgibbon Street, to another rundown terraced house, which was also, he explained, a shelter for men who were homeless.

In the kitchen everyone moved to make a place for me at the big table. Katrina was there. It was a relief to see a familiar face.

'This is Maggie,' Gerard said. 'She's from New South Wales . . . the Grainger Valley, isn't it, Maggie?'

'I was in Sydney, at university. Before that I was at school in Cumberland.'

'Cumberland. So you're . . . you're Lloyd's . . .' A man with a thin face framed by a thicket of beard and hair nodded at me.

'Maggie, this is Lou,' Gerard said.

'Hello.' I nodded back. My cheeks were hot.

'We're all friends of Lloyd's here,' Gerard said quickly. 'And this is Deborah, she's on magazine duty with Lou today.' Deborah smiled: her smooth round face was a start-ling contrast with Lou's.

'How did you go at the clinic?' Katrina said. 'Everything all right?'

'Yes, it's fine, thanks.' So everyone here knew.

An old man in slippers and a stained, shiny suit, the jacket crammed over a jumper, shuffled in from the hall.

'What's up, Stan?' Gerard got up from the table.

'Nothing's up,' Stan said. 'Nothing's been up for bloody years, if you want to know. I just want a cup o' tea.'

'But you had your tea with the others.' Gerard laughed. 'Give us a break, you know we're having a meeting.'

Stan rolled his eyes and sighed extravagantly. 'All I want is a cup o' bloody tea.'

'All right, all right, I'll bring you one, if you go on down to the front room.'

Stan shuffled out. He muttered, 'Terrible bloody service around here.'

When they'd stopped laughing Gerard said, 'Is Stan still on the wagon?'

Lou shook his head. 'Give him a few hours, he'll be well and truly sozzled.'

I couldn't believe he was laughing about someone getting drunk. These people didn't seem worried by anything except the state of the world; they acted as if it were normal to have a house full of derelict men, most of them alcoholics. Here people came in and out all day, it seemed, propping their bicycles in the hall: they held meetings at the kitchen table, they put together a magazine about world affairs and the changes in the church since Vatican II. Stacks of these lined the kitchen shelves. The plainness of the rooms, of the people's clothes, was reassuring: among such humility, such generosity, who could come to harm? In the very air there was an atmosphere of selfless purpose, of common dedication to weighty and thankless tasks.

Katrina said to Gerard, 'Did you tell Maggie about the Sullivans?'

Gerard turned to me, and again I was embarrassed by the kindness in his eyes, in the downward tilt of his head. He said, 'I've been asking around the parishes. There's a family at Gembrook, in the Dandenongs, a big family, they need someone to help out. Mrs Sullivan's pregnant too. You'd have somewhere to live, and they'd pay you something, of course.'

'The Dandenongs?'

'The Dandenong mountains, but it's still part of Melbourne,' Katrina said.

'It's lovely there,' Deborah said.

Everyone nodded. I wanted to stay here, with these friendly people, not with a strange family. But of course I had nowhere to live, and not much money left, either.

'All right, thank you.'

'I'll drive you up there in the morning,' Gerard said.

'Good timing,' Katrina said, 'Ben's coming back early – he's arriving tomorrow.'

There was a pause, then Gerard began to talk about the articles for the magazine. Katrina turned to listen to him; whenever he spoke in his soft voice, everyone stopped talking and looked at him. They talked about Vietnam: about conscription, about plans for a demonstration against the war later that month. I sat on the edge of the discussion, afraid of showing my ignorance.

Deborah and Lou were connected with the university on the other side of Royal Parade, but they were different from the younger students I'd seen at Macquarie: more serious, paler in their dark clothes, their shoulders slightly rounded and braced beneath the weight of some shared responsibility. I saw, from the slight turning of their bodies, almost a flowing towards each other, from the offhand way one listened when the other spoke, as though to be impartial, that they were a couple. I envied them: they were free, while Lloyd and I had to hide.

Deborah caught my eye. I quickly looked away – had I been staring? But she said, 'What were you studying, Maggie?'

'English and French. History and philosophy too, but . . . well, I was, anyway.' It seemed hardly worth speaking about.

Deborah's habitual expression was slightly distracted and perplexed, as though she were inwardly occupied in solving a riddle, but now her frown deepened. 'It must have been hard having to leave.'

The sudden rush of grief stunned me. My eyes smarted, my nose stung, the back of my throat was raw. I shrugged, not trusting myself to speak. Finally I said, 'Are you studying at the university?'

'I'm doing my honours year in English. Lou's tutoring in philosophy. He's writing a thesis for his PhD.'

I nodded. How lucky they were.

Lou said, 'I saw John and Leonie last night. They're going back to India, they know somebody who's going to introduce them to Mother Teresa . . . John's going to try and get an interview for the magazine.'

'Who's Mother Teresa?' I asked.

They all turned to me, incredulous. Katrina explained kindly, but I still felt ignorant and naive.

'I hear Lloyd gives the bishop a run for his money up there,' Deborah said to me.

I nodded. I knew I should say something, but among these people I felt unused to speech, to fitting words to ideas. I wasn't like them. I didn't even have their faith. But Lloyd was one of them: a mate. A member of the group of radical priests and lay people who were trying to change everything in the church. These people didn't live in the same underworld as Jack and Vince. Here it was even possible, for a moment, to think of my pregnancy to Lloyd as a worthy, radical predicament, a part of the struggle to change the world.

Now it seemed that there were several conversations overlapping, as though there were too many important issues to discuss.

'The Australian bishops are frightened of ideas,' Gerard was saying.

'But celibacy wasn't ever seriously on the agenda,' Deborah said.

'What about when they start voting with their feet?' Lou said.

'A lot of them are,' Katrina said. 'Have you heard how many have left already this year? Some of them are applying for dispensations.'

I remembered what Jack had said would happen to Lloyd if he tried to get a dispensation. I wanted to ask about this, but I was shy, and thinking about Jack made my pregnancy no longer seem part of some worthy struggle but something shameful. I didn't belong with these good people in the wholesome atmosphere of their kitchen; I had sat in Vince's lounge room, where Jack had laughed about me being pregnant as if it were a dirty joke, and talked to me about his girlfriend and the abortion doctor, and Vince had stood beside me, hemming me in at the bookcase, and Lloyd had sat pale and quiet, sipping whisky.

Gerard got up from the table. 'I'd better get Maggie back to Park Drive. I'll get us a bite to eat on the way.'

❖

In a small Italian restaurant in Faraday Street Gerard ordered spaghetti bolognese. The food was delicious, I'd only eaten tinned spaghetti before, but I had to force myself to eat. I had no idea where I was or where I was going.

'You and Lloyd've had a rough time,' Gerard said.

'A bit.'

When I heard Gerard say Lloyd's name in his deep, gentle voice, it made me think of him with Jack and Vince in Vince's lounge room, and of how different he was from Gerard and the others. I wondered if they'd have been mates if they weren't both priests.

'Do you know what you're going to do after the baby's born?'

'Everyone except a friend from school thinks I should have it adopted.'

'Is that what you want?' Gerard paused and put down his glass of Chianti.

'It's not what I want, but I don't know what else to do.' I didn't want Gerard to tell Lloyd I was going to keep the baby.

'Well, I'm sure it'll all work out for the best. I'd better get you back or I'll be late at Fitzgibbon Street. I'll pick you up at nine to take you to Gembrook. That okay?'

'How many children are there?'

'Five, I think.'

❖

Already at breakfast Mrs Sullivan's brown hair was trailing in wisps from her French roll, but her smile was determinedly in place, the thin-lipped, weary smile she wore as though to convince herself of an inner calm. On the other side of the wide bench I unwrapped another loaf of bread, and tried not to look at her belly – more swollen than mine – pressing against the tray of the highchair while she spooned porridge into the encrusted mouth of Gus, a chubby child of about eighteen months. The older children were eating at the big table. Through the window I could see, beyond the shallow valley, the trees rising in tier after tier to the horizon in the thinning fog, encircling the house with their linked branches, their matted foliage.

'Larry, you'd better go and clean those shoes. Why didn't you last night? Look how shiny Ian's are.' Larry elbowed Ian in the ribs and there was a scuffle, stopped by Mrs Sullivan's frown.

'I reminded you, didn't I, Larry? You must have forgotten.' I wished I'd cleaned them myself.

Mrs Sullivan looked at us both and shook her head. She said, 'Josie, have you finished breakfast yet? You'll miss the bus. Maggie, have you finished making the lunches? The children'll be late for school.'

'Here you are, Josie.' I handed her a bag of sandwiches and fruit, and watched her pirouette out of the room to catch the bus to the convent school. Josie was a fair-haired version of her mother, but slight, as I had been, too, six years – a life-time – ago. Her uniform was like my old one, only blue. How lucky she was, to use her brain all day, to be with friends!

Matthew, too young for school, grizzled while I buttoned Larry and Ian into coats, stuffed their feet into gumboots, piled them into the van parked outside the back porch, which faced the road. My cheeks smarted, my fingers were numb. It wasn't the sharp, frosty cold of the inland Grainger Valley towns but the damp, clinging cold of the mountains. I drove slowly down the unmade roads into town: a church, a post office, a handful of shops, the school where I dropped the boys off.

At the post office counter my heart skipped: Lloyd's handwriting stood out among the envelopes. I read the letter quickly behind the wheel of the van under the thinning foliage of the trees. *Maggie sweetheart, I miss you so much I get this actual physical ache.* It was strange to feel such intense happiness and misery at the same time. I imagined what it would be like if he turned up on the Sullivans' doorstep one day in his priest's suit and told me to pack, because he was taking me back to Sydney. I imagined the looks on the Sullivans' faces. I knew this was impossible, but I couldn't help hoping he'd find some way to rescue me. When I'd composed myself, I drove the cumbersome van back to the white house perched on its clearing of mud on the ridge above the valley.

Later, as I made the six beds and dusted and vacuumed the rooms, I could see through the French doors that opened from every room upstairs and down the steep slopes of the forest. At midday the sunlight briefly coloured it: I could have put out my hand, it seemed, and stroked the nap, bright green on the ridges and in the shadows smoky blue. Mr Sullivan said the trees were eucalypts: mountain ash. But on most days, when they were grey-green and shadowed black, they reminded me of the trees in northern continents of ice and snow I'd read about, dark by day and night. Every morning fog shrouded the forest, every day low loops of cloud hung over the valley that led down to the hidden stream at the bottom of the property. Nothing ever seemed to dry: not the clothes, nor the mud, nor the long grass and ferns that grew beside the road.

At lunchtime Mrs Sullivan sat at one end of the long table. She looked tired, and I felt guilty. I carried the plates of sandwiches in from the kitchen and called in Matthew, who rode his pedal car up and down the terrace. I stooped to pick up the piece of soggy bread that Gus had thrown down from his highchair onto the floor. To look after my baby when it was born I'd have to live here, and do housework all day and into the night – if they let me stay.

Mrs Sullivan poured herself a cup of tea. She looked at me with raised eyebrows, the absent smile.

'No thanks,' I said. 'Mrs Sullivan? Tomorrow's my next check-up at the hospital.'

The two vertical lines between her brows darkened.

'I told you last week, remember?'

'But it's only a few weeks since the last one, isn't it?'

'Four. They told me to come back tomorrow.'

'You don't really need to go that often. Not until later on.'

'I think I ought to go.' I looked out at the encroaching trees.

'But I've got my parish committee meeting tomorrow. I can't take the children. And we have to change all the beds.' When her smile collapsed I saw the desperation behind it.

'I'm sorry, Mrs Sullivan, I'll change the beds on Friday. It's only one day. Is it all right if I go?'

She got up and unbuckled Gus and took him out of the highchair. She propped him on his chubby legs and wiped his hands and face and straightened slowly, supporting her back with both hands. Without speaking she turned to the clothes rack in front of the window and began turning the limp garments, exposing their damp undersides to the weak, already vanishing sun. I felt sorry for her, but I hung on. After a moment she said, looking away from me, 'Well, if you have to you have to, then.'

For the rest of the afternoon we kept out of each other's way. When I brought Larry and Ian home from school I was glad of the cheerful noise of the boys' voices and footsteps echoing up into the stairwell and throughout the house. Only Josie was quiet, bending over her homework at the kitchen table. She was as studious as I had been and oblivious to the chaos around her, and to all the other kinds of chaos I now knew about. Watching her I grieved for my lost self. Then there was a time of day, between making afternoon tea and peeling the vegetables, when the world seemed to stay its spinning, all celestial bodies to suspend their rotation, the light to pause in its ebbing towards night, and I felt a profound emptiness. While the new life grew inside me, mine was frozen.

Mr Sullivan's arrival home barely altered the atmosphere. He came in tired from his work at the factory he owned in a middle suburb of Melbourne, and the long drive up into the mountains. He was tall and thin, and the dumbbells in his study only gathered dust which I flicked away each week. Something about him, a despondence in his expression and gait, the visible effort he made to connect himself with others, reminded me of my father when he was sober. But Mr Sullivan was never drunk.

At night, after I'd put the children to bed, I sat with Mr and Mrs Sullivan in the lounge room in front of the fire in its cavernous fireplace. When I turned and looked out through the big glass doors that made a flimsy screen between us and the cold, I saw our ghosts sitting outside in the dark: I felt the presence of the trees. Mrs Sullivan sewed. Mr Sullivan read the paper or stared into the fire. Beside his wife he seemed more substantial, as though the weight of her legitimate pregnancy gave him a kind of ballast.

I opened one of my books from university but could only pretend to read; in the unfamiliar room, with these people who still seemed like strangers, the reality of my predicament obstructed understanding.

We sat for a long time without speaking. Then Mrs Sullivan looked up from the button she was sewing onto a shirt and said, 'What kind of school did you go to, Maggie?' The question was abrupt, as though part of some longer, exasperated interrogation.

'A convent school, in the Grainger Valley. I was a boarder there. I won a scholarship.'

Mrs Sullivan glanced at her husband, but he shook out the paper as if he hadn't heard.

'You must have been good at schoolwork,' Mrs Sullivan said. The settled way she sat in the lamplight with her ankles crossed, her head tilted in concentration, slowly drawing the long thread taut, her little finger crooked above the needle, made me feel fidgety even though I had been sitting still, trying not to be noticed.

'Yes I was. I was dux of the school.' I spoke softly, as though this, as well as my sinful pregnancy, were something to be ashamed of.

Mrs Sullivan put down her needle and looked up at me. Her expression was perplexed and grave. She shook her head and clucked her tongue. Mr Sullivan caught my eye now, over the top of his newspaper. I looked down at the black scribble on the page.

'And the baby's father,' Mrs Sullivan was saying, 'did he – doesn't he want the baby? Is that why you can't get married and keep it?'

My face burned. For a while I couldn't speak. *The baby's father.* I could never say his name, never give him an identity. In this good Catholic home, the fact that he was a priest seemed so potentially explosive it felt barely possible to contain it inside me. When I spoke it was hard to sound normal. I said, 'He'd want it if . . . if he wasn't . . . if he was . . .'

Mr and Mrs Sullivan exchanged a quick glance. It occurred to me that they must think the father was married. If only they knew how much worse it was than that.

Mrs Sullivan took up her sewing; she nodded and frowned. Mr Sullivan noisily snapped and rustled his newspaper. I ached with the effort of not jumping up and running from the room. When the silence was smoother I said goodnight and walked, almost ran, to the stairs, the back of my neck prickling under their imagined gazes at me, at each other.

All day I'd looked forward to this moment when I could close the door and, in the comfort of my warming bed, read

Lloyd's letter again and write back to him. I told him how towards nightfall the trees seemed to move closer until they surrounded the house. I told him that I was lonely and that I felt humiliated at the Sullivans', and asked him if he could find me somewhere to live and work in Sydney.

❖

Mr Sullivan's sports car was so narrow and slung so close to the ground that I was always surprised to see how he fitted his long legs into it. Mr Sullivan wore leather driving gloves and a leather jacket and a cap over his thin, sandy hair. The seats of the car were leather, too. He drove quite fast down through the dim, damp forest where thick wads of fog were still caught on the branches. The trees ascended into cloud, long tendrils of bark trailed from their branches, and beneath them the tree ferns unfurled their fronds to make a lower canopy. The road was slippery and black. I watched Mr Sullivan's hand shove the gearstick back and forth with swift flourishes of his wrist: with his other hand he steered around the loops and bends of the steep road. I was glad he was too absorbed in this to speak. He seemed angry that I was leaving his wife to cope alone.

It was better to watch Mr Sullivan change gears than to look at the road: the forest spun around the car, and the leather smelled rancid. I dreaded having to ask him to stop while I got out and vomited in the narrow space between the trees and the car. But soon the road widened and straightened, and the trees folded back to make way for open paddocks. Then, in the middle of the outer-eastern suburbs, where the streets of sand-coloured brick houses crowded around the rectangular shopping strips, we stopped outside Mr Sullivan's factory. Opposite the factory was a station, and I caught the train to the city.

When I stepped onto the platform at Flinders Street, I felt that I'd arrived at the heart of the city, but it was only something to pass through. I stood for a few moments in the gaping mouth under the clocks, and then I went down into the street and caught the tram to Carlton.

I waited impatiently for my examination at the hospital, because I had decided to miss my appointment with the social worker and I didn't want her to see me. The last time, she had said that since the father hadn't come to join me in Melbourne, the responsible decision would be to give my baby to one of the married couples in her file. My only argument was that I was the mother, but this wasn't enough. I was a teenager, and I wasn't married.

I was impatient, as well, to visit the art gallery I'd read about in one of Mr Sullivan's discarded newspapers, when I was cleaning his study. It had just been opened, I read, after its relocation to a new building in St Kilda Road.

I remembered the last time I'd visited a gallery. I was fifteen. I'd escaped from home, guiltily, one Saturday afternoon, and caught the train to Coalport to see the Rodin exhibition. I had walked from the station to the gallery through Civic Park, which was deserted except for a man walking towards me.

When he reached me, the man grabbed me between the legs and said, 'That's a nice little cunt you've got there.' I froze, but he walked on. When I could move again, I hurried on to see the exhibition before it got dark. At home I told my mother, who was distractedly cooking tea while my father shouted from the lounge room. My mother said, 'Did he say anything?' I said that he hadn't, because I was too embarrassed to repeat what he'd said, even though he'd used the word my father often called her. I had felt ashamed, as though I'd done something wrong. My mother shook her head and went on cooking.

Now I was ashamed of being pregnant unmarried, and to a priest. At the same time I felt defiant in the face of the disapproval I saw in the expressions of the Sullivans, and the nurses and doctors and social worker, and in the glances from some people in the street, who looked at my belly and then as if automatically at the ring finger on my left hand.

The new gallery was built like a fortress as though to protect the artworks inside: its stone walls were the colour of the charcoal used in drawings. The pools outside, and the water that streamed down the huge glass wall, reflected the grey trees and sky.

I found the Impressionists on the map and wandered, elated, from frame to frame. In one painting, a naked girl about my own age lay asleep on a dishevelled bed. Her underclothes were scattered where she'd dropped them beside the bed, next to a sleeping dog. The girl lay on her stomach with one leg bent, her profiled face in shadow. Her supple flesh, like the sheets, was silken, velvet in the shadows; her buttocks, the true subject of the painting, were globes of golden light. Naked and sleeping, she looked so defenceless. I thought of Billy sleeping on his back, his little arms and legs askew, while the war raged on outside the bedroom door.

I moved on. And there, right in front of me, was the painting I'd loved to look at, reproduced in the book in the school library, of a Paris boulevard on a late winter's afternoon. I could see the raised stipples and crescents and dots of dried paint, each one mirroring the ghostly movement of the painter's arm and hand, now bones. I stepped back to let some people look, and pass, then stood gazing into the familiar street, along to where the eye was drawn into the mist on the horizon, where the two sides of the street converged. It was a painting of infinity: the mystery of space and time.

The paintings hung like stars, emitting a steady, brilliant light, long after the people who painted them had died. I turned back to the one before me. My fingers itched to hold the pencil again, the paintbrush: I'd forgotten the hunger to bring into being, with quick, instinctive strokes, something that didn't exist before. I had lost the capacity to read or write poems as I had at school, but maybe I could still draw, and even paint.

The painting reminded me of crossing Main Street in Cumberland on my way to the library on a rainy afternoon in winter, wearing my dark green tunic and blazer and velour hat, and old brown gloves. I remembered how the street had been blurred, and beautiful, like the one in the painting: the smudged car lights and traffic lights reflected in the gleaming road, the old buildings shimmering in the pearly light.

Back in the street, I gazed into the wall of water and saw myself, swollen and misshapen. The skeletons of the plane trees, the low, padded sky, the watery air seemed to have this quality of distortion: if I put out my hand to touch the trunk of a tree, I'd feel instead of damp wood the smooth coldness of glass. Everything here – people, buildings, trees – was rooted in this place, and I was drifting like the autumn leaves which clung on till they fell into the gutter.

It was time to cross the bridge over the Yarra. If I missed the train, Mr Sullivan would have to wait. I dreaded the loneliness and the atmosphere of disapproval I had to go back to. I wished I could catch a train to Spencer Street, and another one to Sydney. Who could stop me? But Lloyd would not be happy to see me, he'd be panicked, in case someone found out he was the father. Jack and Vince would put me on another plane. The money I'd earned would soon run out. I had to stay here to look after myself, to look after the baby, to look after Lloyd. And I wasn't truly alone: in my body was the baby; in my mind were all the paintings I had seen.

❖

In Gembrook, winter had occupied the mountains. All day it was twilight. Everyone moved in a hybrid element of air and water. One night I went to pick Josie up from her friend's

house, where I'd driven her after school. I parked the unwieldy
old van in the mud outside the house and kept the engine
running, but when Josie got in, the van would not move
forwards or back. The wheels were embedded in the sludge.
I stayed calm and sat shivering at the wheel while Josie went
back to get help. But inside I was panicking – not because I
couldn't move the van, but because I myself was stuck, trapped
inside the cold and dark of banishment.

When I got to my room that night I wrote to Lloyd again.
I told him that I couldn't possibly stay in Gembrook, or
anywhere in Melbourne, for almost five more months.

❖

Mr Sullivan hunched over the steering wheel beside me,
his profile drawn in bitter downward lines. In the dull mid-
morning light the forest whirled by, a solid manifestation of
darkness. Our enforced physical closeness aggravated the
silence. We reached the lower slopes, the hilly suburbs, then
the flat net of roads in which the brick veneer houses were
caught.

Finally I said, 'I'm sorry I have to leave, Mr Sullivan.' I did
feel guilty for abandoning them, but I was sure they'd find
someone else, someone who wasn't pregnant or a stranger to
the mountains.

'You have to?' It was a hiss, a release of pent-up steam.

'It's so far away from everything. There's an art class I saw
an advertisement for . . .'

'I thought it was university you wanted to go to?'

'I do, but I can't now – now that . . .'

Mr Sullivan frowned sidelong at my convex belly. 'I don't understand you, Maggie, I have to say.'

I stared out of the window. In the yard of an orange-brick house a single eucalypt waved its branches in the wind, as if begging to be rescued from the desolate estate, then fell back and out of sight. The sky sagged with pewter clouds. My throat ached but I couldn't cry, not in front of Mr Sullivan.

'Why didn't you stay at home?'

'My mother doesn't even know. She's a good Catholic, I couldn't tell her.' I didn't say, *especially since the father is a priest.* 'And my father gets drunk all the time, he hits Mum. It'd be terrible for her, if she knew.' I felt like a shelled creature turned on its back, its delicate, quivering flesh exposed. But it would be worse to tell him about Lloyd.

Mr Sullivan's head reared back. He had the startled, alarmed expression of someone who'd just lost his footing on solid ground. Then he nodded several times. At last he murmured, 'Well, that explains a lot. I used to drink too much myself. I was becoming an alcoholic. Then I saw what it was doing to my family.'

Mr Sullivan, an alcoholic? I looked at him. 'Oh.' It was all I could say.

We crossed the Yarra, a tame, urban river, which ran sluggishly between its guard of city trees, and entered a place where mansions lined the wide and wooded streets. We sat then in a smoother silence until we reached the house, a large, two-storey maisonette, where Mr Sullivan lifted my grand-father's port out of the boot, said goodbye, and drove away before I'd rung the doorbell.

❖

I could see Lloyd from the porch. He sat beaming on a shiny white couch. Niels de Lange introduced himself, picked up my port and ushered me inside. Stella, waiting in the hall, put out her hand. I had never shaken hands before. Stella managed to smile into my eyes and take in my clothes and haircut at the same time. I looked past her to Lloyd.

'G'day, Maggie!' He waved extravagantly, wiggling his fingers. He looked pleased to see me, but as if I could have been anyone.

Niels was dark and tall: solid and opaque. Stella, red-haired and small, shifted and sparkled like the surface of water. She smiled at Lloyd: it amused people when his behaviour contradicted his black suit and white collar.

'Hello, Father.' It was torturous to look at him.

Niels led me through the kitchen and out the back door to my room – the maid's room with a separate entrance – in the backyard. The room looked out onto a square of concrete and a wooden pen piled with pieces of brick-shaped coal, not like the lumps they fed their fires in the Grainger Valley. The concrete backyard was unexpected after the lawn and garden in front. Inside the room there was a sink and a triangular shower recess curtained off in a corner. The toilet was in the laundry between my room and the house.

In the dining room I sat next to Max, a four-year-old version of Niels; he dangled his legs from a cushion. From time to time each of us glanced sidelong at the other. His satin skin reminded me of Billy's. We all sat at one end of the big oval table. Except for the table and chairs, the room was bare, as if they'd just moved in or were on their way out. But the fire in the grate made the room, like the kitchen at Parkville, an oasis of warmth in the winter city.

'Would you like to say grace for us, please, Father?' Stella's accent was Australian. Niels's was Dutch: Lloyd had written that he came from Holland.

We crossed ourselves and bowed our heads, while Lloyd prayed aloud.

Niels passed around the platter of omelette and we helped ourselves. I'd never done this before. I took the salad bowl from Stella, and I wondered why there was nothing in it except oily lettuce. I couldn't stop thinking about the moment Lloyd would leave.

'We're so pleased Father found you for us, Maggie. Aren't we, Niels?'

Lloyd grinned at Stella. 'It was good for everyone all round, me meeting you and Niels on the plane that time. I'm glad I kept in touch.'

Niels said to me, 'I hope you will be very happy with us.' He smiled with his eyes but he was half in some other world, or just reserved, I couldn't tell which. This detachment increased his dignity; it matched his height and the way his hair grew back from his high forehead.

'It's not easy to find someone to live in, these days,' Stella said. She was intense, conscious of her effect on other people, alert to their response.

'I think Maggie's pretty pleased, too, aren't you?' Lloyd said.

'Yes, Father.' I looked at my plate.

'Father tells us your baby is due in December,' Stella said. 'He said you were going to have it adopted.'

'Stella,' Niels said.

'I'm just saying what Father told us.'

'It's all right,' I said. 'On the twenty-first.'

Stella shook her head. 'First babies never come on time. Max, don't play with your food like that. Niels! Speak to him.'

'Don't they?' I said.

Max slid his fork from one side of his plate to the other.

'What about the baby's father?' Stella said.

'Stella.' Niels frowned at her and shook his head.

'Well, it must have one,' Stella said. 'Doesn't he want it? Is he a student, too?'

Lloyd calmly forked salad into his mouth. His eyes moved rapidly beneath the lids, but he kept his gaze on his plate.

'It's not that. But he can't . . . we can't . . .' I couldn't go on.

'Never mind,' Stella said. 'Still plenty of time till it's born, anyway.'

Max slid slowly from his chair to the floor under the table. I was relieved to have the attention taken off me. Niels shook his head at him.

'I'm boring,' Max said.

We all laughed.

'Bored,' Stella said. 'Sit up, Max, where are your manners? Maggie has perfect table manners – what will she think of us?'

At the sound of her tone Max sat up.

I said to him: 'If you eat it up I'll read you a story after lunch.'

'There you are!' Stella smiled at Max. 'Aren't you lucky now that Maggie's here to look after you?'

Max looked at me. 'She's lucky too!'

I couldn't help laughing, although I was so miserable. 'I didn't know that,' I said. 'That first babies were always late,'

'Maybe it will be on time,' Niels said.

'They never are,' Stella said. 'If you change your mind about the adoption, it'd be lovely to have a baby in the house.'

'If we're still in Australia.' Niels picked up the bottle of wine and began pouring some into everyone's glass except mine.

Lloyd said, 'Are you going back to Holland that soon?' He glanced at me swiftly and I saw that he was anxious. I noticed as well that he spoke with his mouth half full, that the handles of his knife and fork were resting on the table, and I was absurdly embarrassed.

Niels said, 'I've got some work to do in Europe, but we won't be going back until Stella's feeling well again. And now, with Maggie to help out, you might get better more quickly, mightn't you, darling?'

'I'm sure I will.' Stella's smile crinkled her eyes; her whole face seemed to glow when she smiled at Niels.

Niels put down the bottle and I stared at the label. Ninechateau of the Pope, I translated to myself, Ninechateau of the Pope, to stop myself thinking about how Lloyd had to leave after lunch. He thought I'd be going back to university in Sydney after Stella and Niels had gone to Europe. I knew I wouldn't be, so I didn't know if I'd ever see him again, and I had no idea where or how the baby and I would live.

I noticed that Stella had the almost transparent skin of an invalid, and now it was paler, the shadows bluer beneath her eyes, and between her brows were two sharp lines. She and Niels showed Lloyd to the door and I followed them. Max unexpectedly took my hand in his small one, and I was glad of its warmth.

'Well, I'll catch up with you later, Maggie.' Lloyd held up his arm and spread his hand. 'I hope everything goes all right for you.'

'Yes, Father. Thank you, Father.' If I looked at him, I'd give everything away, I'd run out to the taxi and beg him to take me with him. But he was gone.

❖

'Why don't you come and lie down for a little while, darling?' Stella called out from bed.

Niels pretended not to hear. From Max's room, I could see him sitting at the polished table in the study across the

229

hall, working through a pile of papers. I tidied the books on Max's bookcase and dusted the shelves. Max sat on his bed looking at picture books but swinging his legs.

'Niels, come on, darling.' Stella had been wheedling him for a while. I wondered if I ought to take Max downstairs.

'Not now, darling, I'm working.' Niels spoke in a grave but gentle voice, with the smallest trace of reproach. He sat tall at the table with his white shirt buttoned at the neck and cuffs.

Was Stella joking? Earlier, when I had taken up her tea tray, she had sat propped against the pillows in a blue negligee, her red hair brushed in a smooth frame around her face. I thought that she looked elegant and sophisticated, even sick in bed.

I didn't know what to do; I was still getting used to everything. I plucked a book from the shelf in front of me, sat beside Max and began to read aloud.

'*Cette histoire concerne un petit garçon* . . .'

When I finished, all was quiet. Then Stella called out: 'Did you hear that, Niels? Maggie can read in French. Come in here, Maggie, I want to speak to you.'

Max followed me in and jumped onto his mother's bed.

'Gently, Max,' Stella said. 'Mama's got a headache.'

I noticed that grooves had appeared in her forehead, and that the expression in her eyes was strained.

Max bounced off the bed and onto the floor. Stella winced. 'Where did you learn to speak French?'

'At school. I was doing it at university too.'

'I'd like you to speak French to Max sometimes. We were in Paris, when I got sick. He was speaking much better than I was, so we bought him some books.'

'I can't speak very well yet, but I'll try.'

'That'd be lovely.'

'Have you been sick a long time?'

'Since soon after Margareta died.' She plucked at the hem of the sheet. 'I came down with glandular fever and I never really recovered. But the doctor says I should start getting better soon, if I get enough rest.'

She looked at her hands pinching the hem of the sheet. 'She was only two weeks old. She was the most beautiful child, Margareta. She had red hair, like me. She was born with a bad heart.'

'When did she die?'

'Last year, on the nineteenth of November.'

'Oh, I'm sorry. That must've been terrible . . . oh, but that's my birthday.'

Stella looked up. Then she smiled a strange smile. 'Niels!' she called out. 'Come here!' This time her tone was urgent.

'What is it, darling?' Niels stood in the doorway, looking from one of us to the other.

'Maggie was born on the nineteenth of November.' Stella looked into his eyes. Niels looked away. His expression darkened.

'Was she?' he said quietly. His smile was shadowed, like Stella's.

'Isn't that a coincidence? And her name is Margaret!'

I felt a rush of pleasure, as if I'd just found out I was related to them, but it was sad, too. The grief was still in their faces, like a grain that shows in a surface only in a certain light. What would be worse: to have a baby who died, or to give one away?

❖

Niels came upstairs after work to find me and Max at Stella's bedside. He smiled at us and, as he always did when he came home, rubbed his hands together and said, 'How's my little family?' But when he saw Stella his smile fell.

'She's a bit better,' I whispered to him. 'I gave her some Aspros and it brought her temperature down. But she's still got a bad headache.'

Max wrapped himself around his father's leg, sucking his thumb. We all looked down at Stella. She whimpered and moaned and twisted her head as if evading blows. Her teeth were bared. Her eyes were squeezed almost shut by the force of some pressure inside her skull, but she looked at the little group around her.

'Niels darling. Max. My little treasure. Take your thumb out of your mouth.' Max looked as if he was about to cry.

'Why don't you and Max go to the park, Maggie?' Niels said. 'I'll look after Stella now.'

'I don't want to go. I want to stay with Mama and Papa.'

Niels gently prised Max's hand from his leg. 'You go with Maggie while I look after Mama, and afterwards I'll make us some *pommes frites* for dinner.'

'I want to get into bed with Mama.'

I took his hand from Niels's. 'Come on, Max. Let's go and get our coats. I'll tell you a story when we get there.'

All the way to the park Max glowered and dragged his feet. The horizon here was lifted above the houses and the high crests of foliage. Max looked tiny in the streets of tall fences overhung with taller trees, with glimpses above of long rows of windows, of pediments and gables and vast roofs. He was smaller even than Billy, and I picked him up and hugged him against my protruding belly, but I knew it was his mother he wanted. I put him down and we walked on to the park, holding hands for comfort.

I shared his feeling of abandonment. I'd written to Lloyd and told him what the people in Parkville had said about how many priests were leaving the priesthood and applying for dispensations. I asked him if he'd thought about it, I said that we wouldn't have to have the baby adopted, if he could come and look after us. Lloyd said that it was a big thing to give up a vocation. I said that it was a big thing to give up a baby, too. After that he hadn't written back as soon as usual, and I wondered if he ever would.

When we got back Niels was helping an elderly woman out of her coat in the hall. The woman's smile was stiff; her white hair was sculpted back off her face. Her arched eyebrows made her look permanently disapproving. She kissed Max on the cheek. Niels introduced me to Stella's mother, Mrs Mitchell.

'I don't know why you didn't tell me before this,' she was saying in a rasping voice. 'I don't know why I have to ring up to find out what's going on.'

'But I was out all day,' Niels said. 'Really, it was not necessary to come, Mother. Maggie's been looking after Stella. Sometimes the pain is worse than other days. She didn't want me to bother you.'

Mrs Mitchell glanced at my belly, as though calculating: I was almost six months pregnant. I concentrated on unbuttoning Max's coat, even though he could do it himself. I heard her walk purposefully to the stairs and climb them.

In the kitchen I peeled potatoes while Niels washed a lettuce. Max sat at the table with his crayons, drawing strange, elongated houses and people like skeletons standing beside them.

'That's good,' I said. 'Why don't you do a drawing of the park?'

Max shrugged. 'I don't know how.'

'What about the cannon? Do a drawing of the cannon.'

I watched Niels wrap the dripping lettuce in a tea towel. He went outside to spin it dry.

'I'll show you how to make a French dressing,' he said when he came back.

While he measured the olive oil and vinegar into a jar he said, 'Stella said you were very kind with her today.'

I watched the golden oil rocking on top of the vinegar. 'She was pretty sick.' I remembered how without thinking about it, when I'd seen the pain in Stella's face, I'd stroked her forehead and spoken to her tenderly, as to a child or to someone I loved. 'I was a bit worried.'

Niels nodded. 'Well, I wanted to thank you. Sometimes she has very bad days. But it isn't dangerous.' He shook the jar vigorously. 'See? You have to mix it up like this.'

I said, 'How do you want me to cut up the potatoes?'

'I don't know how do you draw a cannon,' Max said.

'Here.' I picked up the crayon. 'It's like a big fat gun on wheels. And here's you climbing onto it.'

'That's very good.' Niels looked over my shoulder. 'Very thin. The potatoes. Stella said there's an art class in Hawthorn you want to go to? I could drive you there.'

I felt myself flush with pleasure. 'That'd be good. Thanks.'

When dinner was ready, I went upstairs and found Mrs Mitchell sitting on a chair beside Stella's bed, straight-backed but inclining slightly forwards, her hands clamped to her handbag. Stella was lying back against the pillows, her face white but lined now more with irritation than pain. Her smile when she saw me was almost a grimace.

'Hello, Maggie,' she said.

'I came to tell Mrs Mitchell dinner's ready.'

'Will you be all right while I go downstairs?' Mrs Mitchell asked in her rasping voice: everything about her seemed sharp-edged.

'Of course I'll be all right. There really wasn't any need for you to come all this way over in a taxi, Mother.'

I held my breath. I'd never be game to speak to my mother like that.

'Well, if I'm not wanted here . . .' Mrs Mitchell got up from her chair. 'I do know how to make myself scarce.'

'Oh, Moth*er*!' Stella rolled her eyes.

'Niels said to ask if you want any dinner,' I said to Stella.

'Not now, thanks. I might have a boiled egg later.'

'You should try and eat,' Mrs Mitchell told her.

She left the room and I followed her to the stairs. Behind me, I could hear Stella groan.

In the lounge room Niels had lighted the briquette heater, but beyond the double doors in the dining room the fireplace was empty, like Stella's chair. So we ate in the kitchen, which was still warm from the cooking.

After Mrs Mitchell had gone and I'd bathed Max I took him in to Stella. She'd showered and brushed her hair and put on a fresh nightie of cream silk and lace. Her face was shadowed with exhaustion, but she smiled at Max and held out her arms.

Max nuzzled his mother with his head. I took him to his room and tucked him into bed, then went downstairs and prepared Stella's food and carried it up to her.

'Sit down a while, Maggie.' Stella pointed to the chair beside the bed. She began to eat the egg. She didn't seem worried about her mother. This autonomy combined curiously with her perfume to give her an erotic aura. Sometimes when Stella and Niels were together the atmosphere seemed scented like this, thickened, with a trace of quiet exaltation. I understood now that this was connected with their private, physical life together. When Stella was moody, irritable sometimes if in pain or tired, even unreasonable – I could hear her now when we were all busy preparing for a dinner party: *If you want anything done you have to do it yourself* – Niels never raised his voice, he spoke patiently and kindly as if to change her mood, and she became mollified, the air faintly charged. I wondered what it'd be like to have a husband, a lover, like Niels, but it was like wondering what it'd be like to be a millionaire.

'What're you thinking about?' Stella regarded me shrewdly. 'Or should I say who? Stay and talk to me.' She pushed the tray off her knees.

'I haven't done the dishes yet.'

'You can do them later.'

I thought with longing about my own bed, its narrow, solitary comforts, but I sat down.

'I hope you didn't mind Mother, Maggie. Her bark's worse than her bite. I've been trying to make her happy for more than thirty years, but nothing I do will ever make any difference. So now I don't even try.'

How could you stop trying to make your mother happy? Then it occurred to me that if I was doing anything, it was the opposite, even though my mother had no idea what was happening to me.

'Have you been speaking to Max in French?' Stella asked.

'Not much. I'm not very good.' I almost said: not very good yet.

'When we go back he'll have to go to school in France for a while.' She looked me over. 'We'll have to get you some bigger maternity clothes soon.'

I looked down at the cloth of the pinafore she'd given me stretching across my swollen belly.

'I've got some more things you could have. From when I was pregnant with Margareta.'

'Have you? That'd be good. Thanks.'

The day would come when the baby would want to be born, to exist outside my body. For a moment I was breathless.

'Do you really think you might have your baby adopted?' Stella said casually.

'I don't want to. The father . . .' I longed to tell her I had no intention of having it adopted, but what if she told Lloyd?

'Do you love him?'

'Of course I do.'

Stella sighed and smiled. She leaned back against the pillows. 'Did you think he was like a god, when you met him?' Her eyes were glinting in her luminous, wide face. 'I did. I thought Niels looked like a Greek god. We met on a plane. Then I saw him again by accident, on the beach in Perth, where I come from. I was sunbaking one day with my friend Judy. I looked up and there he was.'

I could see Niels towering above her, half-naked, golden in the sun; Stella sprawled in a bikini, lazily opening an eye, and then smiling.

'Did you? Think he was like a Greek god?' Stella looked at me with twitching lips.

The romantic picture faded. 'Ye-e-s . . . I don't know. Not a Greek god.' I thought about Lloyd standing in front of the library window in his black suit with the priest's hard white collar: a broad-shouldered, stocky figure blocking the view.

Stella regarded me with her sharp, narrow-eyed gaze. 'Plenty of time to think about it, anyway,' she said. 'What to do when the baby's born, I mean.'

❖

'Are you sure you'll manage without me?' I hovered in the doorway.

'Of course we will, as long as you don't mind getting a taxi tonight.' Stella stood at the kitchen table, poking the stems of roses into crowded bowls. She looked better after resting all day, though her face still had the pallid, transparent look. Their dinner parties were usually on a Saturday night, and I was always there to help. But it was Wednesday, and I was going to art class. 'Niels made the *blanquette de veau* last night, I just have to heat it and finish the sauce. Birthday cake for dessert. Look.' She took the box from the fridge and lifted the lid. The cake was for Elizabeth, Stella's best friend in Melbourne.

'Thirty candles, are there?' The chocolate-frosted surface was covered with them to the rim. What would it feel like to be so old?

'I don't know if Elizabeth'll appreciate having them counted,' Stella chuckled. 'But it'll be fun watching her try to blow them out.'

'I think she'll like it.'

Stella cocked her head. 'Is that someone at the door? Did you order a taxi? Niels is sorry he can't take you tonight.'

I opened it, and was startled to see Gerard.

'Is there somewhere we can talk?' he said.

'I was just going to my art class.'

'I'll give you a lift.'

'What's wrong?'

'I'll wait in the car.'

I waved to Stella from the hall.

I got into the car beside Gerard: the streetlight suddenly looked sinister, as it had in Abernant while we were outside waiting for my father to stop raging in the house.

Gerard started the engine and drove off. 'Lloyd's in hospital, he wanted me to tell you. In Sydney. He had an operation a few days ago.'

'What kind of operation?'

'Appendix.' He glanced across at me. I was trembling. 'Hey, he'll be all right. They nearly burst, he was pretty crook, but they got them out in time.'

This must have been the reason Lloyd hadn't answered my letter. It was bad enough to think he'd ignored me, but this was even worse.

In Hawthorn I guided Gerard down Chrystobel Crescent to the house whose old-fashioned gables and verandah trimmings were just visible through the branches of the trees. Behind it were the stables where Gunther, a real artist, taught the class in the loft.

'I wish I could go and see Lloyd,' I said. 'It's such a long time since I saw him.'

'He'll be better in no time. You just look after yourself. Drop him a line, that'd be the best thing.'

'I don't feel like going in now.' I sat in the car until Gerard got out and opened my door.

'He'll be fine. Ring me tomorrow and I'll tell you how he is.'

I always hung back before going into class: I felt I didn't belong. After Gerard had driven off, I stood outside for a long time. Lloyd was so far away. It was as if the knife that cut him open had severed the invisible thread that connected me to him.

The cold drove me inside. In the downstairs room, lit by lamps and warmed by an old wood stove, on one of the cushioned couches like beds, Gunther's wife, Vera, sat knitting. Her brown face was wrinkled but her hair was bright blonde. On the walls hung Gunther's paintings, semi-abstract landscapes of the country around their home at Eltham. They were good, but not interesting to me.

'Go on up.' Vera nodded towards the ladder. 'They've started.'

I eased my protuberant body up carefully, rung by rung. At my approach Gunther turned from the easel of a man whose name I couldn't remember.

'. . . it was Man Ray, I think; I read it in a catalogue,' the man was saying. 'It goes something like, "It's the self that matters, it's the fire in the belly with a million rays."'

Gunther nodded, frowning at me. The students came from places I had never heard of: Mooroolbark, Richmond, Black Rock. They looked like ordinary people, they were older than I was, and except for the man – I remembered he was from Greensborough – who talked mostly to Gunther, they chattered more about their children and houses and gardens than about art.

'We thought you weren't coming.' Gunther shook his head. 'The child with child.' He addressed the room. 'More than fire in her belly.' The Greensborough man laughed, but not unkindly. Gunther had the same sun-browned, fissured complexion as Vera, and big brown hands, and wild brown hair that stood thickly out from his skull and emphasised his stockiness.

I was glad the others were too absorbed in their work – their easels angled slightly as though to hide them from their neighbours – to turn and look at me. I went to the rack and lifted out last week's painting, propped it on my easel, and took out my paints. Gunther looked over my shoulder.

'You can put that away again. Here's Molly, tonight we're going to paint from life.'

A girl emerged from the ladder, flicking back her long dark hair like a swimmer climbing from a pool. She called out hello to Gunther and some of the students, slipped behind a screen and, a moment later, dressed in a kimono, walked in bare feet and with lowered head to the chaise longue in front of the rows of easels. She took the kimono off. Gunther went over and whispered to her, squatting on his haunches.

Molly nodded and arranged herself to lie on one side on the blue velvet surface, her back to the room, her head resting on an outstretched arm.

In one swift blue line I traced, the width of the canvas, the round head and dip of neck and sharp ascent to pointed shoulder, the long downward slope to waist and swell of hip, lifted the brush and suggested the buttocks with two crescent moons. With tender precision I painted a figure of voluptuous slenderness. Had I ever been so thin?

My shyness dissolved. I felt weightless, carried out of myself, as when I'd looked at the stars in the bottom paddock. Happiness flooded me like light. It seemed wrong, traitorous to Lloyd, who at that moment lay alone and sick in hospital. But I couldn't help it. I loved the solitariness of the act inside the deep quiet of collective concentration, the removal from ordinary life into the undomesticated space, its rafters, its wooden walls and floor, its smells of paint and linseed oil and turps. There was only the live figure before me, and the other one flowing from inside me through arm and hand and brush onto the canvas.

Gunther was peering over my shoulder. 'You've done this before.'

'No I haven't.'

'I don't believe you.'

'I've drawn people, but I've never painted a nude before. I've never gone to an art class before this one.'

'Bullshit!' He strode off, and everyone turned from their easels and stared.

I painted on. Gunther prowled around the room. 'Too tight,' I heard him saying. 'Look, look at it, look how it flows there . . . see?' He circled back to me. For what seemed a long time a stiffness in the right side of my body registered his presence.

Finally he said in a bitter voice, 'You have done this before.'

'No, I haven't.'

'You're lying.'

I didn't care then whether he believed me or not. 'The fire in the belly with a million rays.' For the first time since I'd been pregnant I felt free from circumstance. This desire, almost sexual, this mysteriously matching ability: nothing else mattered.

Afterwards Vera served coffee from the low table before her couch. From time to time Gunther glanced at me from under the ledge of his brow. Once I caught his eye and he said, looking back at Vera, 'Our pregnant teenager tried to tell me she was a prodigy, upstairs.'

'I didn't. It's true, what I said.'

'I don't believe anything about her,' Gunther said. 'I don't even believe she's pregnant. I think she's just stuffed a football under her dress to throw everybody off the scent. Or else it was an immaculate conception. I don't know who she is, really, what bloody planet she landed here from.'

I didn't care, I was still elated from my work.

Vera said above the puzzled, fizzling laughter, 'Scones must be ready by now.' She went to the stove and slid out the steaming, fragrant tray. She broke the scones open and buttered them hot and held one out to me first, and there was a brief flutter of sympathy in her gaze before it skittered away towards Gunther. But I was still immunised against hurt.

'Pumpkin,' Vera said, and handed around the scones.

I said, 'You can't have pumpkin scones!'

'But they are!' Gunther roared laughing.

I saw that the scones were pumpkin-coloured. I bit into one. It was sweet, and yet it did taste of pumpkin. They were all looking at me and laughing. 'Well I've never heard of it before.'

'There's a lot of things you haven't heard of,' Gunther said.

Now I felt heavy again, and tired. A child who'd never even heard of pumpkin scones, a child who was going to have a child.

I said, 'Do you mind if I ring a taxi? I couldn't get a lift home tonight.'

'Allow me,' Gunther said. 'Where to?'

'Toorak.'

'Toorak!' He looked at the others, shrugged dramatically and raised his eyebrows.

❖

When I entered the dining room the talk broke off abruptly. I saw from Elizabeth's quick sharp smile at Stella, Stella's bland one, that they'd been talking about me. But not unkindly. Of course they must be wondering who the father was, why I'd come all this way to hide.

'Maggie,' Stella said, 'come on, come and join us. So self-effacing!'

But I shrank from their attention, from the completeness of the group connected by firelight. The remains of the food and drink they'd shared were scattered over the table. Friendship linked them visibly, too: it was in their unguarded expressions, the easy way they gestured and held themselves. Elizabeth was the only one of the women who looked like some you saw shopping in Toorak Village, her face enamelled, her hair done up in an elaborate, seamless construction with hidden clips, her fingers heavy with rings. But her soft expression contradicted her glossy appearance. Toby – her companion, as Stella called him – looked elegant in the dark suit he always wore as if, beside Elizabeth, he wanted to provide a neutral foil to the brilliance of her outfits, tonight a strapless dress of gold stuff like crinkled paper. All the kind faces were familiar, and I lingered in the doorway.

'Lucky you,' Diana wheezed, 'studying to be an artist.' She was an asthmatic, always arriving late for the dinner parties and exhausted from getting her children to bed. Her husband, Grant, looked radiant, as though he'd siphoned off her energy. But still, how could Diana envy me?

'I don't know if I'm going to be one yet.'

I saw Stella and Niels exchange a glance.

'It'd be hard once you have the baby, I suppose,' Elizabeth said. 'Unless your family can help out.'

Stella frowned at her and shook her head

'Oh, I'm sorry,' Elizabeth said.

'It's all right,' I said.

Stella and Niels always insisted I join them at the dinner table. Stella seated me between Diana and Grant because they were English teachers, in a private school, but after they'd asked me about the books I'd started to study at university, there had never been much to say.

'Try a sip of Beaujolais,' Niels said. 'Just a taste. Come over and sit here next to me.'

'And some gorgonzola,' Stella said. 'I know you don't like the smell, but you'll acquire a taste for it.'

'No thanks. I think I'll just get started on the dishes.'

Everyone laughed.

Toby said, 'Can I take her home with me?'

Curiosity and loneliness made me linger. I turned to Elizabeth. 'Oh, I forgot to say happy birthday.'

'Thank you.' Elizabeth inclined her head. 'Sure you won't come and help us celebrate what's left of it?'

'No thanks.' It seemed too big an effort, to pass into the circle lit by gentle flames which closed now at my departure – not against me, but because that was the nature of all circles.

I went into the kitchen and filled the sink with steaming suds. Behind me the voices hummed. I hadn't written to Delia. She lived in the past and in a present that existed parallel to mine, across a gulf: further away than in another country. I couldn't send letters there. I wished I could be with Lloyd, tonight, now, beside him in the hospital bed, and in the morning when he woke up.

'Maggie! Isn't it time you went to bed? Everyone's leaving.'

I jumped. Niels set a stack of plates on the table. 'Don't worry about the rest, we can do them in the morning.'

'Nearly finished these.'

'Oh, I wanted to tell you, I have to go to Ballarat for a few days; I've got a client there and something came up suddenly. Stella and Max will come with me, but we thought you could stay here and mind the house. You can have a little holiday. How does that sound?' He smiled his cheerful smile, with rounded cheeks and bright brown eyes, and rubbed his hands together. Sometimes, when Stella was feeling better, he emitted in almost visible waves a pure enjoyment in life.

❖

Lloyd was all right, Gerard said – recovering, but still in hospital. Afraid alone in my backyard room at night, I moved into Max's. Lying in his bed, I could feel the rootling limbs of the unborn child groping in the dark. In the empty house I lay awake thinking about Lloyd and waiting for the darkness to lift for another day. I listened to the sounds – the passing of a car, the creaking of a rafter, or was it footsteps in the hall? – that only deepened the silence.

The next morning I counted the money I'd saved, picked up the phone and booked a seat on a plane. The day after, I packed a small bag, locked up the house, and caught the bus into the city. The air was almost warm, the day was blue and white, the budding elms and plane trees wheeled by beside the windows. Alongside the road the river rippled between the trunks of the trees. On the other side of it the city grew, it swung around to meet the bus. What a joy it was to be in motion, travelling north, turning right out of Batman Avenue into St Kilda Road into Swanston Street! Today the unfamiliar streets and buildings looked benign; they were opening up, falling away on either side of the bus to let me out.

❖

Lloyd turned his head towards me. 'Maggie! How did you get up here?' He sounded weak, and he was as pale as the sheets.

I looked around, then kissed him gently on the lips. I sat down and found his hand beneath the blanket. A colourless liquid dripped through a plastic tube and a needle into his other wrist.

'The de Langes have gone away. Is it all right I came?'

Lloyd's glance flicked back and forth from me to the door.

'Just have to be careful. I wasn't expecting it. But I'm glad you did. Look at you.'

I took his hand. 'Feel this.' I placed his palm on my belly. 'Wait, you can feel it kicking.'

'Ooh, yes, I can feel it.' Lloyd chuckled softly. 'Hello, baby.' Then his hand slipped away.

I sat there for a while and watched him doze. The journey had taken most of the day. The movement of bus, plane, train had given me the illusion that I was finding my way back, but here I was as out of place as I'd ever been with Lloyd.

A bell rang somewhere. I slid my hand out from beneath the bedclothes. A nurse walked into the room. She was a nun. She took Lloyd's blood pressure. In front of her I felt like a dirty secret. Lloyd woke and waved his fingers at the nurse. She swept a smile around the room that vaguely included me, gave him two tablets, switched off some lights and left.

The tip of a long shadow touched the bed. Lloyd's gaze shifted to the door and his face lit up. 'Me old mate!' he whispered.

Vince saw me and mimed surprise, with open mouth and lifted brows. He walked up to the bed and stood opposite me. 'I didn't expect to see you here.' To Lloyd he said, 'Just checking up on you, mate. Anything I can get you?'

Lloyd shook his head. 'Maybe you could look after Maggie here for me.' His voice was slurred, his eyes were hooded. 'Better make sure she gets back to Melbourne before anyone sees her.'

'It'd be a pleasure, mate.' Vince turned to me. 'Where are you staying?'

'Nowhere yet.'

The nurse came back. When she saw Vince she hesitated. 'Oh, sorry, Father, I didn't know you were here. I was just making sure all the visitors had gone.'

'That's all right, Sister – time I got going anyway.' He said to me, 'Come on, I'll give you a lift to a motel.'

Lloyd looked at us from under heavy eyelids and lifted his fingers. 'Thanks for coming.' But he was drifting away. When I looked back from the doorway he seemed to be asleep.

Vince opened the car door with a flourish. 'I thought you might be the impulsive type. You've grown a lot, haven't you?' He looked me over with his insinuating smile.

I was so tired, I didn't even ask where we were going. Vince soon swung the car into the drive of the motel where I'd last stayed with Lloyd. From the passenger seat I noticed how, when he saw the black suit and clerical collar, the proprietor straightened his posture, and deferentially bent his head.

Vince came back and I opened the window for him to speak. He said, 'I'll just take your port upstairs and then we'll go and get something to eat.' I could see the light glinting on the plastic tag of the room key in his hand. I couldn't wait to lie down, but I felt an acute discomfort in my stomach and remembered I hadn't eaten anything but a few snacks since I'd left Melbourne.

In a row of dark shopfronts the window of the Chinese restaurant glowed. Vince ordered a bottle of wine. The food arrived quickly. After he had eaten his prawn crackers and drunk a glass of wine, Vince leaned back and looked at me. He watched me push the food around with my fork, piling the almonds to one side of the chicken and vegetables. He said, 'Why don't you try the chopsticks?'

'I don't know how to use them.'

'Here, I'll show you.'

He leaned across and expertly picked up an almond from the side of my plate and put it in his mouth. I tried to copy him, but the chopsticks scissored apart. I laughed. 'How do you pick up something like an almond?' I was glad I wasn't alone, even if it was Vince sitting opposite me.

He leaned over and placed my fingers in position. I wished Lloyd's hand was touching mine instead. Vince's felt unfamiliar, and I put the chopsticks down. 'I think I'll just use the fork.'

'Tut tut.' Vince shook his head. 'You'll never be able to do it if you don't practise.'

He picked up the bottle of wine and moved it across the table, but I put my hand over my glass. Vince firmly took my hand away and filled my glass. 'I bet you could do with a bit of a drink, to calm your nerves.'

'Just a sip. The de Langes said it's not good for the baby to have more.' I took one and pushed the glass away.

'So you came all this way just for one night?'

He slid the glass of wine towards me and I slid it back. 'I was worried about Lloyd. I was lonely, too: the de Langes went away.' I thought about how vulnerable Lloyd had looked, and I felt hollow and suddenly drained. He was like a compass point, the only one that pointed to where I'd come from.

'Your bloke's going to be fine once he recovers. Why don't you eat a bit more? Shouldn't you be ravenous? How many months to go?'

'Three. Do you mind if we go? I'm a bit tired.' It was too big an effort now to sit upright, holding the weight of the baby above my lap, and to move the food from plate to mouth.

Outside I felt weak and dizzy in the cool air. Vince took my elbow, palm up, lifting me, it seemed, against the weight of the atmosphere. I let him help me and I made it to the car.

When he pulled up and parked I turned to say goodbye. 'What's my room number? Can I please have the key?'

In the flat fluorescent light that slanted into the car I saw that Vince was smiling, as though to himself. He leaned right across to me. I was startled to see he wanted to kiss me goodbye. But he'd been kind, and I didn't want to offend him, so I leaned towards him and offered my cheek. Instead of pecking it he found my lips, and he kissed me with open mouth.

I pulled away. I remembered – my body remembered, I wasn't thinking – standing paralysed among the cabbages in next door's garden, cowering from the circling crows, when I was small and my father had come home roaring drunk. I had a momentary sensation of being outside the car watching myself unable to move. But I was bodily in it beside Vince. I stared through the windscreen at the brick wall as horrified as though the car were speeding towards it.

'Why did you open your mouth?' Vince said.

'I didn't!'

'Yes you did.' He looked at me with exaggerated astonishment. But how could he possibly have thought I wanted to kiss him?

'I did not. You did.' With my open palm I wiped my mouth: the taste of wine from his made me feel unclean. I couldn't wait to brush my teeth.

'You don't know what you're talking about.' Vince was leaning into the space between us. His bulk seemed to fill the car. I shrank right back against the door, then I opened it and swung slowly around to manoeuvre myself out, but before I could stand up Vince was there holding out his hand. I looked at it, not wanting to touch him. His hand was plump and white. He was leaning over me, his other hand on the open door. I felt shut in. For what seemed a long time I waited, and he moved away.

I got out of the car myself, but Vince took hold of my arm. I tried to shake him off. 'I just want to go and lie down. Can you give me the key? Please?'

'I'm going to see you get safely inside.'

No one else was around. The window of the reception office was dark. The other windows, some lit, looked onto the enclosed courtyard and parked cars.

It was all my fault, because I'd turned towards him not wanting to be impolite. But it was more than that. It was a visceral anxiety to be accommodating and compliant.

I knew I hadn't opened my mouth. But I doubted myself. I couldn't work out what was real, except for the grip of Vince's hand on my upper arm. Anyone looking on would see a pregnant teenager, and a distinguished-looking priest of mature years and an authoritative demeanour guiding her towards the stairs. I blamed myself for lacking the proper defences, for not instinctively turning away.

A desert of concrete stretched away to the stairs. On the staircase there was not enough room for us to ascend side by side, but Vince turned side on and squeezed himself beside me, his hand firmly around where my waist used to be.

I climbed the stairs like a sleepwalker. Some automatic mechanism lifted one foot, and then the other. At the top Vince paused to find the key in the pocket of his coat.

'I'll be all right now,' I said. 'Thank you, Father. Please can I have the key?'

'I think I'd better make sure. I promised your bloke I'd look after you.'

He ignored my outstretched hand and unlocked the door, guided me into the room and closed the door behind us and turned on the light. He stood with his back to the door.

I said, 'You can leave now. I'm just going to go to the bathroom. I really don't need looking after.'

In the bathroom I took my time changing into my nightie and dressing-gown. I scrubbed my face and my teeth. When I went back out there he was sitting on the bed, as though it were his room, too, but I hadn't asked him to pay for it.

He stood up. 'You get into bed. I'll turn off the light.'

'Leave the bathroom light on. Just leave the door open a little bit. Goodbye.' I felt the same kind of suspense as when trying not to wake up my father when he was drunk, easing the lit cigarette from between his fingers.

Vince turned off the light. I was pulling my dressing-gown as tightly as I could across my belly, but it was my old one from school and it was too small. I got into bed wearing it and turned my face to the opposite wall. I waited for the sound of the door closing. In my exhaustion my body relaxed automatically the moment it was in horizontal contact with the soft surface of the bed. Had I dozed? But I felt the mattress dip as Vince got into bed beside me. I turned in disbelief. He was naked.

'What are you doing?' I said.

'I'm just going to keep you company for a little while. You really shouldn't have opened your mouth. Look what you've done now.' He pressed himself against me. Then he was inside me, I understood this, but I couldn't feel anything normally. I was screaming soundlessly, as on half waking from a bad dream.

He can't hurt you, I told the baby when it kicked. *I'm looking after you. Go to sleep.* Then at last I slept, but woke again and again – how many times? – to the same nightmare.

When I woke to the light of dawn I sat up. My heart thudded. There was a man in the bed beside me, and it wasn't Lloyd. He was asleep. He lay with his back to me; the back of his silver head. I sat still and waited for the body beside me to evaporate, to disappear. But when I looked again, he was still there. How could I get up and go on from here? I felt a new kind of dread – not for something that was going to happen, but for something that had happened and could not be undone. It was the same: the leadenness of heart and limb.

I got up and went into the bathroom. There was no lock on the door. I stood under the shower for a long time and made an effort to order my thoughts, to plan: I'd leave for the airport before he was awake. But when I came out Vince was sitting up in bed. His expression, bold and triumphant, contradicted the sagging flesh of his chest, his silver hair, his red-marbled cheeks and nose.

'How refreshing,' he said. 'The only other time I was kept awake all night like that was with another convent girl.'

The sound of a child's high, excited voice drifting into the room made me want to burst into tears, but I held myself together. I found my bag and stuffed my belongings into it.

Vince looked offended. 'You could at least stay and have breakfast.'

'It'd make me sick.'

'How will you get to the airport?'

'I'll get a taxi.'

'I'll drive you before I say mass in the cathedral. I can't tell Lloyd I let you get a taxi. He'd want me to see you onto a plane.'

Lloyd was in hospital, and I'd betrayed him. My legs seemed incapable of supporting me. I sat on the end of the bed as heavily as if I'd been thrown.

Vince got up. He was white, and his skin and genitals were slack. Soon the same body would be hidden beneath flowing garments of silk and brocade. When he raised his arms in blessing, the congregation would bow their heads before him.

I could hear him humming in the shower. I noticed that the carpet was frayed where it joined the bathroom tiles, that the paintwork on the door frame was chipped. Vince came out and put on his white T-shirt and underpants. He tied up the strings of the backless vest with the hard white collar attached. The garment looked incomplete; it had the effect of a hastily got-up disguise.

He said, 'As soon as we leave this room, you have to forget anything ever happened. Don't even think about telling Lloyd. If you did, I'd have to tell him how you seduced me. Speaking of the devil, at least I can't have got you pregnant.'

All the way to the airport, the image of Lloyd's face as he lay in the hospital bed – his pallor, his pained smile – was fixed in my mind.

Somewhere in this city Delia would be getting ready for the day's lectures and tutorials. For the first time something had happened that I could never tell her about, if I ever saw her again. I'd be too ashamed.

❖

'God, thank God.' Stella got up off the couch.

I stood in the hall. Niels came in from the kitchen and closed the front door behind me. The car must have been in the garage.

'You're back early,' I said.

'There wasn't any more for Niels to do, so we packed up and came home. We tried to ring you before we left, but there was no answer. We assumed you'd just gone out to the shops or something.' Stella paced the room, puffing in between phrases on a cigarette. She didn't usually smoke except after dinner. 'Until we got back yesterday and there's no sign, nothing. We had to use the spare key and see if all your things were gone. We were about to ring the hospitals and go to the police.'

My face burned at the thought of them seeing the mess in my room. They couldn't know I used to be tidy. I was proud of how clean I kept the house and did all the other housework to perfection because it was my job, but in my own room I didn't have the heart.

'Never mind darling, she's here now.' Niels turned to me. 'We were very worried.'

'I'm sorry, I –'

Stella said, 'We didn't know who to get in touch with. Niels even went to the GPO to look your parents up in the phone book. Why didn't you ring us? I gave you the number.'

'They're not on the phone. My parents.'

'Is that where you were? You only had to say if you were homesick – we'd have been happy for you to go and see them – but just to disappear . . .'

'I know what it's like, to be homesick.' Niels looked at Stella. 'We both do.' But Stella paced and puffed and frowned at me.

'I didn't go home.' As soon as I said this I regretted it. It would have been the easiest explanation: I went home, they sent me back.

'We tried to ring Father Nihill but they said he was in hospital. He's had his appendix out. He's all right, though, apparently.' Stella narrowed her gaze at me over a stream of smoke.

'Is he? In hospital?' It wasn't hard to sound surprised; it had become second nature to pretend.

'Anyway, darling . . .' Niels touched Stella's arm but she wouldn't stand still. Her hair looked flatter and thinner, they both looked older than I remembered.

'I'm sorry.' I went into the lounge room and sat on the edge of an armchair. 'I left everything locked up. I cleaned the house before I went. There was nothing left to do.'

'The house!' Stella said. 'It's you we were worried about. And the baby. Not the bloody house.' I'd never heard her swear before. She sat down on the couch, shifted an ashtray from the coffee table to her lap, and stubbed her cigarette into it without looking. A strand of hair had loosened and fallen onto her face, and she flicked it back with a toss of her head. Without make-up her face was pale and her fine skin puffy around the eyes. 'So where did you go then?'

'The father – I went to see the father.' I could only whisper.

Niels stood looking from me to Stella with the troubled, distracted expression of someone who can't remember where they've left something. 'I'll go and make some coffee, will I?' he said, and went into the kitchen.

'In Sydney?' Stella said.

I nodded.

'But you didn't go home and see your parents.'

'They don't know. They don't know about the baby.'

'They don't know?'

'No one knows except the father. I mean, him and Father Nihill.'

'So what does the father, this mystery man . . . Do you have any idea yet what you're going to do, after it's born?'

'I thought he might be able to come down here, then I could keep it. But he doesn't know, he doesn't think . . .' I covered my face with my hands. I imagined Stella's horror if I told her about Vince. I wanted to hide in the darkness and warmth behind my hands forever.

'Maggie, you can't just go on hoping, you can't wait around for this, for the father . . . I mean, let's face it, if he can't make up his mind by now. Look at you.'

Through the screen of my fingers I saw Niels in front of me. I took my hands away from my face and accepted the cup from him. He sat beside Stella on the couch.

'But he might.' I was admitting to myself, too, that I still hoped for this.

Stella said, 'Is he married? Is that what the problem is?'

'It's not that.'

'There must be something pretty powerful stopping him.'

'There is.'

Stella sipped her coffee. She waited. But I said nothing more. She looked at Niels. There was such a depth of calm in him that his presence anchored the conversation, the rocking vessel of emotion the room had turned into.

Stella said, 'Maggie, it's a baby we're talking about here.'

'I know.' My voice sounded small, as though it had been used up.

'You don't know,' Stella said.

'I told you I was going to have it adopted.' Another lie.

Stella groaned. 'You don't know what it means to have a baby. You don't know what it means to lose a baby. I mean, for God's sake. Niels, you speak to her.'

Niels said, 'I don't think we should talk about it anymore now, darling. Maggie looks tired, and so do you.'

'Where's Max?' I said.

'He's at Mother's,' Stella said.

The mention of him seemed to set us moving as if we'd just come out of a trance. Stella lit another cigarette, then immediately stubbed it out and stood up. Niels collected the coffee cups.

In my room I took stock of the chaos I'd let grow, in layers, always closing the door so Stella and Niels wouldn't see. At home I'd kept my half of the room I shared with Anne tidy and clean, an oasis of order in my corner of the house. I sat on the unmade bed and saw my face in the mirror on the opposite wall above the sink. I stared back at myself. I felt like a survivor of a disaster.

I looked older, the turbulence beneath the surface showing in the expression in my eyes, in the shape of my mouth in relation to the rest of my face. I realised I'd been holding my hands, palms down, on my belly. The baby was growing beneath them, expecting to find a reliable, sensible person on the other side. I wasn't just going to have a baby. I was going to be a mother.

I stood up as if someone had pushed me. I hung up the towels, cleared the floor, untangled and folded the clothes and sorted them and put them away, found clean sheets and made the bed, with the hospital corners the nuns had insisted on at school.

❖

The air brightened and warmed, leaves thickened the trees, flowers coloured the gardens, and life in the house went on almost as it had before, except that Stella was up more often, she prowled around making sure everything had been looked after as she wanted it while she'd been so often imprisoned upstairs. She dressed up and walked to the village, and came back cradling bunches of flowers in both arms. She spent hours arranging them, restoring the atmosphere in the house. Sometimes she went shopping with Elizabeth in the city. When she got home she opened the boxes, and out of frothy layers of tissue paper she lifted garments of sensuous fabrics and pairs of gleaming high-heeled shoes. She held them up reverently for us to admire. 'Norma Tullo dresses,' she said to me, 'and Jane Debster shoes,' in a tone that told me I should never think of wearing anything else.

There was no point in going back to the art class, so close to the birth. When I wrote to Lloyd, Vince's shadow fell across the page, but I wrote as if nothing had happened. I stopped asking Lloyd if he was thinking about leaving the priesthood. He wrote that he missed me, I said I missed him; we said we loved each other, but I knew I was really on my own, because I would never be able to go back.

On my birthday, the anniversary of their baby's death, Niels and even Stella, who was a non-practising convert, went to mass at St Francis'. When they came home Stella went back to bed, though she was almost well. I didn't know what to say to her, so I brought her extra cups of tea. 'I should be waiting on you today,' she said, and turned her face to the wall. Her baby's grave was in another country.

But when she came downstairs at dinnertime her face was eggshell smooth, with tiny cracks of fatigue showing through the make-up. Her dress was a slim black tube, and beside her, in a dress of psychedelic colours falling full-skirted from the neckband, the only one of my old clothes I could fit into and which last summer had hung in empty folds, I felt like a balloon.

Mrs Mitchell arrived to babysit Max, and Stella gave me a small, carefully wrapped present and I unwrapped it carefully, too. 'It's from all of us, Mother as well.'

'It's lovely, thank you! I'll wear it now.' The chain of pink opals glistened on my wrist. I was overwhelmed.

When we got to Maxim's Elizabeth and Toby were already there, seated and smiling and composed. A few minutes later a breathless Diana arrived with an unruffled Grant. Niels ordered champagne. Sitting between him and Stella I opened the presents: a novel by Thea Astley, the lecturer at Macquarie who was a writer, a silk scarf from Elizabeth and Toby, and placed them on the table among the candlelight, the twinkling silver and crystal, the linen made of starched white clouds.

I showed off the opal bracelet, turning my wrist so the light caught all the pearly colours. Only when I'd won a prize at speech night – the last time, when I'd been made dux, a bundle of expensive books handed to me by a smiling Sister Theresa on the town hall stage – had I felt so esteemed. But I was both grateful and ashamed. If they knew the truth about me, they might not think I deserved such generosity. I had to swallow hard before I could thank them. If I started to cry I might not have stopped.

Diana said, 'You must be getting close.'

'When are you due?' Elizabeth said.

'Next month. The twenty-first.'

'What are you going to call it?' Then Diana's hand went to her mouth. 'Oh, I'm sorry, I forgot.'

'It's all right.'

Stella said, 'Nicola for a girl, and Simon for a boy.'

I said, 'I don't think I'm supposed to . . .'

'Stella,' Niels said.

'Oh, bloody hell,' Stella said. 'Maggie, if you're determined to have it adopted out, then Niels and I, Niels and I would . . .'

'Darling,' Niels said. 'We haven't . . .'

'No!' It was not a place for such a raw, animal sound to be let out: the air was burnished with expensive candlelight, the people who shimmered on the rims of the snowy, glittering tables turned and stared. A white-aproned waiter began to walk towards us, then stepped back. Everyone at our table exchanged glances as though they were having a conversation about me which I couldn't hear. I covered my eyes to hide the tears.

Stella put her arm around me. 'Niels and Max and I are a family, we can give it a home. I can't have any more children yet, not until I'm much better, but you can stay and work for us as long as we're in Melbourne, you could see it every day. We'd tell it who its birth mother was.'

'I'm not going to have it adopted. I couldn't give it away to anyone.'

'When did you decide this? Why didn't you tell us?' Stella was astonished.

I took my hands from my face and looked at her. 'Because no one thinks I can look after it on my own.' I couldn't say, and because Father Nihill is terrified someone will find out he's the father. 'At the hospital the social worker keeps pestering me to change my mind. But I don't want it to grow up without me.'

'Well, how *are* you going to look after it?' Diana asked gently. 'It's a big job. Babies need more than milk and clean nappies.'

'Money,' Grant said. 'Forget the milk, they eat money.'

Everyone laughed except me. A waiter approached the table but Niels waved him away.

'Security,' Elizabeth said. 'And two parents.'

'An education,' Diana said.

'One parent is enough,' Niels said. 'The love of one of its parents.'

'It'll need me.' I wiped my hands on my napkin. Stella dabbed my cheeks with a fragrant hanky. I saw the mascara on the white cloth. 'I'm sorry, I'll get the stains out.'

The laughter was a relief.

'I'll get another job.' I looked around at the faces, all turned to me. 'When you and Niels go back to Europe.'

'It won't be easy.' Stella smoothed her napkin back onto her lap. 'Not everyone would be happy about you having a baby around while you work.'

'Nothing is easy,' I said.

I saw the expressions on the faces change from concern to respect. Today I was nineteen. I felt as much an adult as they were, in their thirties.

'I think we should order something to eat.' Niels nodded at the waiter. 'And more champagne.'

'Just like Niels!' Toby hooted. 'Always thinking about food!'

'As long as we remember the important things in life,' Niels said.

'When are you going back to Europe?' Toby said.

Stella looked up from her menu. 'Sometime next year.'

Nobody spoke. On the edge of my vision the waiters swam in the dim streams between the glowing islands of the tables, holding the dishes high above the surface.

Niels said, 'Truffles. I think Maggie should have truffles on her birthday.'

'What's a truffle?' I said.

Toby said, 'It's a lump of mould that pigs dig out of the dirt and carry back between their filthy teeth.'

Everyone laughed again, everyone but me. I was wondering how to start looking for another job. I couldn't ask Gerard in case he told Lloyd.

❖

Now the window frames in the front rooms were crammed with summer-green leaves; the lawn was flooded with the deep green pools of their shade. In the evenings the twilight lingered, the long twilight of the south, while the sky softened and slowly deepened from blue to mauve. It seemed years since I'd seen sunlight and felt it warm my back through my clothes; that each month of my pregnancy had lasted a year, as the school holidays had seemed to at home.

Then a hot wind blew in from the north: it lashed the clouds of foliage to tatters; it burnt the fish ferns and roses in the front yard; it sculpted the washing on the line into an exhibition of plaster dresses and shirts. In Toorak Road, when I went to the shops, the people were blown together in knots: anchored by the weight of my pregnancy, I watched them cower and cringe, as though the sky were full of cracking whips.

'The hot northerly, they call this wind,' Stella said. 'We get hot winds in Perth, but it seems different there, more bearable, I don't know why.' Sometimes she spoke about Perth as though she'd never wanted to leave it. The Melbourne heat sucked the life out of her, it dulled her eyes. And the more engorged with child I grew, the more Stella seemed to shrink – sometimes, although she was much better, lying several hours on the bed inside the silken husk of her nightie. Now she never invited me to sit down beside her on the bed and talk; it seemed the sight of me caused her pain.

When Niels came out of the study one day at lunchtime, I took a tray of food to them upstairs.

'We've got something to tell you, Maggie,' Niels said.

Stella said, 'We want to drive across the Nullarbor to Perth. It's the last chance we'll have for a while. We'll have Christmas with my best friend, Judy. We're like sisters, and I haven't seen her for ages.'

'If you're sure you're well enough.' Niels looked at her gravely. I could tell they'd had a long talk about it.

Stella's eyes were sad but lit with a peculiar light. 'Maggie, there's nothing like driving across the desert and then arriving in Perth, you've got no idea.'

'What about Max?' But I was thinking about the birth. I tried not to show my anxiety.

'Too big a trip for him in summer,' Stella said. 'Much too hot for him in the car.'

'But what if the doctor's right? What if the baby comes?'

Stella shook her head. 'It'll be weeks before that baby's born. We'll come back straight after Christmas.' Her mouth was set in a line, and I noticed her resemblance to Mrs Mitchell.

Later, when I was giving Max his bath, Stella called out from the bedroom, 'Let him play a little while in the bath with his toys. It's still so hot. You can keep an eye on him. I've got some things here I want to show you.'

The wind had decamped. From Stella's window I could see that the heat had set: inside it nothing moved, not one leaf or blade of grass. Clouds occupied the sky: light grey, no rain just yet.

'Come and look at these,' Stella said.

On the white sheet she'd laid out rows of tiny matinee jackets and rompers crocheted in white and lemon and pink; knitted vests, and dresses with smocked yokes.

'They were Margareta's. I want you to have them. I'm sure it's a boy, the way you're carrying it. But you still might need the dresses one day.'

'Oh.' We both gazed at the little garments: surely no human being could be small enough to fit into them? Max was splashing about in the bath, and when I went in to check up on him, he looked suddenly huge.

Back in the bedroom I asked Stella: 'Are you sure you want to give them to me?' The spread-out, waiting clothes made me think about my new uniform hanging on the wall at the end of my bed the week before I started at St Dominic's, how I used to wake up every morning and look at it as if I'd become a new person when I finally put it on.

Stella gathered everything in the layette, she called it, into a pile, and then lay back again on the pillows, as though exhausted by the relinquishing of her dead baby's clothes. 'I can't have another baby. Not soon, maybe not ever.'

'They're so lovely. Thank you very much.' But it was sad.

'We could dress Simon – I mean, dress the baby up in them, and take him to the Village and Como Park. Until we go back.' She looked at me and sighed. 'So, have you heard from him lately? The father?'

'No, he's been . . . he's busy. I'd better start looking for another job soon.' It wasn't exactly a lie to say he was busy; I knew Lloyd would be preparing for the Christmas devotions. He'd written declaring his love, that was all. I hadn't expected anything else, since he thought I was going to give the baby up, and that next year we'd go on in Sydney as we had before.

'No hurry to look for a job. We won't be leaving for a few months yet.'

❖

In the morning I opened the front door to take Max to the park, and stood a moment drinking in draughts of cooler air. The trees, released, shook out their foliage. People strode upright in the street, revived.

When we got back, I set out Max's paper and crayons on the kitchen table, and went upstairs. In their bedroom Stella and Niels were packing. I put down the vacuum cleaner and looked from one of them to the other.

'We're leaving tomorrow,' Stella said.

'But what if I do have the baby? What about Max?'

Stella shook her head. 'Look how high you're carrying it . . . it hasn't even dropped yet.' She frowned and looked away. On her upper lip were tiny drops of moisture. The frown was clamped to her forehead, as when she'd been in pain. I thought about her sitting in the hot car as it drove through the desert for mile after mile, the red dust blowing in through the window.

Niels was folding clothes into the port. He straightened and looked at me. 'Mrs Mitchell will look after Max, if anything happens.'

'She's got Judy's number,' Stella said. 'I can always fly back.'

'What about Christmas?'

'Mother's going to have you over. We'll leave some presents. But we'll have a proper Christmas when we come back, we'll have a lovely dinner. It won't make any difference to Max, as long as he gets his presents.'

I sat on the bed and looked down at the huge mound inside which the baby was getting ready to breathe. Stella and Niels both had a drawn look, the shadowed expression they wore whenever they mentioned Margareta and that they must have worn watching her dying in her crib in intensive care. The closer the time came when I would give birth, the more often they each wore this expression.

'You should have seen me before . . . before Margareta died,' Stella had said once. 'I was full of energy, in those days. I was a completely different person.'

'Maggie, could you please go and iron my blue dress?' she said now. 'I think it went in yesterday's wash.'

'Yes, it did.' I manoeuvred my bulky body downstairs.

The next morning, Max and I waved goodbye as Niels backed the car out of the drive. We stood hand in hand for a moment looking out at the empty street. I gripped Max's hand tightly, and he didn't cry. But he sucked his thumb all day, and I didn't have the heart to take it out, as Stella had instructed me; he hardly spoke.

'Let's lie down for a while,' I said after lunch. 'And when we get up, you can help me make a cake.'

'A chocolate one.'

'All right.' I had learnt to cook, even bake.

We lay on Max's bed. He squirmed and riffled through picture books. I turned on my side, easing the weight off the aching muscles that supported the baby. I dozed, and woke with Max's small hand shaking my shoulder.

'Time to get up,' he said. 'You can't go to sleep now.'

'But I'm tired.'

'But I'm hungry for cake.'

'Just a few more minutes. Please, Max?' Would I ever be able to heave myself upright again?

Max's face crumpled. 'I want Papa. I want Mama and Papa to come home.'

'Tell you what. I'll get up now, and we can make a Christmas cake. We can have some tonight, and keep the rest to have when Mama and Papa come back.'

The late afternoon was darkened by clouds. In the kitchen I turned on the light, lit the oven, and found a recipe. The yellow kitchen was a beacon in the dark house. Measuring out the flour, I thought about Stella and Niels, driving into the desert: I imagined the car as a tiny, dust-covered speck, crawling into its empty heart. I got out the bowl and the sifter for Max, and set him to work. Soon he and the table and floor were dusted with flour. I found raisins, currants and sultanas. No mixed peel: we'd have to go to the shops. No, too late, we'd have to do without. I cut off a slice of butter and put it on the scales, and at that moment I felt the warm fluid gushing between my thighs.

❖

'Are you sure you need to go to the hospital?' Mrs Mitchell unwound the scarf from her hairdo and took off her gloves in the hall. Her eyes glittered, and her mouth had shrunk. 'Are you sure it isn't a false alarm?'

'I think my waters have broken.' In front of Mrs Mitchell this sounded shocking. My body felt huge and out of control.

'Have the pains started?'

'Not yet. But they told me at the hospital it meant the baby was coming soon. I don't think I'd better stay here by myself with Max.'

Mrs Mitchell frowned down at his white-powdered blue shirt.

'Maybe Oma can help you make it.' I squatted down and held his floury hands. 'I think I'd better go to the hospital now in case the baby comes.'

My packed bag stood next to the door. 'I'm sorry I have to go,' I said to Mrs Mitchell. 'I'm sorry I had to get you over like this.' But I felt detached, as if about to set out on a long and solitary journey. My legs trembled, and I could taste the excitement – and fear.

'Well, I suppose it can't be helped,' Mrs Mitchell said.

When my taxi arrived I got in and didn't look back.

At the hospital they gave me a white gown to put on and took away my clothes; they examined me, shaved my pubic hair, inserted a suppository into my anus. They told me to wait in an empty room, with cold walls and floor, and a window too high to see out of. I forgot which floor I was on. All around me the corridors wound in and out of rooms, the stairs led up and down. I could hear people whispering somewhere nearby, the sound of soft shoes shuffling across a floor.

After a shower I lay, passive, on the high white bed, with the chemical dripping into my wrist through a needle in my vein.

'No point in waiting around,' the doctor said. I'd never seen him before. 'Might as well bring it on. All be over by Christmas then.'

There was no daylight in the room. Hours passed. Maybe it was dark outside. It was quiet except for the sound of the soft-shod feet, low voices, an occasional disembodied laugh, and sometimes the screaming of a woman in a nearby cubicle. This was a sound that curdled the blood and left the hairs standing up on the back of the neck.

'It's the Italians.' The nurse came to check on the drip. 'Don't let it get to you. They think they have to scream their heads off when they're in labour. It drives you mad.'

All I felt for a long time was the small ache where the chemical pulsed into my vein. I longed for oblivion: to enter a deep, unbroken sleep. Dull spasms, at first not even pains, woke me when I dozed. I felt a childish yearning for my mother, for the sound of her voice, the sight of her face, although I knew she wouldn't have been a comfort.

Instead, when I once turned my face away from the wall, I saw Mrs Mitchell sitting upright at the bedside, holding her shiny handbag on her knees, her gaze level with the ball of my stomach.

'Oh,' I said.

'Is the pain very bad?' Mrs Mitchell asked, in her matter-of-fact tone.

'It's getting a bit worse. I just didn't expect to see anyone there.'

'I hope you didn't mind my coming. I thought I'd better see how you were.'

'No.' I winced. 'I'm glad you came.'

Mrs Mitchell leaned over and put her hand hesitantly on my arm. It was unexpectedly warm. 'It'll be over soon. It's a terrible business, what women have to go through having babies.' She pursed her lips in disapproval, as though this were a mistake someone could rectify.

'It's all right. What's it like outside?'

'It's cool, starting to rain.'

'It's freezing in here.' I gritted my teeth and clutched Mrs Mitchell's arm. When I let it go, she pulled the cotton blanket up over me and looked helplessly about her.

'Was that fifteen minutes?' I said.

Mrs Mitchell looked at her watch. It was silver; the band might have been made from the scales of a tiny fish.

Now flames were licking at my belly. Mrs Mitchell got up, and came back with a nurse. The nurse stood gazing at her own watch, her head on one side. When the next wave of pain had crested, Mrs Mitchell said she'd better go. She stood looking down at me, her arm hooked through her handbag, her scarf gripped in symmetrical folds at her throat by a sharp-edged stone; what world of elaborate order had she come from, into this region of chaos?

She said, 'Is there anyone you'd like me to get in touch with?'

'No thank you.' I saw Mrs Mitchell and the nurse exchange a pointed glance.

I said, 'Oh, heavens. Oh, bloody hell.'

Mrs Mitchell hurried out of the ward.

The nurse sat down beside me. 'What are you going to do with your baby?'

I turned to her. The words made no sense.

'Have you signed the adoption forms?'

'I told the social worker I'm going to keep it.'

'Are you sure? Are you able to look after it by yourself?'

'I'm sure.' I spread my hands uselessly over my belly. The nurse stood up, shaking her head, and left. I sucked in a mouthful of air and clenched my teeth.

'I don't blame the Italians,' I moaned. 'If I was one, I'd scream the place down.'

The pain had my belly in its jaws. They gave me pethidine. I entered a long, dim tunnel. It took hours and hours to reach the middle. At the other end of it, between the stirrups where my legs were hoisted high and wide apart, there were voices, and faces floating in a white light. More hours passed, I had no idea how many. Not even on those weekends without sleep when my father had ranted and raged on rum had I been so tired.

'Are you sure you don't want to have your baby adopted?' I heard a woman's voice, somewhere beside me. 'Now's the time to tell us, if you've changed your mind. There's a form here you can sign.'

'I'm keeping it.' My voice sounded slurred, I didn't know if they understood what I was saying. I said as clearly as I could, 'I already told everyone I'm keeping it.' I pushed and pushed, and still they told me to push harder.

'I can't,' I said. 'I'm too tired.' It was a different kind of fatigue, my brain in a fog, my body unable to obey its directions.

The doctor eased the baby out with forceps. 'A boy!'

I heard a small mewing sound. Was he crying? 'Where is he?' I was too groggy to hold up my head.

A nurse held up a small parcel, wrapped in a white blanket. The baby was blinking in the light. His hair was red. His face was perfect, with a mark from the forceps like a frown in the middle of his forehead. I closed my eyes, and at last I slept.

❖

I woke up in a long room like a dormitory. I remembered nothing after they'd held up Simon for me to see. It was late afternoon. I saw women in the other beds take their babies from their breasts, or the bottle, before the nurses took them away.

A nurse came over. 'Here, Miss Reed, take these tablets to dry up your milk. All the unmarried mothers take them. Some change their minds, after the baby's born. We normally put you all in the same ward, but there was no room left.'

'I won't change my mind.'

'Take these, you wouldn't want to put up with the trouble of breastfeeding, anyway.'

'I don't know.' But I obediently took the tablets. 'Can I see my baby now?'

'We'll bring him out when it's time for the next feed.'

For the next four hours I waited in fear that I'd never see him again. Then they brought him to me, wrapped in a blue rug. They gave me a bottle. As I held him, it occurred to me that I was holding the warmth from inside my own body. It was the most intimate experience I'd ever had. When he opened his mouth, he looked so defenceless with his tooth-less yawn and his blind, unguarded gaze. It was a shock, the recognition: the rush of love for this tiny stranger. His lips worked busily on the teat while his hands grasped at the air. I couldn't tell if he looked like me or Lloyd. I was scared and proud, and held on to him tightly until they prised him out of my arms and took him away.

That night, from the other end of the ward, I could hear voices singing 'O Come, All Ye Faithful'. It was almost Christmas. The carol singers walked from bed to bed. When they reached mine, I turned my face to the wall. Tears of self-pity and loneliness trickled over my nose and into my hair. Then they brought Simon in again, and I dried my eyes.

I was glad I wasn't home for Christmas; it was always one of the worst times.

❖

In a letter to Lloyd I told him that the baby had been born and I was going to keep him; I told him that he was beautiful, what he weighed, the colour of his hair; that I had named him Simon Reed. On the registration form, next to 'Father', I had put 'undisclosed'. I hadn't heard from Lloyd for a while, and I wondered if Vince had told him what happened in the motel, and that it was my fault. The thought of this opened a trapdoor beneath me: a quick fall, a sudden absence of breath. I didn't know if I'd ever see Lloyd again, once he knew there wasn't going to be an adoption. I told him I loved him. I hoped he still loved me. I felt I was holding on to the hand of someone for dear life, like the people in films before they fell from tall buildings, or jumped. But I knew the baby needed me more than he did, more than I needed him. I told him that I wouldn't be going back to Sydney, that before the de Langes went to Europe I'd find another job. No one would ever know who Simon's father was. It was only a page. One of the nurses said she'd post it, and put it in her uniform pocket.

When the fathers and grandparents came to visit, I got up and went to the nursery and looked in at Simon. I walked along corridors and searched for windows to look out of. The sky was grey, the light was dull. Sometimes the windows were embroidered with rain. I felt empty and light, and disconnected from the world outside and every person in it.

One morning I was laid out on a stretcher with Simon in my arms and slid into one of four slots in the back of an ambulance. No one told me why. I was scared. It was dark and the space was narrow. It was impossible to tell which direction we were travelling in, or how far we were going. Every change in the motion of the ambulance, when it slowed, or stopped, or turned a corner, was without meaning. When they took me out, I asked them where we were. Kew, they said, but I'd never heard of it.

❖

The rest home was like a hospital, except that the women got up when they felt like it and wandered around in their dressing-gowns. There was an atmosphere of deep calm, of languor, as in the aftermath of a storm. Classes were held in bathing babies and preparing formula. I understood that I was here because I was a teenager, and unmarried. The nurses seemed to be watching me all the time, as though waiting for me to make a mistake, so they could take Simon away and give him to strangers. Once he cried for no clear reason all afternoon, and I carried him around the building, whispering in his ear. It was terrible, as though he were crying because he had been born. While I comforted him, I saw two nurses watching me: eventually they nodded at each other, and left me alone.

When Simon slept, I tried to read my birthday book, but it was too hard to concentrate. The reading was only a background to the drama of motherhood. Here the cots were kept beside the beds, and I didn't take my eyes off Simon for long. When the weather cleared, I held him and stood in front of the big windows looking out at the sunny gardens.

When Elizabeth and Toby came to see me, I was sitting up on my bed. They sat on chairs on either side of it balancing one another. In their elegant clothes and with their poised, confident demeanour, they weren't the kind of visitors who usually came to the rest home. Simon slept in my arms.

'He's gorgeous,' Elizabeth said.

'Do Stella and Niels know?' I said. 'Are they still in Perth?'

Elizabeth nodded. 'Mrs Mitchell rang them. They'd be nearly home by now.'

'Have you heard from your family?' Toby said.

'I haven't told them.'

Toby and Elizabeth raised their eyebrows.

'I don't want them to know about the father.'

I saw the glance they exchanged across the bed.

'Have you told the father?' Elizabeth said.

'I wrote him a letter.' I held up the jumpsuit they had brought for Simon. 'I can't wait to try it on him. He looks lovely in white!'

Elizabeth and Toby exchanged another, smiling glance, and I felt myself blush.

❖

Back at Toorak, there was no letter waiting from Lloyd. My mother had sent a Christmas card. I'd asked a nurse to post the one I'd written to her and everyone in the family – nothing about Simon, just a card. My mother said it was a shame I couldn't get home for Christmas.

Sometimes, heating a bottle or hanging out the washing, I thought about Lloyd and felt a swift paralysis, as if my heart had stopped. At other times I realised with a shock that I'd forgotten him for the whole day. Simon preoccupied me, and the housework, and I realised it was possible that one day I might stop thinking about him at all.

I wondered if he was angry that I hadn't had Simon adopted, but at least I'd kept my promise not to tell anyone he was his father. I didn't regret keeping him. Sometimes I peered down from my bed into the little basket, watching him sleep. I couldn't look at him enough: the high forehead sweeping up and around into the curve of skull and red nap of hair, the snub-nosed profile with its fullness of cheek and petal lips, the delicate fist curled beside the jaw. But I still had no plan for when the de Langes would leave.

As soon as she'd recovered enough from the trip home to go out, Stella dressed Simon in a yellow romper suit Margareta had never worn, and Niels drove them to the village. When they came home, I looked up from where I was ironing a sheet in the hall. Beside the board hung a row of shirts on a rack.

'Nobody would believe he wasn't mine, would they, Niels?' Stella said to Simon, 'Your mother irons beautifully – look at your godfather's shirts.'

'No, darling.' Niels was frowning. 'One for you.' He handed me from the pile of mail a letter with the familiar, slanting handwriting. I set down the iron. My heart was pumping hard enough to burst. I put the letter in my pocket, and picked up the iron again.

'I haven't made my mind up yet about the baptism,' I said.

'Aren't you going to read it?' Stella looked at me, then at Niels.

'I want to finish this first, then I'll give Simon his bottle.' I gripped the iron hard, to stop my hand from trembling. This was the first letter I'd had from Lloyd since I'd written to him from hospital six weeks ago.

'I can give it to him,' Stella said.

'No thanks, it's all right.'

I took Simon to my room and sat on my bed holding him in the crook of my arm, the bottle in one hand, the letter in the other. When I had read it, I sat for so long holding Simon over my shoulder, patting him on the back to encourage him to burp, that he went to sleep, and I had to wake him to change his nappy.

Lloyd wrote that he'd been missing me. He hadn't been able to write before because he'd been planning to leave the priesthood and join us in Melbourne, but until now he hadn't been able to give me any details. By the time I read the letter, he said, he'd be on his way, driving down the Hume Highway. He said that he'd become unhappy as a priest, always in trouble with the bishop because of his radical ideas. But what had helped him to make his mind up was when I told him he had a son, and I hadn't given him away. He said that he'd always wanted a son. He said the bishop was ropeable that he wanted to leave, and had made it as hard as he could for Lloyd to get away. So he had decided to pack the car after saying mass one morning and leave.

My room seemed too small to hold all my feelings. I tucked Simon into his basket and I went out and paced between the back gate and the pen of briquettes. I could now name my baby's father. Mixed with my elation and relief there was embarrassment – shame. But all that mattered was the blameless, helpless child asleep inside our temporary backyard room.

When I was calm enough, I went in to check on Simon. He was still asleep. I closed the door gently and went inside the house. Stella rested in the afternoons, she was lying on her bed. Niels was working in the study. Max played under the table at his feet. I stood in the hall, looking into one room and then the other.

'Is he asleep?' Stella said.

'The letter was from the father. He's changed his mind. He's on his way down.'

I looked from Stella to Niels, who was standing now in the doorway, with Max twining around his legs. Stella looked at Niels.

'The father . . . The father's Father Nihill . . . Lloyd.'

Stella nodded. 'I thought he might be,' she said, in a flat voice. 'Niels didn't think it could be true, but I thought so.'

Niels shook his head and frowned.

I was telling them that while I'd been pregnant, and when Simon was born, Lloyd was still a priest, hearing confessions and giving communion. 'I promised I wouldn't tell anyone he was the father. I wanted to tell you but I couldn't.'

I felt unburdened. I saw no unkindness in their expressions and the glances they exchanged, only a profound disappointment, which I knew wasn't directed at me.

❖

A few days later, Lloyd knocked on the door. I opened it, holding Simon. He was crying. When we kissed I was sure Lloyd must have felt the contamination passing into him, through me from Vince. I hadn't expected to feel this; it surprised me and displaced for a moment my relief.

The green car was parked in the de Langes' drive. In his ordinary clothes – they were unfashionable, and they didn't match – Lloyd seemed smaller. He was dishevelled and gaunt.

Niels came into the hall. 'This is unexpected,' he said to Lloyd. He shook his hand.

Behind him Stella said, 'Not entirely, to me.' She didn't look at Lloyd, and she was not smiling.

Stella and Niels retreated to the kitchen and we sat on the couch, the three of us together. It was an ordinary thing to do, and it wasn't.

'He doesn't usually cry like this. He must have wind.' I put Simon over my shoulder and gently patted his back, but he wouldn't settle.

'Give him to me.' Lloyd was all elbows. 'This is your father speaking,' he said in a stage whisper. 'What's the matter, eh? I'm your daddy, did you know that?'

Simon whimpered. He gulped and sniffled, and was quiet.

'I think he does know,' I said.

'D'you reckon?' Lloyd looked cocky. 'How about that?'

He watched me change his nappy. Now he hung back, out of his depth. He said, 'Gee, he's little, isn't he?'

I wrapped him in a cotton rug and laid him on his side in the wicker basket.

Stella came in from the kitchen. She said to Lloyd, 'He was a lot smaller six weeks ago.' She carried a bowl of steaming food to the dining table. 'Why don't you both come and sit down?'

Max was at his Oma's, and I wished he were there to alter, with his child's watchful, vulnerable presence, the atmosphere in the room. We bowed our heads while Niels said grace: Stella didn't ask Lloyd.

'*Bon appétit!*' Stella said.

'*Bon appétit!*' Niels and I said.

Lloyd looked from one of us to another.

'So you're going to get a flat?' Niels said to Lloyd.

Lloyd put his hands on his ribs and filled out his chest. 'Soon as we can. They're going to put me up in Parkville till I find something. If Maggie can stay here for a while longer, a week or two . . .'

'As long as she likes,' Stella said. 'Maggie's always welcome to stay with us.'

She looked at me and I looked down at my plate. My throat hurt. I felt that I could burst out laughing or crying, I didn't know which.

''Preciate it,' Lloyd said, his mouth full.

'It's a pleasure,' Stella said.

'I'll buy a place, soon as I get a job.' Lloyd glanced at me. 'I put the shack on the market, before I came down. Now I've got a family to look after . . .'

'Buy a house?' I said.

'That's what fathers do, isn't it?' He grinned around the table. 'Me and Maggie'll get married, soon as my dispensation comes through.'

'Married!' I said. It sounded so final. But my deferred scholarship, in the back of my mind, was a thread, slender but strong, connecting me to the person I had been. I was determined now to go back and study as soon as I could, even if I had to carry Simon there in his basket. I didn't care anymore what other people might think. But I kept this plan to myself for now.

'Of course,' Stella said. 'You've got a child to think about.' But she sounded unhappy. She said to Lloyd, 'So what sort of job do you think you'll get?'

'There's a job going in a private school, school counsellor. Had a mate put the feelers out. He says I'd have a good chance.'

'It won't be easy for you, starting again,' Stella said. 'It'll be a lot to get used to so suddenly, won't it?'

Lloyd nodded. 'Hasn't been easy so far, that's for sure. But we'll make a go of it.' He smiled at me.

I tried to smile back. It was a relief to have the secret out in the open, to have Lloyd beside me, but I felt a different anxiety about the future. A part of this came from seeing Lloyd, if only hazily, through Stella's and Niels's eyes – not just Stella's disapproval of his manners, but the disappointment in him, or worse, which for my sake they hid as best they could. Of course, I told myself, they'd think he'd betrayed his vows, and had failed them. And I was aware of the contrast between Niels and Lloyd, not only in their manners and clothes: it was something I felt, but couldn't have put into words.

'Well, it sounds like you've got everything worked out.' Niels lifted his glass. 'Here's wishing you luck.'

'Thanks, mate.'

Stella raised her glass in silence. I saw the two vertical grooves in the middle of her forehead: she wasn't usually fatigued at lunchtime. 'What about you, Maggie? Will you go back to your art classes again?'

'I might soon.' I looked at Lloyd. 'When Simon's a bit older.'

'Art class?' Lloyd said.

'I thought I told you. I must have forgotten to, when you were sick.'

'So that's where you were.' Stella's tone was flat. 'You went to visit him in hospital.'

'I think Maggie'll be too busy looking after me and Simon to be going to any art classes,' Lloyd said.

'That'd be a pity,' Niels said. 'She's got a remarkable talent. She showed us some of her work.'

There were several moments then when nobody spoke. In the room was the deep, almost sinister quiet which descends sometimes in those suburbs of thick walls and high fences and padded trees. Simon started to cry again. I picked him up to comfort him, and he loudly burped.

Everyone laughed. Stella got up and started to clear the table.

'I'll do that,' I said.

'No,' Stella said, 'Niels and I can manage. You go and spend some time with Lloyd. You've got a lot to talk about.'

❖

I stowed the little basket beside the bed. Lloyd and I looked down on Simon.

'My son,' he said wonderingly.

'Our son.' For the first time since he'd been born, panic invaded me. 'Do you realise that he's totally dependent on us? That if we don't feed him no one else will?'

Lloyd laughed.

'It's not funny.'

Lloyd took off his trousers and shoes and lay down on the bed. He held his hand out to me. 'Come and lie down, it's been a long time.'

I'd dreaded this moment since I'd seen him get out of the car. I squeezed in beside him. 'Lloyd?' Now, before anything else happened. 'Do you remember that night I came and saw you in hospital, and Vince took me to the motel?'

I felt him waiting. I said quickly, 'That night, Vince went to bed with me.' I didn't know how else to say it.

In the long silence I could hear my breath roaring in my ears. His hand on my waist went still, then withdrew. I felt the bed lift as he got up. He paced back and forth across the room, slamming fist into open palm. 'The bastard. The bastard!'

I sat up. 'Shh. The baby.'

'He's supposed to be my mate.'

'He took me to a Chinese place for tea and back to the motel. He was nice to me, I thought he was being nice. I didn't want to kiss him goodbye but I didn't want to hurt his feelings. He said I opened my mouth but I know I didn't. Why would I? Then he insisted on taking me up to my room, he waited till I got into bed and he turned off the light. I thought he'd gone, but the next thing I knew he was in bed beside me. It was horrible, I hated it, but I didn't know what to do. I didn't know how to stop him.'

'I'll kill the bastard. I'll kill him.'

'I'm sorry.' I wished I could cry, but I held back in case I made it worse.

Lloyd pushed the fingers of both hands through his hair so that it stood on end; his face was red, his socks were different shades of grey.

'I couldn't stand not telling you; it made it worse. All this time I've felt guilty, as if it was my fault.'

Lloyd shuddered, as though he were cold. He turned abruptly and stared into the baby's basket.

I said, 'I love you, you know that.'

He turned back and I tried to sit up, to meet him in an embrace, but he took hold of me, and I fell back onto the pillow under his weight. It was quick. I felt as though he were pouring his fury into me. He moaned, he sighed. I imagined he stifled a sob, but he was quiet. We lay glued together then with his sweat, not speaking, for what seemed like hours.

It felt like a punishment.

❖

From the lounge room I watched my mother get out of the taxi, white-faced and rearing back slightly as she looked up at the building. I knew I should go out and meet her but my feet had taken root. I held tightly on to Simon. I was sick with fear: for Simon, for my mother, for myself. I wished the de Langes hadn't gone out for food for lunch; there was plenty in the fridge. I forced myself to move to the door and open it.

My mother stepped into the hall. She was trembling. 'How could you do this to me?' she howled. 'The minute I read your letter it felt like this great big fist hit me in the stomach.' She bent over, pressing both arms against her middle. She was wearing her good dress. A new brown vinyl port was standing upright beside her. She didn't look at Simon.

'I'm sorry. I'm sorry, Mum.' How could I make my mother suffer any more than she did at home?

Simon was snuffling, although he'd settled after his feed.

'You'll have to get away from him.'

'But I love him. He's his father.'

'Love!' My mother spat the word out. 'What do you know about love?' With a visible effort she looked at Simon. 'Look at him, he's the image of him. You'll have to have him adopted out. And what about your university career?'

I swung around so that Simon was out of my mother's line of sight. 'I'm not giving him away.' It was the first time I'd raised my voice to her. Already I was so used to the weight and warmth of Simon in the crook of my arm I could scarcely remember when that space had been always empty: the small, helpless body against mine strengthened me. But now I'd made him cry.

There was an urgent rapping. I saw Lloyd's shape in the flywire door. He opened it and came in.

'Betty.'

But she went for him and hammered her fists on his chest. 'You bastard, you, you . . . I'll . . .'

'Mum!' I stood behind them.

'What have you done to her?' my mother shouted. She turned to me. 'What am I going to say to everyone? What's everyone going to think?'

Lloyd grabbed my mother's wrists. 'It's all right! Calm down! Maggie, make your mother a cup of tea. With sugar.'

'She doesn't take sugar.'

'Make it with sugar.' He led my mother to the couch and sat her down.

From the kitchen I could hear my mother's voice, now angry, now plaintive, Lloyd's reassuring one, but I couldn't hear much of what they were saying, except when Lloyd said, 'She threw herself at me!' I couldn't believe he thought this. Had I? But the seriousness, the extremity of the situation demanded some rhetoric, I told myself, and was of a kind when people don't mean everything they say. I couldn't stop my hands from shaking.

I cradled Simon, rocked him until he gulped and sniffed, and was quiet. 'Grandma doesn't mean it,' I whispered. 'She's just upset'. With my free hand I turned on the tap and filled the kettle. It took a long time to make the tea. I stood in front of the cupboard, it seemed, for half an hour, trying to remember where the sugar was. The kitchen seemed different, as if someone had rearranged everything in it.

My mother was calmer when I took in the tea, even molli-fied. What had Lloyd said? He had a strange power, a way of getting people to give themselves up to him. I sat next to her on the couch.

'At least you've given him a saint's name.' My mother was looking sidelong at the tuft of red hair, moving her eyes but not her head. 'Better get him baptised. I don't suppose you've had him baptised yet?' She looked quickly at Lloyd and away, her lips drawn. I noticed how tired she looked.

'Stella and Niels've got everything organised for this Sunday. They're going to be godparents. Stella said you can have Max's room till then. Here, why don't you have a nurse?'

I held out Simon. My mother's hesitation made her seem awkward, but then she settled the baby into her arms and rocked him back and forth. Her face softened, the faint lines around her mouth relaxed. 'He's got your grandmother's red hair,' she said. I didn't say, and Lloyd's, whose stubble before he shaved was auburn. I realised I'd been holding my breath, but it was my mother who sighed, and shook her head. She looked up at me with a weary, resigned expression. I stared at a little black flower in the pattern on the familiar dress. She looked down again at Simon. She said, 'He's a healthy baby. He's lovely.' And smiled at him. 'Aren't you?'

The de Langes came in with a freshly baked cheesecake whose fragrance, like their smiles, shifted and settled the atmosphere in the house.

At the table I sat next to my mother, while Simon lay in the basket beside my chair. What a strange thing it was to have grown inside someone, to have someone else grow inside you. Instead of increasing the distance between us, this new life had reconnected us to each other's blood.

'So!' Stella said. At the de Langes' even the smallest meal was a special occasion. Sometimes the act of sitting down together to a meal altered the relations, the feelings, between people. 'Help yourself to salad, Mrs Reed. Maggie, pass your mother the cheese. Lloyd, have you heard anything about your job?'

My mother looked uncertainly at the wedges of cheese arranged on the big wooden board. I picked up the cheese knife and cut her a slice of cheddar.

'Just got the letter of offer this morning.' Lloyd grinned.

'Well, that's a relief, that's wonderful. Now you'll be able to buy a house.' Stella looked at my mother, who nodded, and the look that passed between them was a resigned, forbearing one, with bent smiles. I guessed this news – the first I'd heard of it – was one of the things Lloyd had told my mother while I was making the tea.

'Congratulations,' Niels said. 'So tell us more about it.'

Lloyd began to explain, and my mother turned to me. She whispered, 'You know I didn't mean what I said about the baby, about having him adopted out?'

'I know.' I felt older. A mother beside a mother.

'You won't ever tell him?'

'Of course not. Of course I won't.'

❖

'I baptise thee Simon William . . .' Gerard wore the silken vestments, but he performed the ceremony in a natural voice. Simon only winced when he poured the cold water over his head. Lloyd hovered beside me, as though he wanted to perform the ceremony himself. On the other side of me stood my mother, and Stella and Niels with Max between them, the others around us in a circle. I dried Simon's hair with the end of Margareta's baptism shawl.

At the de Langes' afterwards, I was overwhelmed – it was a long time since I'd been among so many people in a room – and escaped into the dining room on the pretext of filling my plate. From the double doorway I could see the foliage of the maple tree framed by the lounge room window. In front of it Mrs Mitchell stood talking to my mother. Mrs Mitchell talked and talked – what about? – while my mother bent her head and nodded or spoke and smiled, sometimes with her mouth turned down. I almost laughed: usually it was while my mother talked that no one could get a word in edgewise.

Niels, a bottle of champagne in each hand, and Max at his elbow, in a tiny suit and blue bow tie, balancing a plate of savouries on his forearms, moved among the little crowd. Watching them I realised that there were a lot of people who'd never met each other before. Only Lloyd and my mother were from my old life.

Stella was showing Simon off to everyone, as proudly as though she really was his mother. When she reached Elizabeth and Toby she handed Simon to Elizabeth, who was wearing white linen and clucked and cooed before quickly handing him back to Stella. On the wall behind them was the painting Stella and Niels had just bought of a woman standing at a window, leaning out of its frame and almost of the picture's. The woman was young, and she gazed out of the picture with a look of such hopefulness, such joyful expectancy, that I turned away.

Lloyd was entertaining Gerard and a couple I didn't know. Gerard looked up and beckoned me over.

'Maggie, this is Julie, and Brian, Brian Tobin,' Gerard said. 'Brian's one of the priests we talked about in Parkville. He's left and he's applying for a dispensation to get married.'

'Hello.' I was surprised that they looked like any ordinary engaged couple. Brian wore modern, matching clothes. Julie wore a miniskirt and white boots. They were holding hands. They were about the same age, and Julie didn't look pregnant.

Lloyd said to Brian, 'Good to have a mate in the same boat. Hope we'll be seeing a lot more of each other.'

'I think us refugees should stick together,' Brian said. 'It won't be easy to adjust to civilian life.'

'Have you found a job yet?' Lloyd said.

'I'm going back to university. To finish my psychology degree. Julie's a social worker, she's already got a job down here. I'm going to be a kept man for a while.'

Julie smiled back at Brian. 'We've been looking at flats.'

'How did everyone take it back in Brisbane?' Gerard said.

'Mum and Dad were a bit shocked at first,' Julie said, 'but they got used to the idea. They're right behind us now. But they're glad we're coming to live down here. Because of all the gossip.'

'You've already found a flat, haven't you, Lloyd?' Brian said.

'A one-bedroom in Murrumbeena, just till we move into the place in Springvale.'

'What place?' I said.

'It's a new house, on a new estate. All young couples like us, with kids. I borrowed the deposit from my old man till the sale of Lantic Bay goes through.'

'But I haven't seen it.'

'You'll like it there. It's near the school I'll be working at.'

Gerard said, 'Are you looking forward to it, Maggie, having your own home?'

After a small silence, I said, 'I don't know.' I saw the look on Lloyd's face. 'I'm just getting used to Lloyd being here.'

I excused myself and went to my mother, who was alone now and looking lost. Katrina joined us.

'Mum, this is Katrina. Katrina told me I had to book into the Women's Hospital to have Simon. She told me where it was.'

'I suppose I should thank you, then,' my mother said. She sounded embarrassed, and I felt guilty that I'd put her in this position.

'Not at all.' Katrina smiled, and my mother smiled back.

'Katrina and Gerard and other friends of theirs look after homeless men.'

'Oh yes?' My mother looked dazed.

I looked around the room. An unpleasant lightness seemed to lift me from solid ground. In this room full of people I felt cut off even from Lloyd, as though the intimacy of our connection still couldn't tolerate exposure, belonging only to closed rooms, to the dark. I could hear the loud ascending octave of his laugh: now he was swanning among the guests, cracking jokes, now prising Simon out of someone's arms, everyone laughing at his pantomime of pride with jutting jaw and exaggerated grin, at his awkward cradling of the baby in both arms, elbows high, the shawl disarranged and trailing to the ground. He was wearing his priest's black jacket over a white shirt still creased from the packaging, a navy tie, and a pair of borrowed brown trousers. It occurred to me that I should have ironed the shirt, that this was now my job.

'They've gone to a lot of trouble, the de Langes,' Katrina was saying to me. 'They must be very fond of you.'

I sipped champagne. 'They're that kind of people. They're generous.'

'So are you going back to university?'

'I'd like to, one day, but there's no one else to look after Simon yet.'

'You'll find a way.'

'I hope so,' my mother said.

'I want him to have an educated mother,' I said.

'You are educated.' Lloyd was suddenly there, between us. He held Simon out to me with mock ceremony. 'I think Mummy'd better take over now. Bit of a bad smell in there.'

I went out to my room and changed Simon, heated his bottle and took him back inside. Elizabeth and Toby had asked Stella to say goodbye to me. I could hear Niels and Max in the kitchen, laughing among the clatter of plates and the chink of glasses. I joined the circle the others who were left had made.

My mother stood beside me. 'At least I'm not worried you've got nowhere to live. I heard about the house.'

'I don't want you to worry about anything.' I still wanted to protect her, though she wasn't in any more danger here. The worst had already happened.

My mother nodded and smiled her painful-looking smile.

A block of panic, like ice, filled my chest. A house. Marriage. Lloyd at work all day.

Gerard said, 'Lloyd, there's a feature coming up in the magazine on dispensations. What you have to go through. Maybe you'd like to do something, from a personal point of view?'

'Be glad to, cobber,' Lloyd said. But I couldn't imagine him working with the collective on the magazine. I didn't know why exactly. This afternoon beside Gerard and the others he seemed insubstantial, almost to float from group to group where he made himself the focus, but without their core of gravitas. He looked as familiar as my own reflection in the mirror, and yet like someone I'd just met. We loved each other, I reminded myself, we had a child to care for together. But nothing would sink in. I looked around at everyone. Their smiling faces seemed distorted, their voices too loud. 'Excuse me a minute,' I said. I handed Simon to my mother and hurried from the room. Behind me I heard the puzzled silence, felt the looks exchanged.

When Lloyd found me I was sitting on my bed.

He sat beside me. 'What's the matter?'

'Nothing. Everything. I don't know.'

'I thought this is what you wanted. Me coming down here to be with you and Simon.'

'I'm sick of hiding, I'm sick of running away. Couldn't you get a job in Sydney? I could go back to Macquarie.'

'But who'd look after me and Simon? Anyway, I've just bought us a house.'

'I didn't know about that. I haven't had time to think about it. I can't imagine ever feeling at home here. It's like I left a part of myself back there, and if I stay here there'll always be a part of me missing.'

Lloyd's eyes were glazed. 'You'll feel different when you've settled down. Brian and Julie are going to start a family too, when Brian finishes his degree. We've got friends here, we won't be on our own.'

My mother came in, still holding Simon. 'What are you talking about? What's the matter?'

'Nothing. Maggie just wants to go back. But it's too late now.' He said to me, 'We're better off down here where no one knows us.'

Stella called out from the back door, 'Maggie? Lloyd? What are you doing out there? Everyone's starting to leave.'

'You can't come back home,' my mother said. 'There's enough gossip going round already, from what I've heard.'

'I wasn't talking about that.'

'What will I tell everyone? I don't even know how to tell your father.' She sat heavily on the bed beside Lloyd, as if she'd been struck behind the knees.

'I can't go back now,' Lloyd said.

'He's right,' my mother said. 'And neither can you.'

❖

On a grey Sunday afternoon the next summer, I watched from the lounge room the two women get out of the taxi. They looked about them at the bare street, at the small, new brick veneer houses squatting in the bald earth of the yards where tiny leaves grew on the twigs of trees, and where thin spikes of grass pushed their way out into the light.

Sister Theresa and Sister Bernadette walked along the concrete path towards the porch. On either side of the path the soil, which a mate of Lloyd's had ploughed with a rotary hoe, had turned to the hardness of rock. The nuns' faces were grim inside the white coifs, their wide cream sleeves and scapulars and their black veils rippling and waving in the hot wind. They might have just walked out of medieval Europe, into this suburban wasteland. There was no front fence. I looked up and saw the sky, heavy with heat. When I pushed the pram up the hill to the milk bar and the phone box a mile and a half away, at the end of our new estate where the older part of the suburb began, I felt its weight.

Sometimes, before the de Langes left for Europe, I used to ring Stella and tell her about Simon, how he rocked and swayed to the music I played on long afternoons while waiting for Lloyd to come home, how he loved 'Puff, the Magic Dragon' and 'Morningtown Ride'. I told Stella how Simon grabbed onto the couch and hoisted himself up, and stumbled along sideways before falling on his bottom, then heaved his unwieldy little body up again; how he loved company, calling out and waving when he saw older children riding their scooters and dinkies in the street, how he tried to leap out of my arms when I took him there, but I couldn't let him crawl about for long in the mud in winter, the dirt in summer. There was no park, and no shade, so most of the time we stayed inside. I told Stella how sometimes I could have eaten Simon, when I kissed his chubby feet. I didn't tell her how each morning when I made the bed, I wanted to get back into it and never get up again. But I was still glad I'd kept Simon.

Now there was no one to ring, I sometimes went to the shop and bought a bottle of milk, though Lloyd could pick some up on the way home from work. Without a purpose or a destination, I couldn't bear to walk around the estate in the labyrinthine streets, which ended in blocks of land, some empty, some occupied by the fragile frames of houses, through which I could see the landscape where the market gardens had been razed, a landscape as ravaged as ones I'd seen in photographs of battlefields.

Each weekday morning all the men in our street drove to work. The women stayed home with toddlers and babies. A lot of them were pregnant. They shuffled to their letterboxes in dressing-gowns and fluffy slippers as late as lunchtime. They were all older than I was, and some had grown up together. They wore engagement rings and proper wedding rings: I wore my two-dollar one although I wasn't yet married.

My next-door neighbour had worked as a secretary in a bank and married a teller. She had a photo of their wedding on her sideboard, and she looked as happy now as she had that day. I heard her cheerfully scolding her children, saw her take down her terylene curtains to wash each week and sometimes the venetian blinds to hose down on her rotary clothesline. All the houses except ours had terylene curtains and plastic venetian blinds in every window.

When we moved in, Lloyd had said that soon there'd be a bus route along the main road at the end of the street, and a phone box on the corner, but there was no sign of either. Lloyd said we couldn't afford to have the phone connected.

The two nuns reached the concrete porch behind the triangle of birch trees I'd planted, which were sparsely leaved sticks stuck in the dirt, nothing yet like the shaded grove I'd imagined.

'A thousand welcomes!' Lloyd greeted them from the narrow hall with open arms and loud, cheerful laughter, his smile fixed inside the beard that made him look even older. Behind him I held Simon, who beamed, and squirmed to get a better look: he loved visitors, and we didn't get many. When Lloyd behaved like this I was sometimes embarrassed, as teenagers can be by their parents.

In the lounge room the nuns sat side by side in the second-hand chairs. I served tea and biscuits and sat beside Lloyd on the couch. Simon crawled over everyone's feet. I saw the room through the nuns' eyes: it looked small and ugly with its low ceiling and narrow skirting boards. The curtains of cheap brocade I'd had made and tied back with tassels looked ridiculous.

The person I had been the last time I'd seen the nuns no longer existed. I was Simon's mother, Lloyd's 'non-wife'. The three of us were the scandal personified. I was proud of Simon, who wobbled on his plump legs, clutching the knees of my jeans. But in front of the nuns my feelings for Lloyd were complicated. I felt exposed in my involvement with him, as though caught in a forbidden, shameful act. I felt uncomfortable imagining what the nuns must have thought of him, and of me, too.

Every afternoon I waited impatiently for him to come home, but when he did he was tired and had work to do. Most nights he went out after tea, to meetings of other ex-priests applying for dispensations, or something political, where he could feel purposeful and important. He seemed to miss his old life as much as I did mine. The only things we did together were eat, and make love, late at night, when he finally came home.

I had nothing to read. It didn't occur to me that there might be a library in a place like this: driving around the suburb with Lloyd I hadn't seen one. But I lived in an intellectual vacuum, and had almost lost my desire for books. The night before the nuns came, Lloyd was out as usual. Bored with television, I'd sat at the kitchen table reflected in the triangle of black windowpane between the parted curtains, and forced myself to read Lloyd's copy of *Newsweek*. It was like reading in a foreign language, but I ploughed on through article after article, to occupy my mind.

Only a report of the My Lai massacre in Vietnam had got through to my capacity to understand. On a Sunday morning, after feeding Simon, I went back to bed: I didn't want to begin the day. I picked up the copy of *Newsweek* from Lloyd's bedside table. Simon was wriggling about happily beside me with his toys. Lloyd was in his study. I finished the article and started to cry. Lloyd came in and wanted to know what was the matter. When I told him he said, 'Gee, you get upset easily, don't you?'

I was thinking about these things while the nuns and Lloyd and I sat in silence. It felt as though the nuns had come to say something that could not now be said.

'I didn't think you'd come all the way out here,' I said to them. 'From Camberwell – is that where you're staying? It's really nice of you.' I'd never spoken to them like this, as an adult.

'Yes, at Siena,' Sister Bernadette said. 'But we're flying to Sydney tonight.' She looked at me and Lloyd. Her smile seemed to exhaust her.

Sister Theresa didn't once smile or speak to Lloyd or even look at him. She said, 'What happened to your scholarship, Maggie?'

'I just deferred it again, Sister. For another year.'

'And after that?'

'Monash isn't far from here. I'll get a babysitter.'

'We'll have to wait and see,' Lloyd said. That morning he'd heard me vomiting: the doctor had said I couldn't get pregnant in the week between changing brands of the pill, but we both knew I was.

Sister Theresa was quiet when she looked away, her face animated with what she wasn't saying. I had written to tell her about Simon and Lloyd, because otherwise she'd have heard only the gossip I knew was everywhere in Cumberland, about how I'd run away with Lloyd. Since I couldn't bear to describe any details, or the machinations of Jack and Vince, what I had to say wasn't much different. But I needed to tell her myself. I couldn't forget the part of her reply where she'd written, 'You have been handed early in life its weightier responsibilities.' The tone of the letter was so formal, and abrupt in its restraint, that I was surprised she'd wanted to come and see me.

It seemed a long time since anyone had spoken. I jumped up. 'Listen to this!' I held up the cover of *The Pastoral Symphony*. 'I'll put on the slow movement.'

Sister Theresa still frowned, she glowered, even when Simon, sitting at my feet, rocked from side to side on his padded bottom and gurgled as if singing, and waved his arms about. The music made the room seem smaller, it turned the ceiling into a lid, it brushed against the walls and when it found the gaps in the open windows it slipped away. We all sat looking at the windows as if watching the music escape. Above the fence were the tops of two aluminium-framed windows in a brick wall, and a triangle of roof tiles, and the grey sky above. Lloyd was smiling as at a private joke or as though something was on the tip of his tongue to say if the music would stop.

I got up and lifted the arm of the record player: my hand shook and the needle scratched. 'Don't you remember, Sister?' I said to Sister Theresa. 'When you played that to us in second year? That was the first time I ever heard a symphony. You told us how that bit was the sun coming out after the storm, and about the birds.' Sister Theresa looked across at me, her eyebrows almost touching. How could she have forgotten? That sunny afternoon in the first-floor classroom with the blue sky outside the window and the fronds of the Cocos Island palm, almost close enough to touch, glittering inside the top half of the frame, and Sister Theresa gazing out of the window listening to the music that might have been written to describe all this, the light and air . . . the peace. 'That's why I picked it.'

'Well, Maggie' – Sister Theresa looked away, her face contorted – 'I suppose that makes it all worthwhile.'

Did she mean it? I stood, confused, in the middle of the room. Simon tugged at my jeans and I lifted him onto one hip, proudly, but I was shy, too, of making this motherly gesture in front of the nuns. They had travelled to this room from another time and place in which I still saw myself walking in the garden in my green uniform.

I saw a flock of crows flap into a window frame and perch in a row on the side fence, uttering the cries of creatures intent on injury and death. I was suddenly frightened, as though I'd had a premonition.

The nuns had ordered a taxi in advance to take them to the airport. When she said goodbye, Sister Theresa looked at me for a long moment, in a way that made me feel that I was still the blameless person she had known, who could be whatever she wanted.

I waved to the nuns from the porch and then from inside, to bring Simon in out of the heat. I saw the image of myself they must have seen from the taxi: standing behind glass, framed by the window – with Simon in one arm, Lloyd behind me – growing smaller and then disappearing.

Simon grizzled and writhed and bucked against my hip. He was hungry. Lloyd asked me what was for tea. I held Simon out to him and he took him from me with the lifting of the elbows, the little backward step, as if he'd expected a heavier weight.

In the kitchen I saw on the table the lemon in the bowl among the apples. I stopped and held up one hand and covered the lemon as Sister Theresa had done when she'd looked over my shoulder in the library one afternoon at the reproduction of the Matisse painting in the book I was reading. The rest of the painting – the striped red and orange wall, the flowers, the woman's purple coat – had dulled, and glowed again when she'd uncovered the lemon. Now when I dropped my hand there was just a lemon in a bowl of apples. Only in a painting could one lemon make such a difference to the light in a room. Above the table I'd hung, unfinished and unframed, the blue nude I'd painted at Hawthorn. I turned the light on, and started to peel Simon's pumpkin and potato.

Lloyd came in. 'So you're going to take up your scholarship again next year?'

'The year after. I just found out I can defer it for one more year. If I don't I'll lose it. I can still look after you and Simon.'

'Who'll look after him while you're at uni? And the new baby?'

'It'll be six months old. They'd let me go part-time, on a Commonwealth. A teacher's wife from your school knows someone near the university who'd babysit for the extra money. And there'd be a playmate for Simon. He gets lonely and bored stuck in here all the time. So do I, sometimes.' I put Simon's vegetables on the stove and started to peel ours.

'You never said you were lonely and bored.'

'Only sometimes, when you're not here. And when you are we never talk about things like that.'

'Sounds like you've got it all nutted out.' His voice went up a notch.

'It'll be my last chance.'

Simon whimpered. I took him from Lloyd and put him in the highchair and gave him a slice of cheese. I felt the anger grow, a seed sprouting in the dark. 'You do whatever you want. I never complain when you go out every night. And on weekends you just go and play golf. You've never asked me what I think about anything, like where to live. You knew I always wanted to go back to university.'

'I'm the one who works hard to earn the money. I'm entitled to a bit of relaxation.'

Simon started to cry. I finished mashing the vegetables and when they were cool enough I spooned them into his mouth. 'We're upsetting him.'

He lowered his voice. 'If you have to go back, you can give up the Commonwealth and get a studentship from the education department. It's more money.'

I turned to Lloyd in amazement, the spoon of vegetables poised, and Simon complained. I turned back to him. 'But then I'd have to study full-time. And I'd be bonded to the education department. I never wanted to teach in a school. I told you that. A long time ago.'

'What's wrong with being a teacher?'

'Sister Theresa said I could be a scholar. I could get my master's, and a PhD. I could write books and teach in a university. I'd earn more money, eventually. That's why I took the Commonwealth in the first place.'

Lloyd's face was scarlet. He looked angry and scared. 'You're not going to have a better job than me.'

I finished feeding Simon. I picked him up and took him to the bathroom. There was no way to answer this. Not now. Not yet.

To calm myself, I imagined the nuns' journey home, the long drive to the city and then the airport, the flight above the mass of land, the landscape now swollen, now flat, or cloven; forested, or bare; the Murray River at the border cutting it into two parts as distinct and as connected, earth to water, water to earth, as present and past. In my mind I built the bridge across the river, an extension of the road that was fixed in the landscape and yet moved mysteriously between one city and the other, connecting mile by mile each place, leading both forwards and back.

EPILOGUE

There is the story . . . and then, thanks to the intimate
connexion of things, the story of one's story itself.

HENRY JAMES

'Aren't you the girl who ran away with the priest?'

'I'm not a girl, and I didn't run away with a priest.'

The man's wife tugs on his arm. They say goodbye and leave. Colleen introduced them to us when they recognised her and came over to say hello. We are at a cafe on the Grainger River, in Cumberland.

'Good on you, Maggie,' Delia says.

'I'm so sorry.' Colleen smiles with her eyes. She's a nurse, a mother, a grandmother. She has known heartbreak: bereavement worse than any loss of mine.

Our other old classmates look at each other or pretend not to have heard.

'So I'm still the scarlet woman around here.' I make this sound like a joke. I know it's not appropriate, to be ashamed,

313

but for a moment I have the shrinking feeling of wanting to hide.

'Rubbish.' Delia stands up. 'Come on, time to go back.'

❖

Only one of the old palm trees beside the central cloister is still there: it was one of a pair, and the imbalance is part of the strangeness of what was once so familiar. The missionary nuns who travelled here from Ireland, to build the convent and open the school, planted it when they arrived one hundred and fifty years ago. It's not a convent anymore, it's a Catholic high school. No one has lived here for years, but today we're celebrating the arrival of those Irish nuns. And it's fifty years since my class left school.

We sit at one of the trestle tables on the lawn. Girls and boys – *boys!* we say to one another, wearing blue uniforms, not green, serve tea and sandwiches and scones.

The woman beside me, who wasn't at the cafe earlier, turns and says in a low voice, as though inviting a confidence, 'Are you still with him?'

She doesn't say his name or even 'the priest'.

'Not since nineteen seventy-five.'

The woman drops her conspiratorial expression and looks disappointed. 'But I heard you ran away together. I thought it was this big romance.'

'It wasn't really like that.'

After tea we disperse to inspect the place. On the cloisters I see the tessellated tiles as well as the red concrete they've replaced them with. I hesitate at the door into the Georgian building which opens at the other end of the hall onto the street, at the formal entrance to the old convent. My legs feel heavy; I can scarcely move. If I walk in and enter the front room on the left, I'll see where Lloyd used to eat breakfast after mass. I walk, I propel myself into the hall. Only the marble tiles and the doors are the same.

Opening off this hall were the reception rooms, of high ceilings and marble fireplaces and polished wooden floors. In the one where I used to meet Lloyd, the fireplace has been boarded up, the ceiling lowered, and partitions of grey fabric divide the space into office cubicles. The room seems much smaller, whether because of the clutter or because memory had enlarged it, I don't know. For so many years I've kept an image in my mind of the illicit, orgiastic ritual that was performed here. I saw myself in uniform lying on the floor under the priest in his black suit, the remains of the half-eaten breakfast on the table in one corner, the woman in the picture pouring milk into the bowl.

Now I'm appalled at the destruction of the room's proportions, at the ugliness of the furniture and of the materials tacked over its elegant features. But unexpectedly I'm relieved. Here is physical evidence of the passing of time. Seeing this room it's impossible to hold on to that image, and its significance fades. The room has been repurposed to good use, to serve the education of the girls and boys who study here now. My sensibilities, my memories, have no place here.

I walk outside and see that the chapel cloister is shorn of the jasmine vine that blossomed every spring and summer. Where it grew the old bricks are a brighter colour, and I imagine what the building looked like when it was new and the vine was planted. So many times the scent of other star jasmines has unlocked in me the happiness of the years here before I met Lloyd, and then the grief of the loss of my younger self. Now standing here in spring, with the fragrance gone, these feelings are remembered, but not real.

In the garden a couple of the old shrubs grow, and one rose arbour still stands. They've replaced the gravel with grey concrete paving stones. Only the pattern remains of the paths I used to walk around in the early morning, studying French and Latin grammar. Instead of flowerbeds, the lawn borders the paths. In my mind I see the garden as it was, superimposed on this ruin. Beyond the lawns I can see the old junior school building, and the science block built while I was here, but newer buildings crowd the grounds, and I can't see where the path I'm on used to lead to the bottom paddock. So I don't go down there, or to whatever is there now. Instead I walk back towards the boarders' wing.

The big dormitory with its high ceiling and Georgian windows has been made into a library. I can see the narrow beds here against the wall where I slept one year, and there in the middle row where I slept the next, but each step brings me further into the present. Other spaces in the building have been divided up to make classrooms, or closed off where before they were open. Then I remember the back stairs at the other end of the dormitory – the library – that lead to the attic. At the bottom I bump into Delia and we climb them together. The door at the top is closed: it seems permanently locked. We can find our way around only by going back to the main staircase, which is all that's familiar: its terrazzo steps, its wooden banister worn shiny and smooth. We climb to the top landing and remember the small flight of steps around a corner and follow them up to the attic. It's like navigating our way in the orderly disorderliness of a dream.

This room seems also to have shrunk. A false ceiling hides the vaulted beams. Stacked shelves disguise the dormer windows, cutting off the view of the crown of the old mulberry tree far below, and the town beyond. The only light enters from the window at the end wall. We go down to where we sometimes talked leaning on the railing overlooking the back stairs, although the stairs have been boxed in against the railing, and there's nothing to lean over now.

'Why did they have to build that ceiling?' I say.

'Don't go to the bottom paddock – they've cut down the willows, and some of the camphor laurels.'

'Did you notice they've totally destroyed the jasmine on the chapel cloister?'

Delia smiles at me. 'We had a lot of deep philosophical conversations up here on rainy afternoons, didn't we?'

'And I told you my shocking secret.'

'You told me two.'

'That's right, about Dad. He stopped drinking years before he died. Only because the doctor told him it'd kill him otherwise. Mum had left him, but she took him back on condition he never drank again. And he didn't.'

'What was he like then?'

'Intelligent. Witty. He used to paint and do carvings. Before he died he gave us all a painting. It was his way of saying sorry. It wasn't enough for Mum, of course. She wanted him to say it, but he could only make gestures.'

'What about the other secret? Did you still see Lloyd, until he died?' This is how we used to talk, as though listening to each other's thoughts.

'You were right when you said it'd only get me into trouble. Years and years of it, even after I'd left.'

'I wonder if I should have told someone.'

'If you had, I wouldn't have had my children. And I wouldn't be me.'

Delia moves over to the window and I follow her. We don't say anything for a while. Then she says, 'Will you send me another story?'

'I've just had one published, I'll send that.'

'The one I read, it was like you were talking to me again up here.'

In this last, repurposed room, now late in the day of the occasion I dreaded at first, declining to attend until curiosity and shame at my cowardice propelled me here, I feel reconciled with the naive, ambitious Maggie who told Delia her secrets in this attic. She might have been disappointed I don't have more letters after my name – impossible to do post-graduate study married to Lloyd, impossible on my own – but she'd approve of my single-minded efforts, despite obstacles she couldn't have imagined, to keep the 'fire in my belly' alight: of how I've used those obstacles as raw material, as a sculptor uses clay.

'What about you?' I say. 'What are you going to tell the OECD in Norway next week?'

❖

Delia and I are almost the last to leave. We walk towards the gate in the high brick fence between the grotto at the bottom of the garden and the end wall of the chapel. A jacaranda I've either forgotten or that was planted after I left leans over the fence, into the honey-and-lemony light I remember of a late afternoon in spring. Everything else I've seen today has changed except this light, and the particular peaceful, linger-ing quality it had, it has, on a Sunday afternoon. Once Delia and I would have been in the bottom paddock at this hour while the shadows of the willows grew in it until they almost touched the fence, and the bell rang for benediction. Now I'll remember how it catches on the branches of this jacaranda. This will now be what I remember.

We step out through the gate. One of the students closes it behind us. Soon the school will be empty and quiet: a place where no one sleeps.

We say goodbye and Delia wraps both her arms around me. She doesn't let go for a long time. When we part, walking in opposite directions, I still feel the warmth, inside me.

There's nothing left back there. I can go home.

ACKNOWLEDGEMENTS

I'm enormously grateful to the late Dr Don Lewis of CFS discovery, and to Susan Bassett, for their professional guidance over many years in the management of ME/CFS, which has been essential to my work.

Special thanks to my agent, Clare Forster, at Curtis Brown: I'm honoured by her belief in my work, and her commitment to getting my late debut published: I thank her for suggesting the title – and for her warmth and professionalism, since she first read the manuscript and gave me a valuable and generous appraisal. Also, on her team, Caitlan Cooper-Trent for her wise and thoughtful comments, and Benjamin Stevenson.

At Hachette, special thanks to former publisher Robert Watkins for his enthusiastic, careful guiding of my book almost out into the world, to Vanessa Radnidge, publisher, for similarly, and with great sensitivity, continuing and completing this work, and to indefatigable senior editor Karen Ward (thanks to

Karen and Robert, too, for their insightful feedback). Thanks to the Hachette sales, marketing and publicity team.

Thanks to the freelance editors Alex Craig and Ali Lavau, whose expert, respectful counsel helped to shape and polish the book into its final version.

I'm grateful to Jenny Lee, former editor, and Gerald Murnane, former fiction editor, of *Meanjin*, as well as Andrew Sant, former editor of *Island Magazine*, for publishing my first and only stories: this sustained me through some difficult years and indirectly provided encouragement to persist with what became *Maggie*.

I'm especially grateful to Gerald Murnane as well for his generosity in reading, and writing invaluable comments on, two earlier drafts – also for allowing one of these to appear on the cover.

For reading, discussing and providing often written comments on earlier drafts I thank:

Les Harrop, convenor of the former Melbourne Writers Group, and its members including my friend Sally Rippin, and Nelly Zola, Llewellyn Johns, Anne Neumann, Richard Moir, Clive Mitchell, Adrian Costigan, and Pam McCasker.

Janey Runcie, Renata Singer.

For their friendship and feedback, Elisabeth Hanscombe, Gemma Schooneveldt, and Michael Galvin.

In our Queenscliff/Geelong writers' group, Pam Baker – as well as for her unwavering friendship – and Kim Waters, Ann Abrahamson, and Susan Kruss.

Big thanks to my elder sister, whose feedback was particularly important, and whose unconditional support I can always rely on. I don't know what I'd do without her.

Heartfelt thanks to Catherine de Saint Phalle: writers' writer, writerly reader, and true friend, whose suggestions are always both sensitive and spot on, and who has fiercely championed my work. Thanks also for the quote on the cover.

I'm grateful to my niece, Emily, and to Katherine Matthews, for their support and help with technical practicalities.

Thanks to Matisse Mitelman – who stepped up to take some interim photos – and to Scott Kluwer, for their support, and to Matt Sleeth for his important part in setting *Maggie* on the journey to publication.

I'm grateful for the unfailing support of my other siblings, my younger sister – forever inspiring, forever missed – and my four brothers, who generously encouraged me to write this novel, and waited patiently for me to finish it.

Gratitude is an inadequate word for what I owe my daughters for their loving, generous support of too many kinds to describe.

hachette
AUSTRALIA

If you would like to find out more about Hachette Australia,
our authors, upcoming events and new releases, you can visit
our website or our social media channels:

hachette.com.au

HachetteAustralia

HachetteAus

Catherine Johns has taught English and French in Melbourne secondary schools, and English in TAFE. Her short stories have been published in *Meanjin* and *Island Magazine*. One of these was shortlisted for *The Age* short story competition. *Maggie* is her first novel. Catherine lives and writes in Melbourne.